THE FALLEN BLOODLINE

MAGDALÉNA GAVLASOVÁ

Copyright © 2024 Magdaléna Gavlasová

All rights reserved.

ISBN: 9798342448079

To all the tangled knots of insecurities—may you one day realize the power you hold within, and may your journey untangle the strength you never knew you had.

A special thank you to those closest to me for not losing it after hearing about my book again and again (and again), for tolerating the constant beeping of your phones, and for your endless patience as I obsessed over the perfect book aesthetics.

Matthew 10:28

"And fear not them which kill the body, but are not able to kill the soul: but rather fear him which is able to destroy both soul and body in hell."

chapter 1

BLOODLINE OF TEMPTATION

The sky grows dark as evening arrives, marking the moment I've been eagerly anticipating yet dreading for some time now. I slip into one of my favorite dresses—a simple, yet pretty, emerald green sundress that flares out slightly at the waist. The color enhances my green eyes, making them sparkle with a vibrant intensity, while the deep hue contrasts beautifully with my tanned skin. My rather long brown hair rests against my back in soft waves. Standing a little above average height, I step back from the small mirror to get a better view, admiring how the dress accentuates my silhouette. I'm satisfied with my choice. It's a small gesture to ensure that if, by some unfortunate twist of fate, I meet an untimely end in a sacrificial ritual tonight, at least I'll go out looking pretty.

Just a few weeks ago, life was predictable. The summer had just begun, bringing with it the promise of freedom from my Ph.D. in criminal law and part-time teaching duties. Morning meditations, afternoon workouts, outings with friends, and quiet evenings at home with my cat, Cerberus, were my daily routine. That was until the storm broke, not in the clouds, but in my life.

One quiet night, while watching an old favorite show in the comfort of my home, the rustling of wings disrupted my peace. At first, I thought it was just a scary moth, preying on my lepidopterophobia, but I soon realized it was something far more extraordinary. A woman, with fiery red hair and an ethereal presence, appeared in my room. Her name was Yabbashael, and she revealed to me that she was my guardian angel.

In a surreal conversation, Yabbashael explained that I am Nephilim, the daughter of a fallen angel, and that my ability to see and talk to angels is my birthright and my only power. Apparently, it took me 26 years to truly open myself and break the veil that conceals the world of angels from human sight, but I finally did it—all thanks to my dedication to self-improvement.

Or, perhaps, I've suffered a bad head trauma and am now living in my own dream, in a coma, and none of this is real.

Soon after, Ethan—the fallen angel claiming to be my father—showed up, tempting me with an array of powers and the promise of immortality if I choose to accept them.

Like an angel on one shoulder, Yabbashael urged me to embrace my mortality, while emphasizing the sacredness of the afterlife. Despite Yabbashael's warnings, the allure of supernatural powers and eternal life—the devilish offer on my other shoulder—seemed irresistible. The panic attacks that seize me whenever the thought of death crosses my mind would become nothing more than a faded memory.

Yabbashael painted fallen angels as monstrous beings driven by selfish motives, desperate to avoid eternal solitude. She argued that my father—whom she called Peliel, since she didn't know the name he took after his fall—was manipulative and dangerous. She insisted I should listen to her, given she is an angel who's never done anything wrong.

But despite her arguments, the prospect of living a life free from the fear of death, with abilities beyond my wildest dreams, seemed undeniably appealing. I couldn't shake the feeling that Yabbashael, though well-meaning, might also have her own agenda, her own reasons for keeping me in the dark about my true potential as she first tried. She, too, enjoys having a friend different from angels, one she can only keep if I stay human. Her protective nature and the rules she followed were clear, but so was Ethan's offer of something extraordinary.

After several hurried discussions fitted around Yabbashael's duties protecting numerous other charges, coupled with Ethan's vows to aid me in combating malevolent forces and safeguarding human lives, I made my choice.

Ethan, as my biological father, is the only one who can grant me my full powers and make me a true Nephilim. It took him some time to figure out exactly how this transformation is supposed to happen, but here we are.

Finally.

chapter 2

INTO THE DARKNESS

As I arrive at the designated spot, I see Ethan standing under a streetlamp, its soft light mingling with the last traces of daylight. The sun is nearly set, casting the sky in deep hues of purple and blue, while the lamplight creates long, stretched shadows around him. His tall frame is outlined in the gentle glow, accentuating his chiseled features and the slight smirk playing on his lips. His dark hair falls casually over his forehead, almost covering his piercing dark eyes, adding to the aura of mystery and menace that surround him.

He casually fiddles with his fingernails, not even glancing at me before pushing off the lamp, as if sensing my presence. He strides toward me with easy confidence, arms outstretched for a hug. I tense, instinctively stepping back. His bold approach feels intrusive; we've barely spent any time together, and to me, he's still practically a stranger.

Casual physical contact has never been my thing, especially with someone I hardly know. My guard is always up, only lowering when a genuine connection breaks through—but this is different, and I'm not ready to let him in that easily.

"I have questions," I say, keeping my gaze as sturdy as possible. I need him to understand that I won't be rushed into anything and I won't be participating in any rituals without knowing the details first.

"And hello to you, too," he replies with a chuckle that quickly fades as he catches the serious expression on my face. "Alright, I'll answer any questions you have on our way. Let's go." Without waiting for my response, he points in the direction we need to go and starts walking, giving me no chance to protest.

His eagerness to make me like him—to make me immortal—strikes me as strange. Despite our biological connection, we're strangers. I'd expect him to take the time to get to know me before inviting me into his eternal life, but maybe he's just like me. Impulsive and impatient. The apple had to have fallen from some tree, after all.

"Where are we going?" I inquire as I follow him.

"There's an old cave near the beach, about 20 minutes from here."

"A cave?" I repeat, my voice trembling slightly. The word

echoes in my mind, bringing with it images of darkness and isolation. I hardly know him, and the idea of being alone with him in some cave feels like a scene ripped from a horror movie. What if he's not truly Peliel, my father, but someone else masquerading as him? A demon, perhaps, with sinister intentions of sacrificing me.

Yabbashael claimed she sensed my father's presence, but she's never met him with me and she couldn't confirm the name he's been using after his fall. And the timing of his appearance—just a day after I discovered my ability to see angels—seems too calculated, too deliberate.

But perhaps I'm allowing my imagination to run wild. I'm scared of what might happen tonight and I'm scared I might be making a really bad decision, the worst I could actually make in my life, but I can't help it. I feel a strange sense of familiarity with Ethan, a connection that feels genuine.

Fear prickles at the edges of my thoughts, but so does a stubborn sense of curiosity. I've always had a strong intuition, and it whispers now, beneath the cacophony of my anxiety, that I can trust him. I take a deep breath, trying to steady my racing heart. This has to be Peliel, my father, and he wouldn't plot to lure me into some cave to harm me.

"Don't worry," Ethan says, likely sensing my concern from the furrow in my brow. Or perhaps he's reading my thoughts. I've been told fallen angels can enter people's minds and even affect what they see or hear, but I hope he wouldn't dare using these powers on me. "It's an old cave used for rituals. My friend assures me it has everything we need," he adds, addressing an issue I'm not really worried about, which might indicate he's really *not* invading my mind and that he's being honest.

However, his words do little to soothe my nerves as he reminds me of a ritual I know nothing about, and for a moment I give in to my anxiety and try to find out more about who he truly is. "Okay, Ethan, I trust you," I say, trying to sound convincing, though my high-pitched voice probably wouldn't fool a child. "You know, Ethan doesn't sound very angelic."

"No?" He chuckles humorlessly. "Good."

"What do you mean?" I ask, not catching the joke.

Ethan looks away, his jaw tightening. "Ethan is my chosen name now. As an angel, I was known as Peliel." He glances at me, as if checking to see whether his answer has satisfied me, whether it has dispelled my doubts. Sometimes, he doesn't seem so different from the angels—it's clear he sees right through me, sensing every doubt and fear I try to hide. Then his voice drops, almost to a whisper. "But after my fall, I didn't feel worthy of that name." He runs a hand through his hair.

At least he said the same name as Yabbashael; that's a good sign. "Not worthy?"

"The 'el' in Peliel means God. But I failed to live up to that, to God's standards, because I didn't believe there was a good reason behind all the rules."

"So, how did you settle on Ethan?" If I could choose my own name, it would be something elegant like Victoria or Valerie. Why pick a plain name like Ethan?

"Well, after my fall, I started going by Aition, which means guilty. But it felt outdated, and people often misheard it as Ethan.

Eventually, I stopped feeling guilty and found comfort in a name with a more positive meaning."

"Ah." I nod, though I'm still puzzled. "What does Ethan mean?"

"In Hebrew, it means strong, enduring," he explains.

"I see," I reply, though I'm not entirely sure I do. Why all the fuss about names? Do they really matter that much? After all, it's people who assign meaning to them.

I pause, trying to gather my thoughts. So many questions swirl in my mind, and it's hard to choose which one to ask first. I should want to know why he fell, what the ritual will include, and whether I can truly trust him. But the one thing that's been on my mind ever since I found out about what I am is how my mom could have cheated on my father with him.

"How did you… Did my mom… How did you become my father? No, that's not what I meant to ask," I stumble over my words, trying to find the right way to phrase my question without prompting an awkward lesson on sex education.

"I know what you're getting at," Ethan saves me from saying something more embarrassing. "When I fell, I wasn't myself." His expression darkens as he begins his explanation. "I was stripped of my wings, many powers too. I couldn't control the new ones yet. My deception powers allowed me to infiltrate people's minds, making them see and think what I wanted. As an angel, I could only guide people, but falling changed everything. It felt like they were in my head, every passerby… I felt their emotions, saw what they saw. I felt like I was going crazy."

His words paint a vivid picture, but it's not the answer I'm looking for. Still, I appreciate his willingness to open up, to share his struggle. The more he reveals, the more I see the fragments of a once-mighty angel now grappling with his fallen state.

"I was also overwhelmed by human emotions I never experienced before. It took about a hundred years after my fall to regain control of myself and my powers. I started to see human women differently, not just as beings we guard. And then I saw her. She was the most beautiful woman I'd ever laid eyes on," Ethan reminisces, his tone softening with adoration. "Her green eyes, her long curly hair... that smile," he trails off, lost in his memories. "And her body, perfect in every way," he adds with a suggestive grin, biting his lip.

"Whoa, hold on. You're talking about my mother, right?" I interject, feeling a knot of unease forming in my stomach.

"Sorry... Yes." He quickly gathers himself. "To make it short, I couldn't resist her," Ethan continues, his voice turning cold and detached. "But I couldn't seduce her as myself. She was devoted to your father. I liked that even more about her. She seemed so pure, so good, so happy and she was always so merry. I couldn't help myself and I... deceived her. She thought she was with your father that night."

"What?" My voice rises with disbelief and horror. "So you... you actually raped my mom," I cry out loud, the words bursting forth from the depths of my emotions.

"Shh!" Ethan looks around nervously, checking if anyone has overheard our conversation, but luckily for him, there's no one around.

"I can't believe you did this!" I stop walking, unable to move. The shock and revulsion make my legs feel like lead. "What kind of person are you?"

"I'm not perfect, I know that. At least I'm trying to be honest. I was really confused. I'm not like that anymore. You can't imagine what it's like to fall and be stranded here on Earth, becoming more like a human than an angel. Losing everything and everyone. I can't put into words how I felt. One moment I was up, the next I was down. I felt crazy. No, I actually *was* crazy." Ethan continues walking without looking back at me as if that explanation alone should convince me to do the same.

For a moment I consider turning around, getting back to the safety of the known. But then I ponder his words. My mother's story might not be as simple as I thought, but at least now I know she's an honest person, not a cheater. Perhaps it was the angelic desire of purity that twisted into something darker, corrupted. The allure of her innocence may have drawn him in, warping his celestial instinct to protect into a selfish, destructive force.

Despite my revulsion, there's a sliver of understanding for the guilt he has carried for so long, evident in his self-proclaimed name Aition. It's clear he has been tormented by his actions for a long time. If he's learned from his mistakes, shouldn't that be enough? I'm not sure. I've been trying not to judge, but aren't there things that deserve to be judged? Should I give a second chance to anyone, regardless of their actions? Or perhaps I should just try my hardest to understand them before I pass judgment? Where are my books on Buddhism now that I need them?

I take a deep breath, steadying myself. "Still, I don't know what kind of person you are," I say, feeling the need to say at least something a bit judgy. Yet, I take a step forward, choosing to follow him into the unknown, fully aware that my commitment to self-growth and openness—to seeing beyond initial judgments, to understanding others' feelings, motives, and capacity for change, as the Buddhist philosophy I embraced this summer taught me—might be my downfall.

Ethan halts abruptly, his shoulders tense as he slowly turns to face me. His eyes lock onto mine, wide and pleading. His jaw tightens as if he's wrestling with the words, struggling to express what he's about to share—yet he tries. "I'm a good person. I care about humanity, I care about the good, and I want to fight against the bad with you." There's a raw honesty in his voice that tugs at something deep within me. But what if it's just his superpower, the power of deception, mastered into masking any hints of dishonesty? What if it's just my trust in the good in people projecting onto him, blinding me to the truth?

"You do, huh? But the things you are telling me tonight, they're not exactly painting you in a good light." I place my hands firmly at my sides, lifting my chin defiantly, inviting him to convince me of the kind of person he truly is. "The ultimate question remains: why did you fall?"

He pauses, his gaze drifting downward as his fingers absently trace patterns on the edge of his shirt. A deep breath follows, his shoulders sagging slightly before he finally speaks. "I told you before how we felt about humans as angels. We guarded them and adored them. When I said Yabbashael wouldn't tell you about your true powers because she wouldn't want to lose you, I was speaking from experience. I also guarded the soul of a Nephilim. He realized who he was when he was sixteen years old—very early. He was the kindest person I have ever met. After all those years, I could finally talk to one of them. I loved it. But he never met his father. He was never given his powers. I tried to find the angel who fathered him, but that was not according to the rules, of course. His father didn't want to be found, and he didn't want to give his son any of his powers. I spent the guy's whole life with him, we became close friends, and then he died. I was supposed to let the angel of death take him away to the other side, but I couldn't bear to leave him. I thought I was better suited to take him there; we knew each other well, after all. I wanted to comfort him, not leave him with a stranger. I disobeyed the orders for the second time. I fell."

As he speaks, his jaw clenches, and though his voice remains steady, there's a faint tremor beneath the surface, as if he's holding back a torrent of emotions long buried. One thing becomes clear to me—his actions were driven by compassion, a fierce loyalty that runs deeper than most. Instead of painting him in a negative light, they portray him as someone who cared too much. What kind of twisted rules would demand such severe consequences for an act of kindness? I'm glad I didn't go for the option the angels wanted me to choose. They only know rules—rules that are wrong. They must be, if they caused Ethan's fall for something so pure.

I refrain from voicing these thoughts aloud, not wanting to reopen old wounds or add more salt to them. Instead, I search for the right words, but all I can manage is a quiet, "I'm sorry."

Ethan gives a small nod, but his expression remains unchanged, a mask of practiced calm.

"So you know who his father was?"

"Yes, Ezra. He was the first person I found after my fall." Ethan's eyes light up with a rare flicker of warmth. "I wanted to hurt him, but instead, we became friends. I love that guy. You're gonna love him, too. Not when he's serious, though," he adds, a brief smile breaking through the gravity of our conversation. Before I get a chance to ask more about this Ezra, Ethan points towards a hill about a hundred meters away. "We're almost there."

As we reach the base of the hill, Ethan stops in front of some massive boulders.

"I don't see any entrance," I observe, scanning the rocky surface for any sign of an opening. I half expect—and secretly hope—for doors like those that lead to Moria.

He looks at me with a huge, cocky smile. Moving effortlessly, he approaches one of the massive boulders—easily two or three times my size—and with a swift motion, he pushes it aside.

I stand there, astonished, unable to comprehend the sheer strength he just displayed. The boulder scrapes across the ground with a sound that reverberates through the still night air, revealing a narrow passageway leading into the hill.

Thinking it might be some sort of illusion, I cautiously attempt to push the boulder further, but it remains unmoved.

"Don't worry, on your way out, you'll be able to do that," he tells me while tapping my shoulder.

I don't like being tapped on my shoulder.

Actually, I *hate* it.

Touch my back, touch my arm if you have to, but keep my shoulder alone.

It feels grounding, but in a bad way—like an anchor dragging me down into the depths.

He notices my slight flinch, his eyes narrowing for just a moment as if he senses the shift in my feelings. But he chooses to let it go, redirecting his attention back to the entrance as he steps inside.

As I follow him into the black hollow space, Ethan effortlessly replaces the boulder, effectively sealing me in. The darkness envelops us like a suffocating blanket. I fumble for my phone, the cold device slipping slightly in my clammy hands. Finally, I manage to switch on the flashlight. The narrow beam cuts through the pitch black, revealing multiple corridors stretching out before us. I count seven in total.

Ethan carefully grabs my elbow, pausing as if to gauge my reaction. When I don't respond, he confidently guides me down one of the corridors, despite not having a flashlight himself. It seems his abilities extend beyond mere strength; he navigates the darkness as if it were daylight. The surface beneath my feet is crunchy and uneven, and each step echoes ominously in the confined space.

"Wait, how do you know where to go?"

"I know the way," Ethan replies confidently.

With the narrow beam of my phone's flashlight as my only guide, I can see just a small portion of the cavern at a time. I'm completely reliant on Ethan to navigate through this maze, unsure of how many twists and turns we've already taken or how I would find my way back if left alone.

"This is a very old place," Ethan explains, as if sensing my need for distraction. "Legend has it that it's enchanted—making it impossible for anyone to find their way back if they don't know the path."

Not exactly comforting. Goosebumps rise on my arms, fear creeping in. What if he's wrong? Or worse—what if telling me this legend is a warning, meant to keep me from trying to run? It's not like I could outrun him, but maybe he doesn't want to bother catching me and bringing me further by force. The thought of him leading me here for some nefarious purpose flickers through my mind again. Yabbashael's warning suddenly crashes into my thoughts: *As your guardian angel, my sole desire is for your soul's safety and purity. Your father has fallen for a reason; I have not.*

How could I have been so stupid? Her reasoning for why I should trust her and not my father now seems more logical than ever. Anxiety claws at my chest, making it hard to breathe, but I force myself to keep moving, the ground crackling beneath my feet.

As my foot catches on something, I stumble, nearly falling. I quickly sweep my flashlight to the ground, and my breath freezes in my throat. Skulls—not all of them human—litter the path ahead. Their hollow eye sockets seem to stare up at me, accusingly for disturbing their peace and destroying their forms.

A chill of horror races down my spine, and I struggle to keep my composure. I instantly regret the wish I made; I had hoped for the enchantment of the Doors of Moria, not the grim depths that awaited the Fellowship within.

I can feel Ethan's gaze on me, even though I can't see him through the darkness. His audible sigh suggests he's aware of my fear and discomfort, yet he offers no words of reassurance. Instead, it feels like my unease bothers him, making me feel even more isolated in this eerie place.

"We're almost there," Ethan announces after few more minutes, as though it's meant to reassure me—which it doesn't. Fear grips me, tightening like a vise around my chest, and I can't push aside the worries anymore. Every nerve in my body screams that I should turn and run, but there's nowhere to go. His words replay in my head again and again. *This place is enchanted.* If he wants to kill me, he will.

Finally, Ethan comes to a stop. "Wait here," he instructs me, his voice carrying a harsh edge as if I were nothing but an object to obey. Or perhaps my fear is making my imagination run wild. Who knows?

I watch as he moves a few steps forward and effortlessly shifts another massive rock aside. He disappears into the passage he opened, and moments later, light spills out from within. He emerges from the opening and gestures for me to follow. Switching off my flashlight, I step forward, my heart pounding in my chest as if it's trying to finish me off before someone else can.

chapter 3

OF GOATS AND PAIN

The sight that greets me in the dimly lit chamber is astonishing. It is round in shape, and the first thing that hits me is the heady scent of incense, rich and ancient. The walls are draped in curtains of blue, purple, and scarlet hues, giving the space an ethereal, almost sacred, atmosphere. Small stools are spaced around the perimeter, each adorned with lit candles that flicker and cast dancing shadows across the room.

In the center stands a square wooden altar, its corners adorned with bronze horns that catch the light. Bronze vessels and utensils rest atop it. Behind this altar, a smaller wooden one gleams with a layer of gold, holding various liquids in modern glasses. The blend of ancient and contemporary elements strikes me as both surreal and unsettling.

I glance at Ethan, who is watching me intently, perhaps gauging my reaction. The serene, almost reverent look on his face only heightens my unease. I take a deep breath, trying to steady my nerves, and step further into the chamber, the scent of incense growing stronger and more irritating with each step. Every detail of the room seems designed to overwhelm and awe.

What kind of ritual is about to take place here? And what role will I play in it?

As I approach, my eyes land on a goat tied up behind the altar. A sinking feeling grips my stomach, heavy and foreboding. I turn to Ethan. Suddenly, all the fear I had for my own life evaporates, replaced by a fierce worry for this innocent creature.

"Why is there a goat in here?" I ask, though a part of me dreads the answer.

"It's a necessary sacrifice," he with a cold detachment.

My heart clenches at his words. "You're going to kill it?"

"No, you are," he says seriously, his eyes locked onto mine. Then, after a few excruciating seconds, he bursts into laughter. "No, sorry. You should have seen your face. Don't worry, I'll do it."

"No way," I protest, my voice rising with a mix of panic and anger as if I wasn't afraid of Ethan just a minute ago.

"Pandora, it's part of the ritual," he says as if there's no room for debate.

"I don't care. I don't want any powers or immortality if it comes at the cost of an innocent life," I declare, my conviction solidifying with each word. The thought of such a sacrifice turns my stomach, and I know I'll never budge.

Never.

"It's just a goat," he argues, a smile playing on his lips as if I'm the one who's being unreasonable, even absurd.

I stare at him, my mind racing. The casual way he dismisses the goat's life horrifies me. "I won't be a part of this," I say firmly, taking a step back from the altar. "If this is what it takes to gain powers, then I'd rather remain powerless. It's over." I tip my head toward the exit.

Ethan's smile falters, his lips pressing into a thin line as his brows knit together. He exhales sharply, "People kill thousands of animals every day."

"Yes, and I hate that fact. But somehow I can cope with it knowing it's for survival, mostly. People could actually eat less meat—" I start, but stop myself, realizing this isn't the time for a lecture on vegetarianism. "But that's not important right now. You know what I mean. This is different—it's selfish, it's murder, and the animal would be wasted. I don't want any part of it."

"What if I kill it and then eat it or give it to someone else for meat?"

Automatically, I step between him and the goat, blocking his way just in case, though I know it's futile. He's ten times stronger than I am—no, not ten times, a hundred times. Still, I plant my feet firmly, refusing to budge, even if he challenges me. "Seriously, I just don't want to be the reason for another being to die. I don't want to stand here and watch you kill it. I want out."

"Look, Pandora, I've spent the whole week searching for this place. I went through a lot to gather the information needed to guide us here," he says through gritted teeth. "I had to prepare a special oil made from myrrh, cinnamon, calamus, cassia, and other stuff I don't even remember the names of. Do you know how hard it is to get some of those things? And I had to find the perfect goat. Not just any goat—the *perfect* one. Don't tell me it was all for nothing," he sighs.

"Had I known, I would have told you not to bother."

"We have two minutes before the sun sets completely. In that moment, I'm killing the goat, and you are going to accept the powers. If you don't, then its death will truly be a waste." He plays his cards well, capitalizing on my reluctance to waste the animal. He is as stubborn as I am.

"If you do this, you will lose me anyway," I say roughly, though my eyes plead desperately. Animal lives are one of the most important things to me. The thought of this innocent creature being slaughtered tears at my heart.

But he ignores me, trying to go past, but I shift, blocking his path again, determined not to let him through. Without a word, he pauses, then leans down and, with effortless strength, picks me up as if I weigh nothing more than a feather. The gentleness of the gesture contrasts sharply with the gravity of the moment. He places me aside with ease, never breaking his stride, then bends to pick up the goat, checking the time as if my defiance were an inconsequential detail in his mission.

My breath catches in my throat as I watch him. The room seems to close in on me, the scent of incense now suffocating. The goat's wide, frightened eyes flash before me, amplifying my sense of dread.

Suddenly, a tall figure looms behind Ethan, casting a long

shadow that stretches across the chamber.

"Don't kill the goat!" a voice suddenly shouts.

Ethan spins around, his eyes as wide as the goat's. "Ezra? What are you doing here?"

The newcomer steps into view—a tall, muscular figure with dark eyes and the same chiseled features. He could almost be Ethan's mirror; the resemblance is uncanny.

Wait, did he say Ezra? As in the fallen angel who refused to give his powers to his Nephilim son?

"I tried to call you, but it didn't go through. I was afraid I wouldn't get here in time. There were some kids in front of the cave, and I had to make them leave before I opened the passage. It took longer than expected," Ezra explains.

A deep line forms between Ethan's eyes. "In time for what?"

"In time to stop you from killing the goat," Ezra laughs. "It was... well, it was a joke. The whole ritual... all you need to do is ask whether she will assume her Nephilim powers, and she just needs to accept. Anywhere, anytime," he continues, still laughing. "I was just hoping you wouldn't have killed the poor animal before I could get here."

I stare at them, my mind swirling in a whirlwind of confusion. These past weeks have been an onslaught of new information, leaving me struggling to process it all. And now, faced with what feels like a bizarre joke from an alleged fallen angel, my thoughts spiral into chaos.

Nothing makes sense. What should I make of them? What should I make of myself? Am I really just a fool, believing in these supposed supernatural beings? My gaze shifts to the boulder at the entrance of the chamber, wondering if even that was part of some elaborate trick. My pulse quickens, a cold sweat breaking out on my forehead. A supernatural being, a former angel, wouldn't make such bad jokes—would they? In my mind, they hold a kind of grace, elegance, and wisdom, even if they are fallen. They are still ancient and powerful.

"You think this is funny?" Ethan's voice is low, laced with a dangerous edge.

"Well, yeah. Kind of. A lot, actually. The picture of a fallen angel performing a ritual sacrificing an animal to God in his own house is hilarious," Ezra almost chokes on a chuckle, seemingly unfazed by Ethan's growing anger. At least it seems all of this is not a joke on me and they too believe they are fallen angels. We might all be crazy though.

Ethan steps closer to Ezra, his jaw tightening, his fists clenching at his sides. His movements are slow, deliberate, as if each step carries the weight of barely contained anger. There's no trace of humor in his eyes, only a cold, hard glare that makes my blood run cold.

"Whoa, calm down, my friend. I gave myself a good laugh, but now I'm here to tell you what you need to do." Ezra's tone is light but cautious, trying to defuse the tension.

Ethan huffs, shaking his head slightly. "All of this just to give yourself a good laugh? You must really be bored." I had thought Ethan said I would like Ezra's fun side, but his humor doesn't amuse me, nor does it seem to amuse Ethan himself.

Ezra's tone shifts to serious, his face devoid of any traces of laughter or even a hint of a smile. "You, better than anyone, know how I feel about giving a Nephilim their—our powers. Immortality is a punishment, not a gift. I wanted to give her more time to think about it. You've rushed her enough to make a decision. Maybe I also wanted to give some time to your beloved Yabbashael to persuade her not to do this. To be honest, I was hoping she would get through to her." Ezra looks at me pensively, then turns back to Ethan. "I know you don't want to hear this, Ethan, but I just wanted to help keep her soul as it is, let her have her happy afterlife we could never have."

"And there it is, his serious side," Ethan retorts, annoyed, but his fists finally unclench.

Ezra turns his gaze towards me again and continues, ignoring Ethan's remark, "But if you have already decided this is what you want to do, then I won't try to stop you. That is why I came. You have free will, both of you, do what you want and I will help you."

He redirects his attention back to Ethan. "I will always help you, my friend, with *anything*."

When he speaks, Ezra sounds a lot like an angel, like Yabbashael. Unlike Ethan, he exudes a calm patience, untainted by impulsive desires. Yet, he supports Ethan despite their differences. I can't help but wonder what they must have been through together to forge such a bond. But their intense gazes lock onto me, and the pressure of their stares makes my skin prickle.

"I already made up my mind," I announce, my voice steady despite the turmoil inside.

Ethan checks the time again, a nervous habit perhaps, even though Ezra had insisted that time held no significance in this ritual. He turns to me, his eyes piercing through the dim light.

"Do you accept your Nephilim powers, Pandora, my daughter?" he asks, his tone oddly formal.

This is it.

This moment feels like the fulcrum on which my entire destiny balances. After days of relentless contemplation, I am resolute. The thought of eternity, watching loved ones age and die while I remain unchanged, gnaws at my heart. But the desire for strength and power drives me forward.

Perhaps it's my origin, the blood of a fallen angel coursing through my veins, that's pushing me to embrace my true self. From the moment I got the offer, I felt its allure like a siren's call, impossible to resist. Maybe all of the decision-making wasn't even real, and the sole desire to unlock my full potential has been guiding me all along, an intrinsic part of my very being.

"I accept my powers," I declare, my voice echoing through the chamber, sealing my fate.

Ethan's lips curl into a satisfied smile, his eyes gleaming with approval. We exchange a meaningful look, but still, I feel no immediate change.

"Did it work?" Ethan asks, his voice breaking the short silence, laced with both hope and doubt.

"I don't know. Maybe we should try killing her. If she survives, we'll know it worked," suggests Ezra, a wry smile tugging at his lips. I just hope he's kidding.

Ethan's eyes flash with irritation. "You're full of good jokes today, aren't you?"

I glance between them, the gravity of my decision sinking deeper into my bones. Adrenaline courses through me, mingling with the remnants of fear and anticipation for what's to come—if anything even does. Each second stretches into an eternity, and I wonder if this is what infinity feels like—an endless wait for something monumental, something life-changing.

But nothing life-changing will ever come again, not after this. After one or two lifetimes, everything will blur into sameness. Why am I only realizing this now, when it's too late?

Finally, an unfamiliar force surges through me, igniting a searing heat that intensifies with each passing moment. The heat pulses through my veins like molten lava, rendering me weak and helpless.

Collapsing to my knees, I'm engulfed by the relentless agony coursing through my body. My mouth opens in a silent scream, but I can't make a sound, as I can barely breathe. The air feels like an iceberg sliding down my throat and lungs, cutting them open. My skin feels like it's blistering from within. I try to cry, but my body is so hot that the tears evaporate before they even reach my cheeks.

I glimpse Ethan's futile attempt to approach me, halted by Ezra's restraining grip. Their figures soon blur, swallowed by the overwhelming intensity of the inferno consuming me. The world around me fades, leaving only the searing pain and the pounding of my heart in my ears.

Desperation overtakes me. With trembling hands, I claw at my eyes, removing my contact lenses in a frantic bid for relief. But even this does nothing to alleviate the burning. My vision swims with tears that never fall. And as if the pain wasn't enough, a high-pitched ringing starts in my ears, drowning out all other sounds.

Every muscle in my body seizes in spasms, locking me in a vice of torment.

Time loses all meaning as I am adrift in a sea of agony.

I was wrong. This is eternity.

chapter 4

WHISPERS OF DESTINY

I cautiously inhale, bracing myself for the familiar torment to flare up once more, but instead, the lingering scent of incense fills my lungs, soothing rather than searing.

Slowly, I open my eyes. The soft candlelight bathes the room in a warm, golden glow, revealing the intricate details of the chamber. Delicate patterns of flowers adorn the curtains, their woven petals swaying gently in the unseen breeze as if alive. Etchings carved into the wooden altar catch my eye, the ancient script whispering secrets of the past.

"Are you okay?" a voice breaks through my awakening.

I turn my gaze to Ezra as he leans to get a better look at me, and for a moment, I'm caught by the subtle green hue of his eyes, a color that seems to shift with the light. His expression is laced with concern, yet there's a glimmer of relief in his eyes.

Beside him, Ethan watches me intently, his raised eyebrows betraying a worry. The confident demeanor he usually wears like armor has slipped, revealing an uncharacteristic vulnerability, though ever so slight. The memory of his earlier question surfaces, and I feel a knot tighten in my throat as I struggle to find my voice.

"I think so," I mean to whisper, but the words come out louder, more forceful than I intended, resonating through the chamber. It surprises me—not just the volume but the firmness in my tone, mirroring the newfound strength coursing through me.

As they help me to my feet, I'm struck by the sudden absence of pain, as if it has been completely swept away, leaving behind an unexpected surge of strength and vitality.

With each steady step I take, the weight of the ordeal begins to lift, replaced by a growing resilience that feels both new and empowering. It's as though I've shed an old layer of myself, emerging renewed and stronger than before.

The sound of rustling wings fills the chamber, and red curls shimmer in the dim light as Yabbashael appears before us, her usually radiant presence dimmed by an aura of exhaustion. Her ethereal glow is dulled, shadows playing across her features, highlighting her fatigue.

"Why would you do that?" Her question is directed not at me, but at Ethan, her tone tinged with reproach. Her stance is steady, but there's a subtle slump in her shoulders, as if resignation has quietly settled in. Her expression remains composed, though her fingers briefly tighten at her sides.

Ethan meets her gaze with a tender expression, his eyes softening. "Leave, before you fall," he says gently.

She holds his gaze, her breath subtly hitching, before turning to me. Her eyes search mine, calm yet full of unspoken sorrow. I meet her stare with a silent plea for understanding and forgiveness, my heart aching for her approval as if she were an important figure in my life.

I've only known about her existence for a few weeks, yet somehow, I felt her presence my whole life. I hadn't realized it until now, when the bond is gone, broken, and for the first time, I know what it's like to be truly alone. Even with people around. Even with her here and now. Because I know she'll leave.

Her face remains impassive, but the weariness is etched in the subtle lines around her eyes. The silence between us is thick with things left unsaid, and it's clear she feels the loss too.

Without uttering another word, she spreads her wings, each feather like a small flourishing garden, beautiful and intricate. She disappears into the shadows of the chamber, leaving behind a bitter sense of melancholy.

She's gone.

Never to return, not without the presence of one of her charges. And I am no longer one of them. Those are the rules.

Being left alone by my now former guardian angel, a sense of emptiness settles over me. It's like a small heartbreak, an unexpected void where her comforting presence once was.

Doubts begin to creep in, whispering uncertainties about the path I've chosen. I can't help but wonder what my next step should be. The fear of the unknown tightens around my chest, and I feel on the brink of panic.

But before I can delve deeper into my nervous thoughts, Ezra pulls me back to the present. "We haven't been officially introduced." He extends his hand with a warm smile. "I'm Ezra."

"Dora," I respond, taking his hand.

"You prefer to be called Dora rather than Pandora?" Ezra asks as if he preferred the latter.

"Well, Dora's my name. I don't know why Ethan calls me Pandora, I thought he was just teasing me," I explain.

"What? That's not possible," Ethan blurts out. His brow furrows, and his eyes narrow, flicking back and forth as if he's trying to connect invisible dots but failing.

I arch my brows, refraining from voicing the obvious question. "After your birth, I visited your mother and you in the hospital. I... 'persuaded' your mother to give you the name Pandora," Ethan says.

"Oh, God. This obsession with names again," I mutter under my breath. "Well, she didn't—" I begin, but Ezra cuts me off, his jaw tightening.

"So you gave her the name; it wasn't her parents' idea," Ezra concludes, sounding almost cryptic.

"Yes, I knew it was her true name when she was born," Ethan adds, his tone matter-of-fact, yet layered with an undertone of significance.

Placing my hands on my hips, I ask, "What do you mean, true name?" This is starting to sound too serious, too destiny-like. All I want is to be a stronger version of myself, a super-Dora, nothing else. Just a girl who means nothing, but can now do great things to protect humans from malevolent forces. Like Sam and Dean Winchester, only stronger—and without the dying-over-and-over part.

"When a baby is born, I can kind of feel its... purpose in the world, and I know the right name that reflects that," Ethan explains, his eyes distant, as if recalling countless moments like that.

Oh great, he really is talking about a purpose in the world. I don't want any purpose. If it's a bad one, I'll be sad. If it's a good one, it will be an enormous pressure to fulfill it. And the idea of having a predestined role alone makes my stomach twist.

Avoiding the important question, I focus on the first thing that comes to mind, "Is it like an angel or a fallen angel superpower?"

"No," he shakes his head. "It's a gift, my gift since the beginning of my existence."

"Beginning of existence... so you're not born?"

Ethan rolls his eyes and sighs.

Devoid of fresh ideas and finding my distractions ineffective, I ask the inevitable question at last, my nerves tingling as if on high alert. "So what does my name reflect?"

Ethan and Ezra exchange a look that seems to convey a thousand unspoken words. The suspense is almost unbearable. I can feel my pulse quickening. What if my name holds a destiny I'm not ready for? What if it's something I can't escape? I was only barely ready for one change tonight.

Ethan takes a deep breath, his eyes locking onto mine with a gravity that sends another shiver down my spine. "When I first saw you, I knew you'd be a great person. I knew you'd release hope," he begins, his tone heavy with significance. But he doesn't smile, and I sense there's more—something I don't want to hear. After a short pause, he adds, "But also, misery."

The words linger in the air, thick and suffocating, pressing down on me. I feel the usual knot tightening in my stomach—dread—but I quickly remind myself of what I became today, and I fight it with resolve. Whatever this so-called destiny is, I'll face it. I have to.

But a cold truth seeps in, one I can't shake: the life and choices I thought were mine now feel like the scenario in a book that's already been written. Does this mean that nothing we do matters? Is everything about the future already determined?

"What does that even mean? What's going to happen?" I ask, my voice taut.

Ethan looks at me, his expression softening, though his eyes still hold that unreadable depth. "I don't know, really. I just had this feeling; I can't explain it. I don't know the future. I don't think there *is* a set future. It's just a possibility. Don't worry about it, Pandora."

"Stop calling me that!" I snap, the name tightening around me like a chain, choking me with every utterance. I don't want this destiny. I want to make my own future, my own choices, my own life. And my own damn name.

"But—"

I square my shoulders, feeling a spark of defiance ignite within me. "No, I don't care what you felt. My name is Dora, period," I assert, my voice steadying as I reclaim a piece of myself. This is my life, my identity. I won't let some prophecy dictate who I am.

He said not to worry about it, so that's exactly what I'm going to do. Apparently, he doesn't know what my future holds either—it was just a feeling. That could mean a lot of things, and most of them might not be as bad as they sound. I don't need to be pulled toward the worst of them by being called a name that isn't truly mine. Maybe there's a reason my mom resisted his urge to name me Pandora. Maybe Ethan was wrong when he 'saw my purpose' or whatever. I may not control my destiny, but I control my name—my sense of self. For now, that has to be enough.

"Let's get out of here," Ezra suggests, untying the goat with a gentle touch. Its soft bleat breaks the tension in the air, grounding us back to the present.

After Ethan and I extinguish the candles, their smoke curling upward like whispers of the past—or perhaps warnings of the future—we head out, with Ezra leading the goat alongside us.

"So, what's going to happen now?"

"Now, you're gonna go home and rest while I get rid of the goat," Ethan replies casually.

I shoot him an angry glance.

"And by 'get rid of,' I mean return it to the guy I bought it from," he quickly corrects himself, raising his hands in a gesture of peace.

"Don't think for a second that I'm not furious with you for wanting to kill it as a sacrifice..." My mind flashes back to the fear that clawed at me earlier, before I got scared for the goat's life, when I thought I might be the one offered up tonight. I take a steadying breath, my voice quieter but firmer as I add, "At least from now on, I know I'm off the table."

"You know, death isn't something to fear," Ethan says casually, as if he wasn't the one who persuaded me to give up my own mortality. "Life isn't as important—the souls are better off in the afterlife."

My mouth falls open, disbelief crashing over me. Is he serious?

"I thought all those talks about the afterlife being the soul's salvation were just exaggerations! You actually believe that?" My voice rises with each word as the absurdity sinks in. "Then why did you push me to accept my powers? Why make me give up my mortality?"

"It's not the same thing. Afterlife in heaven or hell is meant for humans; there is nothing better for them in this world than ascension, living as souls without bodies. Humans are fragile and afraid of death their whole lives. They need to be protected so that demons don't steal their souls. But Nephilim—you—can actually achieve so much more."

He pauses, drawing a deep, almost dramatic breath. "When you accept immortality, demons won't be able to take your soul. You don't need to be afraid of a burglar killing you, of being hit by a car or getting cancer. You can exist without such fears that make humans miserable and bad."

Ethan's gaze shifts to the ground, his shoulders tensing as he continues. "I wasn't planning on having a child, and after I realized what I'd done and saw your mother pregnant, I still wasn't planning on giving you the powers. But then you were born, and I felt it. I knew what you had to become to fulfill your purpose."

Oh, here we go with my purpose again. If he felt I'd cause misery, why would he want me to fulfill this so-called destiny?

It's all so overwhelming. I can't even begin to process everything that's happened in the past few hours—the revelations, the rituals, the talk of powers and destinies. It's too much to take in at once. Wrapping my arms around myself, I try to hold on to some semblance of control as the world tilts beneath my feet.

I need time. Time to sort through it all, to make sense of it. Maybe rest will help. I nod slowly, more to myself than to anyone else. Yes, a good night's sleep to clear my head and gain some perspective.

"By the way, did you notice?" Ethan interjects, his voice carrying a hint of excitement that slices through the fog of my thoughts.

"Huh?"

"We're not using any flashlight," he points out, a wide smile spreading across his face which I can actually see.

"Oh my God, you're right. I didn't even realize I could see perfectly in the dark!" For the first time since the excruciating pain of accepting my powers and discovering a strange, unknown purpose in life, I actually feel a spark of enthusiasm.

I've been walking without any light or contact lenses this whole time, ever since we left the chamber, and I didn't even notice. This is awesome. My vision is sharp, every detail clear despite the absence of light. The walls of the cave, the uneven ground, all the different skulls, even the subtle expressions on Ethan's face—all of it is as clear as day.

As we approach the concealed entrance hidden behind the imposing boulder, Ethan and Ezra motion for me to be the one to move it aside. Instantly, a wave of nervousness washes over me. What if I fail? What if I'm not as strong as they expect me to be? Will they laugh? Leave me here until I manage to do it myself?

"Come on, Dora," Ezra urges, shifting impatiently from foot to foot with the goat's lead in his hand.

I take a deep breath, trying to steel myself against the mounting pressure. With hesitant steps, I approach the boulder, silently pleading with myself to succeed. I place my hands on the rough surface, feeling the cold stone beneath my fingers. Leaning against it, I push with all my might, the weight of the rock resisting my efforts.

My muscles strain and my heart races, but I refuse to give up. Then, centimeter by centimeter, the boulder begins to yield to my determination. Sweat beads on my forehead as I pour every ounce of strength into the task. Thirty seconds feel like an eternity as I persevere, pushing until finally, with a triumphant heave, the boulder shifts, allowing us passage.

Breathless and trembling, I step back, my lips curling up. I glance at Ethan and Ezra, their faces lighting up with genuine smiles, their eyes shining with pride.

"See, you did it," Ethan says, his hand aiming for my shoulder before quickly landing on my arm, where it rests reassuringly.

"Yeah, but it was so hard," I murmur, feeling a bit embarrassed at how long it took me compared to how easily he did it before.

"You will get stronger as the years pass," Ethan assures me.

I follow them out into the open air as Ethan pushes the boulder back into place, sparing me the effort, likely sensing that I need to regain my strength. A gentle breeze brushes against my skin, soothing the lingering tension from the cave. It feels as though the weight of everything inside is already fading, becoming an old, distant memory—almost as if we had never entered at all.

Ezra claps his hands together, as if sealing the decision. "Now, let's go home."

I pause in my tracks, a sudden impulse, my inner child, seizing me. "Can I play with the goat for a while?" I blurt out, surprising even myself with the request. I just can't resist the little creature's innocent eyes and gentle bleats. I just love animals so much.

Ethan tilts his head, a smirk forming as he turns back to me, barely choking back a laugh. "You want to play with the goat?" he repeats, drawing out the words.

I nod eagerly, a broad smile tugging at the corners of my lips. The simple desire to connect with something pure and uncomplicated feels like a balm to my frazzled nerves.

A moment of hesitation passes before Ethan's features soften, his disbelief fading into reluctant amusement. "Alright, but only for a few minutes," he sighs, shaking his head with a resigned smile. "I feel like I've gotten myself into a different stage of parenthood than I ever planned."

I laugh softly as the goat nuzzles my hand, its gentle affection offering a brief moment of calm after the intensity of the day.

As I step into the comforting embrace of my home, Cerberus, or Berry for short, my ten-kilogram black-and-white feline friend, greets me with a cautious approach, his eyes wide and wary as he peers out from under the furniture.

With a soft sigh, I lower myself to the floor, coaxing him out from his hiding spot beneath the bed. "What's wrong, Berry? It's me," I reassure him with my familiar voice, but even I can hear the different edge it carries now. Slowly, he comes closer, his nose twitching as he sniffs tentatively at my hand. He's a cat, he can never resist to smell an outstretched finger. Finally, he nuzzles against my nose with a gentle lick.

"Sorry I left you alone for so long, buddy," I murmur, burying my face in his fur. "It's been a crazy day."

Berry seems to understand, his purring growing louder as he rubs his head against my cheek. His soft fur and rhythmic purring create a cocoon of comfort around me, easing the day's tension.

Climbing into bed, I find myself longing for the solace of Ben's embrace, his absence keenly felt in the quiet of the room. We've been seeing each other for just about two weeks, but I'm head over heels for him.

Though there's nothing special about him at first sight—he's of average height, with light brown or maybe even blond hair—one look at his cute smile makes me lose myself. His eyes, though, are what captivate me the most. There's something different about them, something more, something mysterious. It's as if he knows much more than anyone else, yet he's too modest to let it show. He carries a wisdom beyond his years, even though he looks younger than his claimed 27 years. I wouldn't be surprised if he was truly somewhere between 20 to 25. Despite his maturity, he radiates a positive and fun energy that makes him incredibly magnetic.

Unfortunately, he lives in a different town, making our

moments together rare and precious. The distance means I can't see him every day, or every night.

And so I close my eyes, allowing my mind to drift into the realm of imagination, where his comforting arms await me. In my thoughts, I can almost feel the warmth of his embrace and the steady rhythm of his heartbeat against my cheek.

chapter 5

EMERGING POWERS

I look around, taking in the serene landscape. Dozens of sheep with fluffy white coats dot the lush, green pastures, their soft bleats blending with the whisper of the wind. The sky above is a clear, endless blue, stretching out to meet the horizon.

As I gaze across the expansive fields, my eyes fixate on the distant sight of a solitary wooden house, its weathered facade standing in contrast to the vibrant greenery.

Just as I take a few purposeful steps forward, the grass crunching softly underfoot, a firm grip seizes my arm from behind, halting my progress.

"What are you doing here?"

As I turn around to face the familiar voice, I'm met with the sight of Ben standing in front of the house I'd been watching from afar just a second ago. His sudden presence feels both comforting and disorienting, even a bit grim as I find the gravestone next to him, bearing the word "Anushtan."

"What are you doing here?" he repeats his question in a serious tone, but his lips twitch before eventually curling into a warm smile.

"I'm not sure," I admit, glancing around the unfamiliar surroundings.

But as I stare into his calm, sky-blue eyes, I can't help but return his contagious smile. I remember the last time I looked into them—it was right before he left for a meeting.

"How did the meeting go?" I ask him while heading to the house without thinking, as if pulled by some invisible thread, as if I'm not in control of my movements at all.

As I push the door open, I step into a small apartment cluttered with boxes, the scent of dust and cardboard filling the air. Ben follows close behind, the wooden floor creaking softly under his weight.

"It went well actually. I've been offered a job. I'm moving next week, so you'll be seeing much more of me from now on." His smile stretches wider, his eyes sparkle, the news clearly lighting a fire within him.

Mirroring Ben's infectious smile, I exclaim, "Really? That's great!" I was afraid he'd get sick of riding the bus for an hour every time just to see me, and break it off before it could become serious between us. Now, if he ever tires of me, it will be because of who I am, not the distance between us. The thought is both comforting and terrifying. Let's hope that doesn't happen.

A sudden impulse to kiss him overtakes me. I lick my lower lip, my feet almost moving on their own as I lean in, but lingering insecurities hold me back. I hesitate, still too self-conscious to be sure it's what he'd want. What if he doesn't like me anymore and decides to move away if I lean in? What if he's already changed his mind about me and I'm mistaking friendliness and politeness for affection? Maybe moving to my town will force him to take a step back, so I don't get any wrong ideas.

No, I can't initiate a kiss yet. I need it to come from him so that, at least for one day, I can be sure it's what he wants. That I'm what he wants. That's just who I am—a tangled knot of insecurities.

However, as I contemplate the possibility of his kiss, a sudden wave of confusion washes over me as I glance around. I don't recognize this place. And what is Ben doing here, wherever here is? He's supposed to be away in another town.

The absurdity of the situation finally dawns on me, leaving me grappling with the unsettling feeling that nothing here makes sense.

As I connect the dots, the surreal nature of the situation becomes undeniable. First, the gravestone with its cryptic inscription, the distant house I reached in a blink of an eye, and now this unfamiliar apartment with its alien surroundings. It's as if the fabric of reality itself is unraveling before my eyes, each thread dissolving into the bizarre. This has to be a dream. Nothing else could explain the twisting logic and fluid transitions of this world.

I glance out the window and confirm my suspicions—the

bustling cityscape outside is a far cry from the pastoral scene I encountered mere moments ago.

But for the first time in my life, despite realizing I'm dreaming, I don't wake up. Instead of being pulled from this strange reality, I remain within it, fully aware.

My heart flutters with excitement. In this dream world, born from the depths of my imagination, anything is possible and without consequences. The boundaries of reality no longer constrain me; I can shape and mold this realm to my will.

I can do anything.

Encouraged by the realization that I hold the reins in this surreal realm, I decide to seize the moment. Closing the distance between us, I wrap my arms around Ben's neck, savoring the warmth of his body, the smell of his hair, the depth of his eyes. This dream feels vividly real. More real than any other dream I've ever had.

I lean in, my lips meeting his in a slow, deliberate kiss. The softness of his mouth envelops me, each second stretching out as I lose myself in the sensation. His hand slides down to my waist, moving lower until he grips my butt, pulling me against him. The contact sparks something deeper, a boldness I've never felt before, as my insecurities melt away. In this dream world, nothing holds me back.

A sharp pain jolts me awake.

I blink rapidly, disoriented, and find Berry perched on my chest, his claws kneading my face with insistent precision.

"Nooo," I groan, the remnants of the dream slipping away like sand through my fingers. "Thanks a lot, Berry," I mutter, rubbing my eyes and gently pushing him away. Ben's arms vanish, the excitement evaporating into the cold reality of my bedroom.

I let out a heavy sigh, sinking deeper into the bed as if trying to bury myself beneath the covers, willing the dream to come back. My fingers curl into the sheets where his touch once lingered, but there's nothing. Frustration wells up, an ache spreading in my chest as I stare at the ceiling, the emptiness of the room swallowing the remnants of the beautiful dream. I had hoped to squeeze much more from it.

Berry rubs against my leg, his soft fur brushing my skin as his wide eyes lock onto mine. He lets out a low, drawn-out meow, his gaze almost pleading, tail flicking impatiently as he pads toward his empty bowl.

"You'll have to wait," I mutter. "You can't keep waking me up and get away with it." I roll over, trying to fall back asleep, clinging to the hope of reentering the dream. But just as I begin to drift off, a loud beep from my phone shatters the silence. I always forget to set it to night mode.

Groggily, I reach for my phone, squinting at the screen. But as soon as I see Ben's name, any remnants of sleep are gone. I roll onto my stomach, propping myself up on my elbows, a smile spreading across my face. My eyes snap open, fully alert now. His message reads: "I just had a dream about you." Curiosity surges through me. I quickly type back, asking him to describe it. His reply comes almost instantly: "...well, it was a very, veery nice dream!" A winking emoji follows, and I can't help but grin wider.

The implication is clear—his dream matches mine. The connection between us feels even stronger, and despite the rude awakening, a sense of comfort and happiness fills me. Excitement bubbles up inside me, making it impossible to stay still. Even though Berry doesn't deserve a reward for waking me and I know he's not starving, I jump out of bed and feed him anyway.

After a few texts laced with innuendo, his tone shifts, and he reveals that he's relocating to my town for a new job. I freeze at the message. That's exactly what he told me in the dream. How could I have known? Could my dreams be more than random images?

It's probably just a coincidence. But it feels too uncanny, too perfectly aligned with reality to dismiss. I didn't even know he was looking for a new job; all I knew was that he had some kind of work meeting in my town the day before.

I frown, the phone suddenly feeling heavier in my hand as I reread his message. Then my gaze shifts as I remember the gravestone I'd noticed in the dream, with the word 'Anushtan' engraved. Could that mean something too? I type the name into a search bar, watching as the letters fill the screen. A result pops up: just a name.

I tilt my head, a deep furrow forming between my brows. That's it? It feels like there should be more—like the name should mean something important. Weird. How could I dream of something so specific and unfamiliar? Is my subconscious mind trying to tell me something? But what?

I'm probably reading too much into this. It was just a dream. Nothing more. And the fact that it matched Ben's message is likely just the result of my overactive imagination and sharp perception.

I pick up my phone again, fingers tapping nervously as I dial Ethan's number. He answers after the first beep. "Hey, Pandora, I was just about to call you."

"Hi. Can we meet? And it's Dora," I assert.

"Of course. Time to start your training. Come over, I'll show you my place—you're gonna love it."

chapter 6

THE OTHER SIDE OF DARKNESS

I drive to Ethan's house, situated on the outskirts of town. After a few attempts, I manage to park my car in a place that's a little further down the road, worried that spots closer to his place might already be full. Feeling a small sense of victory, I walk the remaining ten minutes to his house.

Soon, I arrive at my destination, where a grand, white mansion stands before me—well, maybe not a mansion, but it certainly gives off that impression. The house exudes an air of antiquity, as if it belongs to a wealthy and esteemed family. With its two stories, towering front porch columns, and a balcony spanning its entire length, it commands attention and respect.

This is not quite what I expected. This house doesn't exactly scream 'fallen angel'. A bunker, maybe. Honestly, a cave wouldn't have surprised me.

Ascending the steps, I approach the massive door, searching in vain for a doorbell. Just as I'm about to use the old door clapper, my phone buzzes with a text from Ethan: "Come in."

I push open the heavy door and step inside.

The interior matches the opulence of the outside of the house. My eyes are immediately drawn to the magnificent staircase in the center of the hall, its banisters intricately carved and gleaming in the sunlight streaming through the enormous glass windows. The air smells faintly of polished wood and old books.

The entry hall leads into what appears to be an expansive library on the right, rows of bookshelves filled with volumes that hint at a lifetime of secrets. The door on the left remains closed, hiding whatever mysteries lie behind it.

Before I can explore further, Ethan enters the hall, his presence immediately drawing my attention. His eyes sparkle with a mix of anticipation and satisfaction, as if he's been waiting for this moment for a long time.

"Welcome home, Dora," he says warmly, stretching out his arms before quickly pulling them back to his sides.

"It's Do-," I start to correct him out of habit, but then I realize he actually called me Dora for once. I guess he's really trying to play nice today. "Thank you. So this is your house?"

"Indeed. I'll give you a proper tour another time. But for now, Ezra is waiting downstairs. Let's go."

"What's downstairs?"

"You'll see." He replies mysteriously, leading the way to a door I hadn't noticed before. Curiosity piqued, I follow closely behind.

"How can you afford a house like this? Do you even have a job?" I ask, shaking my head in disbelief as I glance around the luxurious surroundings.

"Well, I know how and where to invest money." He shrugs, a casual grin tugging at the corners of his mouth, but the mischief in his eyes betrays him, hinting there's more to the story than he's letting on.

I get it. With abilities like his, manipulating the stock market or influencing wealthy investors must have been child's play. "And how did you get the money to invest in the first place?"

"I worked. Hard," he replies simply, though I can't tell if he's being serious or just growing bored with my endless questions.

"Oh, of course, you worked hard," I backtrack, realizing I may have sounded harsh.

Ethan pauses, a flicker of amusement in his eyes as if deciding this story is worth sharing. "I was kind of like... Robin Hood, you know? Stealing from the rich what they didn't need."

"And giving it to the poor?" I raise an eyebrow, my voice dripping with doubt as I cross my arms.

"Yeah... sometimes," he says, a ghost of a smile playing on his lips. His casual admission confirms my suspicions. It seems my initial impression of him was correct; he is no hero.

He leads me down a narrow, spiraling staircase. The walls curve tightly around us, as though the very structure is closing in. The further we descend, the darker and more oppressive the air becomes, until we reach—well, I don't even know what to call it.

The space is filled with a variety of workout equipment and an array of weapons: shields, spears, swords, and other items I can't even name. As I take in the expansive surroundings, it becomes clear that much of this enormous area is empty. Absolutely empty. It could easily accommodate a basketball court, tennis court, or virtually any other court. Curiously, half of it is filled with sand. Maybe for beach volleyball. But why is there no net? Adding to the peculiarity, there's a bar stocked with alcohol on the side.

The scent of sweat mingles with the aroma of wood polish from the bar, and the hum of a refrigerator stocked with drinks fills the air. A flickering neon sign over the counter casts dancing shadows, creating an atmosphere of both relaxation and tension. The bizarre combination of elements makes me feel as though I've stepped into some kind of warrior's playground.

As my gaze wanders, I finally notice Ezra seated on a bar stool, nursing a drink—despite the early hour. Behind the bar stands a girl, unremarkable in appearance, serving him. She is of average height, with blond hair that falls somewhere between long and short. She's neither strikingly beautiful nor unattractive—just ordinary. Yet, there's something about her that seems slightly off, as if she doesn't quite belong here. It's becoming clear that normalcy is not a trait to expect in this place.

Ethan nudges me forward, and the girl's lips curve into a small smile. She steps lightly around the bar, her movements unhurried and graceful, as if the world moves at her pace. Extending her hand, her gaze holds mine—steady, yet warm. "Hi, I'm Marvedeme."

"Dora, nice to meet you," I reply, shaking her hand before

turning to greet Ezra.

"Do you want a drink, Dora?" Marvedeme asks.

"I'm supposed to be training," I decline.

"One little drink," she insists with a playful wink, her smile making it hard to refuse.

I don't want to offend her, but I really need to stay focused. The last thing I want is to make a fool of myself in front of everyone. I'm well aware of my limitations. "Thank you, but my tolerance for alcohol isn't very high."

The room buzzes with their laughter, light and infectious, spilling over like an inside joke. Ethan leans in, a grin tugging at the corner of his mouth. "I bet that changed."

"Well then, maybe just one," I give up.

"What would you like?" Marvedeme asks, gesturing to the well-stocked bar.

"Something... sweet?" I say, uncertain about the options.

"I'll whip up something special for you," she promises with a smile, deftly selecting bottles.

"So, you keep a bartender down here?" I quip, turning to Ethan.

"No." He chuckles. "I can mix my own drinks. We just like hanging out here. Marve is Ezra's girlfriend, and she enjoys playing bartender."

Ezra's girlfriend. Interesting. I wouldn't expect Ezra to have a human girlfriend, and she doesn't look like an angel either—all the angels I've seen so far have a sort of Elvish quality, with soft yet sharp features and ears that, though not pointy, give an ethereal impression—so I don't think she is fallen or Nephilim. "I don't mean to be rude, but..." I pause, choosing my words carefully. "What exactly are you, Marve?"

Their eyes flick to each other, brows knitting ever so slightly. One shifts on their feet, the other's lips parting as if to speak, but they hesitate to share the truth with me.

"I'm a demon," Marvedeme declares, her voice unwavering. She holds my gaze, but her fingers tighten ever so slightly around the edge of the bar. A fleeting twinkle dances in her eyes—a tiny crack in her composed facade.

"A demon," I repeat, the word heavy on my tongue. I release a loud sigh, my gaze snapping to Ethan. My brows shoot up, silently demanding an explanation. Memories of his warning flood my mind—demons, soul-devourers, the worst of the worst. I swallow hard, stealing a glance at Marvedeme. He warned me that they are creatures I should never wish to cross paths with. How could he hang out with one?

Ethan raises his hands defensively, palms out, as if fending off an unseen blow. His eyes dart to mine, wide with the urgency of someone bracing for a verbal barrage. "She's not like the demons you've heard of," he says, his voice firm but with a trace of pleading. "She doesn't kill for pleasure, and she doesn't take orders from anyone." His gaze flickers to Marve, slowly winking with both eyes—a silent apology for my unspoken accusation.

Though it does make her sound better, it doesn't change her nature. "But what does she live off of?" I demand.

Ezra steps forward, his expression tightening with irritation at having to defend his girlfriend to me, the newcomer. "She sustains herself on souls, yes," he admits, his tone grudging, "but a single soul can sustain her for a human lifetime. She doesn't consume more than necessary to survive. This limits her strength, but it keeps her alive."

"But they're human souls! How can you, former angels, not care about that?" The accusation spills out before I can stop it. Yabbashael made it clear, in the short time we had after my ability to see angels awakened—souls are the only thing that truly matters. Their fate is everything. What happens to humans in life means little, as long as the soul remains untouched. And Ezra had me believed he cared about that too.

I know it's probably not smart to challenge one of their own my first time in their circle, but I can't help it. Ethan should have told me all of this before bringing me here to face her. He could have explained, and I wouldn't have had to feel so blindsided.

Ethan's response is measured, but his eyes hold a hint of defensiveness. "It's only the worst criminals."

Marvedeme stands silently, her shoulders slightly hunched, eyes fixed on the bar. Her fingers trace the rim of the glass in front of her, lips pressed into a thin line.

I know demons are supposed to be inherently wicked, but something about hurting her, assuming she's cruel just because of her nature, feels wrong. "How do you know they are truly guilty?" I ask her directly.

The idea of condemning someone without absolute certainty troubles me deeply. While I support justice for murderers, the slightest shadow of doubt makes me wary. Few cases offer complete certainty; it's often about reasonable doubt. But to justify taking a soul, I'd need absolute certainty.

Her eyes widen slightly as they lock with mine, and for a brief moment, a spark lights in their depths. Her breath seems to catch, as if she's daring to believe in something she hasn't allowed herself to hope for. Maybe it's the act of simply listening to her that might already be more than what many others have done.

"When I reach out for a soul, I sense its essence, as dark as the night," Marvedeme explains softly. "Bad souls like this don't taste good, pure bitterness, and they're not even very powerful. In a way, I grant them mercy, sparing them from eternal torment." The justification sounds a bit forced, but I get it.

I nod, silently accepting her explanation. A few minutes ago, I was ready to condemn them all for associating with a demon. But now, seeing the vulnerability in her eyes, I feel a pang of sympathy. She's barely surviving—lacking in strength, power, and even a decent meal. Her life existence sounds far from the monstrous image I had conjured up in my mind.

"With people like that, I'd rather see them burn," I say, my voice dropping to a low, icy tone. My jaw tightens, eyes narrowing. But with a slow breath, I ease the tension from my face. "But at least this way, they serve a purpose," I add.

A quiet sigh of relief escapes the group, as if they'd all been holding their breath, waiting for my reaction.

I tilt my head slightly, eyebrows lifting as I meet her gaze. "Are there others like you in the world?"

Marve's eyes drop, her expression clouding over, not with shame this time but with something deeper, more painful. Her lips part, barely a whisper escaping. "There used to be."

Before I can fully process what she's said, Ethan's sudden clap cuts through the tension. "Alright, let's begin training." He rises, striding toward the sandy area at the center of the gym with a focused, determined look.

I glance between Ethan and my drink, the pull of unfinished questions gnawing at me. Setting the glass down, I take a step toward him, hesitation swirling in my gut. "Wait," I call out, unable to let it go. "I need to know more."

Ethan turns back, his casual shrug betraying impatience. "Can't we save that for later? Let's get into something fun now."

"Fun for you, maybe," I mutter, meeting his gaze head-on. "But I need answers. What exactly have I gotten myself into? What kind of world is this, and what kind of dangers are out there?" My voice sharpens, pressing him for clarity.

Ethan's grin stretches wide, showing all of his teeth as his eyes light up with excitement. "For answers? I've got just the thing—my trusty friend, the library," he says, his voice practically bubbling with pride. His expression is smug, like he's just come up with the perfect solution, one that's not only clever but convenient for him too.

"You're kidding, right?" I shoot back, my patience wearing thin. I stop dead in the middle of the sand, planting my hands on my hips. "You wanted me in your world, but now you're dodging a few simple questions?"

"Hey, one question leads to another," he says as if that's a valid excuse for dodging me. "I'll answer them, I promise. But let's see what you've got in terms of skills first."

I narrow my eyes, not letting him off that easily. "Just a few questions, then we can train," I propose.

"Three questions, five minutes max." Ethan glances at his watch to set a time limit as he adds, "Go."

I don't waste time. "You mentioned Marve doesn't take orders to kill. From whom? And is there really a Lucifer? Was he the one who killed the others like her?" The questions spill out faster than I intended.

Ethan raises an eyebrow, a sly grin playing on his lips. "Those were three questions—well done," he teases. I bite my lip, realizing too late I'd burned through my limit in one go.

Before I can argue, he starts answering, leaving me no room to protest. "There is a leader, Baal. He's essentially the king of demons, and he doesn't tolerate the existence of beings like Marve. To him, they represent a different way of life, one he cannot allow, especially because they refuse to follow his orders and serve his purposes. As for Lucifer, he's the ruler of hell, where bad souls are sent. He's entrusted by God to oversee these souls, serving as God's right hand and most trusted angel. Contrary to popular belief, Lucifer has never fallen and has nothing to do with demons."

Ethan flicks his wrist to check his watch, a smirk tugging at his lips. He doesn't say anything, but the slight raise of his eyebrows and quick, satisfied nod tell me everything—I can almost see him patting himself on the back for not losing too much of his precious time on explanations.

"Who is Baal?" I try my luck, pushing for more given we still have a couple of minutes left from the limit.

"Someone you don't want to meet," Ethan replies curtly, his tone making it clear that's the end of the conversation.

"Alright, let's get started."

"Okay, so what exactly are we doing?"

Ethan rolls his eyes, a gesture I've learned is more for show than real frustration—likely just his dramatic response to yet another one of my questions. "I'm going to teach you Kalaripayattu."

"Kala-what?" Never heard of it.

Ethan launches into an explanation, detailing how it's one of the oldest Indian martial arts, incorporating techniques that range from barehanded combat to wielding various weapons—sticks, swords, spears, daggers, and other things that sound like they're straight out of ancient warfare. He also emphasizes the importance of daily practice, physical conditioning, studying, and honing my other powers.

While he talks, I can't help but wonder if he realizes I still have a job to maintain. Sure, I'm mostly free for the summer, but I'm not about to master all of this in a couple of months. Does he expect me to drop everything and dive into his training boot camp?

His enthusiasm for teaching catches me off guard. It's obvious that combat is his comfort zone, the first thing he gravitates toward. Me, though? I'd rather dive into the intricacies of this new world, get some answers about what's happening around me before I'm thrust into physical training.

But then again, I've always wanted to learn how to fight—though I imagined someone more like Ra's al Ghul as my master.

At first, Ethan guides me through what seems more like a stretching routine than actual combat stances. We practice leaps, jumps, and twists, but it's clear from the start that I'm completely out of my depth. Each movement is a glaring reminder of my inflexibility, a sharp contrast to Ethan's effortless fluidity.

When we move on to kicks with our arms raised above our heads, I find myself struggling to swing my leg straight, let alone reach my hands. The more I try, the more obvious it becomes just how far I have to go.

But progress takes time. So I push through, repeating the motions over and over for what feels like an eternity. Each kick, each awkward attempt, becomes a small victory. I still can't touch my hands, not even close, but I can feel myself improving—if only by a millimeter at a time.

Throughout it all, I'm painfully aware of Marve and Ezra watching from the bar. Their eyes never leave me, observing every misstep, every failed kick. Every time I stumble, I wonder if they're silently judging my abilities.

A ridiculous thought crosses my mind: Would they abandon me? Find or create a new Nephilim daughter if they decide I'm too bad at this to complete their circle? I shake the idea off—it's absurd.

Yet, the longer their eyes linger on me, the more the doubt creeps in. Maybe I'm not supposed to be this clumsy. I've always been good at sports, quick to pick up new skills, but here, I feel like I'm flailing. Am I failing? Maybe it's not me, maybe Ethan's just starting too hard on me...

My legs ache, my muscles burn, and my breath comes in short, ragged bursts, but I keep going. I have to prove that I can handle this—even if I'm the only one doubting it right now.

chapter 7

BACK TO SCHOOL

After two hours of intense exercise and stretching—more than I've ever done in my life—I finally collapse at the bar. My muscles scream for rest, and all I want is to enjoy the drink I never got to finish earlier. As I sip, I watch Ezra and Ethan sparring together for a change, eager to see them in action instead of being the one struggling.

"Do you fight with them, too?" I ask Marve, noticing her crouched behind the bar, sorting through bottles or maybe just keeping herself busy.

She pauses for a moment, her hands stilling before she

answers. "No," she replies, a hint of sadness threading through her voice. "I can't."

"Why?" The question slips out before I can stop it, curiosity edging past caution.

She straightens up, rising from behind the bar. Her eyes lock onto mine with a seriousness that catches me off guard. "I haven't eaten properly in a long time."

The raw honesty hits me, a chill running through me, but I hold it in, not wanting her to see the effect she has on me. "I see," I say softly. "I'm sorry." It's not her fault that her nature requires her to consume human souls to live. It seems like those who try to be good often face the harshest struggles.

Marve's eyes follow Ethan and Ezra's every movement, the slightest twitch of her lips betraying the tension she's trying to hide. Her hand hovers over a bottle for a moment longer than necessary, fingers tracing the edge of the glass before she pours the liquid with slow precision. The rhythmic clinking of bottles is the only sound she makes, but it's clear her attention is far from the task at hand.

Instead of feeling sorry for her, I shift my attention to the guys. They start by removing their shirts, revealing perfect six-packs that glisten under the basement lights. Standing barefoot in the sand, they look like they belong in an ancient arena. They exchange a bow, a subtle smile playing on their lips—almost as if they're putting on this show for me, silently demonstrating what years of dedication can achieve.

Ethan takes the offensive stance. They both move with such speed that it's hard to see what they're actually doing. If I didn't know any better, I'd say they were dancing. They traverse the gym with lightning speed, almost teleporting from one end to the other. After a few moments, they each grab a sword and shield, seamlessly incorporating them into their routine.

It's mesmerizing; I've only ever witnessed such prowess in movies. Now, I'm torn between the fear of letting them down and never mastering this art as they do, and the thrill of trying.

"One day, you'll be as good as them," Marve reassures me, almost as if she's reading my thoughts. IS everyone around here capable of that?

"You really think so?"

"I'm certain of it. I've seen you train, and you have the potential."

"Thanks." I smile, genuinely grateful for the encouragement. "Do you enjoy fighting?" I'm treading on sensitive ground, but with the guys still occupied and my social skills lacking, I'm grasping for conversation.

As an introvert, making small talk is hard enough, but finding the right questions for a demon I've just met feels almost impossible. My mind scrambles for something—anything—appropriate. What on earth could I ask her about. The taste of souls?

Her lips slowly curl into a wicked grin, as if savoring the memory of countless battles fought without restraint. "Every demon does. It's in our nature." The playful malice in her smile catches my attention, but something else makes my breath hitch— a flicker of yellow dances in her eyes, a brief, almost imperceptible shift. I blink, unsure if it was a trick of the light, but the chill that

I'm suppressing tells me otherwise.

"Then it must be hard to fight one," I muse.

"It is. I hope you never have to find out just how much."

I shake my head. Like that's possible after choosing to give up mortality to fight supernatural monsters. "But I want to. I want to battle demons."

"Why?" She blinks, taken aback.

"Because they're bad... in general," I quickly amend, realizing the unintended slight. I didn't mean to offend her personally. "I want to stop anything that harms others."

She narrows her eyes, her lips curling slightly, but her expression is anything but humorous. "Then you should start with humans," she replies, her voice laced with disdain.

She's right—humans do cause harm to one another, to animals, and to the planet. "But humans have laws, law enforcement," I counter. "As far as I know, there's no judicial system for soul-killing beasts," I wince at my choice of words—'beast'—hoping she doesn't think I'm lumping her in with the rest. *God*, I really shouldn't be allowed to talk to other 'people'.

"I don't think it's wise to start a—" she begins, but before the rest of the sentence can escape, Ezra strides over, silencing her with a gentle kiss on the cheek. Her shoulders stiffen briefly, betraying her frustration, but she lets it go, eyes flicking toward him with reluctant acceptance. It's obvious she doesn't want the guys involved.

"One well-deserved drink, please," Ethan says a bit too loudly, reaching for the glass Marve has already prepared and set on the bar.

"Did you win?" I ask, noticing the triumphant grin plastered across Ethan's face.

"Duh, I always win. I'm the best fighter you'll ever meet." I glance at Ezra, expecting him to challenge Ethan's claim, but instead, he nods in agreement.

"And the most humble one," Ezra adds playfully, nudging Ethan with his elbow.

"Excuse me," Marve whispers abruptly, her voice a little too sharp, before turning and walking away. The tension that follows is palpable, and I can't shake the feeling that something I said hit a nerve. Maybe it was my careless remark about soul-killing beasts, or perhaps it's the quiet frustration that if she were stronger, she'd prove herself the best fighter in the room.

Worried the guys might get upset if I told them about my conversation with Marve or asked if they thought she was mad at me, I quickly steer the conversation in a different direction.

"Oh, I've been meaning to ask," I begin, my voice a little too casual, "do I have any other powers besides strength and fast healing?" My gaze locks onto Ethan's as he savors the last sip of his drink, then lazily heads back to the bar for a refill without a word.

I wave my hand, hoping to pull Ethan's focus back, but he barely glances my way, a faint smirk tugging at his lips. "Don't look at me. I don't know much about Nephilim," he replies with a shrug, his words tinged with that familiar teasing edge. "Ezra's been fallen much longer. He's the expert here."

Typical. Even if he knew something, I'm sure teaching me would bore him to death, unless it involved kicking or punching.

With a sigh, I shift my attention to Ezra. He stands a little off to the side, seemingly lost in his own thoughts, but I know he's listening.

"Ezra?" My voice softens as I approach him. "Would you, please, teach me something about Nephilim? About... myself?"

Ezra nods, setting down his glass as if he'd been waiting for this moment all along, just playing it cool. "Indeed, there's much to learn about your heritage and your abilities. But it's not just about powers—it's about understanding who you truly are. You possess the traits of both angels and humans," he begins, slipping into the role of a mentor with a quiet, practiced ease.

"Humans are deeply emotional, they have a sixth sense, but they have no supernatural abilities. Angels, on the other hand, have many powers, but they are only allowed to use some of them. Fallen angels keep only a fraction of their former powers, but we have the freedom to use them however we want. Sometimes, both angels and fallen angels possess unique powers that set them apart from others. In your case, as a descendant of a fallen angel, there's a good chance you've got some hidden talents waiting to pop up when you least expect it. Being part human, it's likely that your powers are tied to your emotions. You must be careful and not let your emotions drive your actions."

Ezra pauses for a moment, his eyes narrowing slightly as if mentally reviewing a checklist. A small nod follows, confirming his thoughts. "Yeah, and your perceptiveness is remarkably high as well."

"Speaking of heightened perception and special gifts, something weird happened." I pause, glancing at Ethan as I prepare to venture into a personal territory. Even though he's not my father in the common sense of the word—he didn't raise me, wasn't there for all the milestones—in the corner of my mind, I know he is *biologically* my father, and I feel a twinge of discomfort sharing something so intimate with him. For some reason, I don't like sharing details about my personal life with my family unless it becomes something serious. And yet, here I am, crossing that line.

I clear my throat, pushing through the awkwardness that only I feel. "I had this dream about the guy I'm seeing," I say quickly, hoping to breeze past that detail. "In the dream, he told me something I hadn't heard before, and when I woke up, I had a text from him... saying the same thing. Could it mean something, or am I just reading too much into it?"

My dating life, however, doesn't seem to be the earth-shattering revelation it would be with my real parents. Ethan barely acknowledges it, swirling his drink like it's the most fascinating thing in the world, while Ezra, on the other hand, nods thoughtfully, clearly weighing the possibilities. "It could mean something," he muses, his gaze distant, "but then again, maybe not. What place did you dream about?"

"There were several places," I clarify, the images still sharp in my mind. "I remember them perfectly, but I couldn't place where they were."

"Couldn't place them because you've never been there, or because you didn't recognize them?"

"I've definitely never been there," I confirm. "But maybe I've seen them in a movie or something. It's hard to say."

"You can trust your instincts," Ezra says softly, his gaze steady, like he's willing me to believe. "As a Nephilim who's accepted her powers, your perception is heightened. With focus, you'll learn to distinguish what's real from what's imagined or even planted by someone else. Your senses, your brain—they're working at a level beyond what you're used to, even your memory."

I close my eyes, concentrating, sifting through the vivid images in my mind. My breath steadies as I reach deeper, past the surface memories. "No," I murmur, opening my eyes slowly. "I don't think I've ever seen those places before."

Ezra raises his hands slightly, palms up, as if presenting me with the only logical answer. "Then it looks like you wandered into someone else's dream." His voice carries a note of impressed surprise, eyebrows lifting slightly. "Not bad for a newbie with fresh powers."

Ethan, leaning back against the bar, flashes a grin. "Well done."

I catch their proud glances, but they only make me feel uneasy. I didn't mean to do it, and it's not something I have control over yet. It doesn't feel like a real achievement. "Thanks," I murmur, shifting uncomfortably, "but how does it work?"

"That's for you to find out; it's your power. I haven't met many Nephilim in my life, and they haven't exactly consulted their powers with me, so I have no idea whether it's just your special gift or something typical for a Nephilim," Ezra says.

I chew on his words for a moment before venturing, "Maybe I'm like a Jedi... you know, some are stronger with the Force, and some are better with a lightsaber. Maybe mind powers are my thing," I add, half-joking, half-hoping for some extraordinary abilities.

Ethan grins, catching onto my playful tone. "Do you have your lightsaber with you?" he asks, turning to Ezra, who shakes his head with a mock-serious expression. "Me neither. I guess we'll never find out then."

I chuckle, the absurd image of these two ancient, powerful beings sitting down to watch Star Wars flashing through my mind. But somehow, it makes them feel more real—more like me.

As the day drags on, and with Ethan showing little interest in delving deeper into the mysteries of the otherworld, I decide to take him up on his earlier suggestion. "Mind if I explore your library?" I ask, eager to uncover more about my new reality.

"Go ahead," Ethan waves me off casually.

I jump to my feet and stride toward the staircase, passing through the breathtaking entry hall before reaching the library.

Stepping inside, I'm immediately struck by its sheer scale—easily three times the size of the small living space I share with Cerberus. Shelves upon shelves of books stretch upward, each one holding the promise of countless realms, eras, and answers. Ethan had mentioned these books could help me grasp the intricacies of this new world. But now that I'm here, I'm not quite sure where to begin.

I let my fingers trail over the dusty spines, each book a relic of its own time. Some are so coated with age that I can hardly make out their titles, while others show signs of recent use—less dust, edges softened by eager hands. My gaze lands on one such volume, its dark leather cover worn but not forgotten. The title *Defeating*

Mystical Creatures catches my eye.

I pull it from the shelf, the weight of it heavier than I expect. The emblem on the front, a warrior brandishing a fiery sword, seems to shimmer faintly in the dim light.

I flip the cover open, revealing pages filled with intricately detailed drawings of creatures—werewolves, shapeshifters, vampires, and wraiths. Each figure seems to leap from the page, their colors vibrant, their textures unsettlingly real. I swear, for a moment, the wraith's hollow eyes blink. Elaborate script flows alongside the illustrations, explaining their weaknesses and how to defeat them, but my attention keeps returning to the hauntingly alive images. It's as if the creatures are waiting to be unleashed.

As I continue skimming through the pages, the door creaks open, and Marve steps into the library. Her timing couldn't be worse.

Before I can close the book, her eyes flick to the title. Without missing a beat, she strides to another shelf and pulls out a thick volume. "You might want to start with history first," she says, her tone light but firm as she hands me the book. "Understanding life, the world, and its creatures is key before trying to destroy any of it."

I glance at the title. "*Genesis?*"

"Lots of things in it are inaccurate, but there's also a lot of truth. It's a good starting point to grasp the basics. Once you're done, let me know what you think of God. I'll show you other books you should read when you finish this one."

I nod, taking the book from Marve's hands. My fingers tighten slightly on the plain cover that seems less thrilling than the intricate, ancient tomes surrounding us. "Alright, thank you," I say, though starting with something I could easily buy at any bookstore feels so... anticlimactic.

Still, I appreciate Marve's guidance. Despite the unsettling reality of her diet and nature, she's been the warmest toward me, more so than anyone else here. Maybe she feels she has to try harder than the others. Or maybe she's just a much nicer person.

Marve slides a few more hefty volumes in front of me—*Exodus*, *Leviticus*, *Numerus*, and others. My lips part, but the sigh gets stuck somewhere deep in my chest, too stunned to even make it out. Or maybe bored before it has the chance. I glance at the pile, my shoulders slumping. "I'll never finish all of this," I mutter, half to myself. I thought summer meant a break from the mountain of reading I usually do for school and work. My eyes flick up to Marve. "Are these all part of the Bible?"

"Yep," she says with a playful glint in her eyes, clearly enjoying the sight of the towering stack of homework she's just handed me. She really is devilish. "Take it one book at a time. You'll get through it," she adds with a wink, her tone light but teasing.

With that, she leaves me to my fate, the door clicking softly behind her as I stare down at the daunting pile of ancient texts.

I realize this will take weeks to even skim through. Feeling slightly overwhelmed, I grab *Genesis* from the pile and dash downstairs to ask Ethan if I can take it home. I find him just as he was when I went upstairs, sitting on a bar stool with a drink in hand, not the one I left him with, though. Without even looking up, he waves dismissively, as though the request isn't worth his attention.

Taking that as permission, I hurry home with the book tucked under my arm, Cerberus curling up beside me the moment I sit down. Before I know it, I'm lost in the ancient stories, the hours slipping away until the clock strikes midnight.

Exhausted, I close the book and crawl into bed. With my mind full of ancient stories and a heart eager for more, I drift into sleep, anticipating another day of discovery.

chapter 8

PRYING

I glance around the old wooden house, its age softened by the warm glow of sunlight streaming through the lace curtains. Dust motes dance in the golden beams, casting everything in a dreamlike haze. The familiar scent of aged wood and lavender wraps around me, but something feels off.

My gaze lands on Ben, who's standing by the window, locked in conversation with a woman I've never seen before. She's dressed in a flowing beige gown that brushes the floor, her beauty almost unreal. Long, curly brown hair spills down her back like a waterfall, so thick and full that it conceals more than just her shoulders. Her striking blue eyes, bright and clear, seem focused on Ben, though they flicker with something unreadable. A slow, nagging unease curls in my gut.

Even through my confusion, I can't help but be mesmerized by her presence. Her aura demands attention, but what unsettles me most is that she hasn't noticed me standing there. Not even a glance. Ben's gaze, however, shifts to me almost immediately, his expression tightening as if my arrival disrupted something important.

I take a hesitant step forward, my foot creaking on the old floorboards, breaking the silence. Still, the woman doesn't react. It's as though I'm invisible to her, or maybe, I think with a chill, she's choosing to ignore me. I open my mouth, ready to ask who she is and why I feel like an outsider in this house, but something stops me. A knot of uncertainty tightens in my chest, holding my voice back. Or is it jealousy?

"What are you doing here?" Ben's concerned voice snaps me back to the present. His grip is firm but gentle as he takes my arm and leads me towards the door.

"Who is she?" I blurt out, the question escaping before I can stop it.

Ben's expression doesn't change as he glances over his shoulder, as if the answer should be obvious. "Just my wife," he says, casually, like he's telling me the sky is blue.

His wife? How could he say it so casually? My chest tightens, a strange mix of anger, hurt, and curiosity bubbling up, swirling inside me like a storm ready to break. How could he keep something like this from me?

"You never told me you were married."

Ben sighs, running a hand through his hair, his face a mixture of discomfort and something else—regret, maybe? "We're not together anymore. Haven't been for a long time."

He opens the door, and we step out onto the beach. The salty breeze washes over us, carrying with it the rhythmic sound of waves crashing against the shore. The tension that had been coiling inside me begins to loosen, the serenity of the ocean working its magic.

With the change in scenery, a change in the topic comes just as naturally. "I thought you were ignoring me," Ben confesses as he joins me on the pebble beach, where I'm already seated. I don't even remember sitting down.

"Why would I ignore you?"

Ben sinks down beside me, his legs stretching out so that they barely brush against mine, but the contact sends a jolt through me. His presence feels solid, warm, and yet distant at the same time. "I texted you," he continues, his voice quieter now, almost drowned by the sound of the ocean, "but you never replied."

Oh no. My mind races back through the whirlwind of recent events—discovering the supernatural world, encountering an actual demon. In the chaos, I had completely forgotten about Ben. I hadn't even checked my phone.

"I'm so sorry," I say, my voice filled with genuine regret. "I've been... overwhelmed. I meant to respond, but I was so exhausted I just... crashed and—"

But mid-sentence, a cold wave of realization hits me. *I'm dreaming.* The last thing I remember was falling asleep, tangled in thoughts of Nephilim powers, demons, and ancient rituals. And then I found myself in that old wooden house.

As I gaze into Ben's beautiful eyes, an idea slowly forms, something that makes all of this feel suddenly worthwhile. If this is a dream, then I should be able to control it. But a nagging question stops me: Whose dream is this—mine or his?

The beach feels familiar, but the house and the woman in beige? She's a stranger to my memories, a puzzle I can't solve. This must be his dream. The thought tightens my chest. I shouldn't take the lead. The idea of navigating someone else's dream feels intrusive, like flipping through the pages of a diary not meant for my eyes.

I glance at Ben, his gaze full of something between confusion and hope, and I know I have to tread carefully. This is his space, his subconscious laid bare. The beach, the house, the mysterious woman—they all belong to him, parts of his mind I'm only a visitor in.

"You're incredibly pretty," he murmurs, his voice soft and intimate, drawing me closer with each word. Before I can think, his lips find mine, and the kiss feels astonishingly real. His touch is electric, sending tingles through my body as his fingers trail softly along my arm, moving with a gentle grace that makes my breath hitch.

His hand slides from my arm to my shoulder, then traces the delicate curve of my neck. Each touch is like a soft current, igniting my skin, making me acutely aware of every sensation. My heart races as his fingers weave into my hair, tugging lightly, anchoring me in this strange, surreal moment.

When his lips leave mine, they graze my jaw, and then the sensitive skin of my neck, leaving a path of warmth and yearning in their wake. Every inch of me tingles, consumed by the softness of his touch, the heat of his breath against my skin. My mind feels heavy, clouded, as if every thought I had moments ago is slipping away, lost in the haze of his kiss.

God, what was I even thinking about before?

"I can't believe I've finally found you," Ben whispers, his breath brushing against my skin. "The girl I've been looking for my entire life."

He leans in for another kiss, and this time, the world dissolves completely. All that remains is the beating of my heart and the intensity of his touch, each second stretching out as if time itself has been erased. It's like we're suspended in this perfect, impossible moment—his dream or mine, it doesn't seem to matter anymore. But somewhere, deep inside, a voice whispers: *The girl he's been looking for? Please, he barely knows me.*

He has no idea what I really am, no clue about my plans to fight demons, to step into a war most humans can't even comprehend. And the worst part? I can't tell him any of this. Not because I don't want to, but because I can't. The Spell Yabbashael warned me about binds me. It's not just some arbitrary rule—it's like gravity, woven into the fabric of reality. Unbreakable, inevitable.

Yabbashael explained it once: After God realized that His presence and that of the angels caused more harm than good in human lives, He decreed that they should protect and guide only from a distance. Angels could influence human instincts, nudge them, but they couldn't directly interfere unless the human was truly open to sensing them. And even then, humans could never fully perceive their existence unless they physically manifested, and even that could only happen under rare, specific circumstances.

Unlike angels, humans can see and hear Nephilim and fallen angels, but they can't *know* what we are. Since we originate from angels, we can't reveal our true nature to them. If we try, the Spell ensures they won't hear it. The words will vanish, lost in the air before they reach human ears. How could Ben and I ever be together when everything between us would be built on a lie?

"You barely know me."

His eyes meet mine, full of certainty, unwavering. "One look into your eyes, and I see everything I need to know. I know you're good, and that's all that matters." His hand rests on my cheek, thumb brushing lightly against my skin.

"But how?"

"I just do," he says, his voice steady, as if the answer is the simplest thing in the world. "I've never felt this way before. You're special."

His words should soothe me, but they don't. Instead, they stir something uneasy inside me. Once more, I remind myself of the ethical line I'm toeing—invading his dream, actually engaging with his subconscious, when he has no idea. He's revealing thoughts and feelings he might not be ready to share with me, not if he were awake and in control of his words.

Yabbashael's warnings echo in my mind. Prying into someone's thoughts—that's the behavior of fallen angels. The temptation to know, to dig deeper, to uncover what lies hidden in the hearts of others—it's a slippery slope.

But how do I get out?

Feeling as if I were being pulled from deep water, heavy and with an unnatural resistance, I wake up. I blink into the darkness of my room, my body heavy against the sheets. The familiar sound of Berry's rhythmic purring fills the quiet space, grounding me in the present.

So that's how it works. I hadn't known I could leave like that, slip out of his dream so easily, wake up by my own will.

Berry is sprawled across my legs, a soft, warm weight that pins me in place He stirs but doesn't protest as I gently lift him up and shift him beside me, my fingers absently running through his fur. I settle back into the pillows, trying to coax myself into sleep again.

But Ben's words echo in my mind—*I texted you.* The memory nags at me until I reach for my phone. The screen lights up, revealing three unread messages. I set it back down on the nightstand, deciding I'll respond in the morning. The last thing I want is for him to think I've been up all night doing who knows what.

No matter how hard I try to calm my mind, I can't shake the thought of falling into Ben's dreams again, uninvited. Ezra warned me to never be driven by emotions. Yet, my feelings for Ben are overpowering. How do I regain control over myself, my powers, my mind?

I let out a breath, remembering the peace I once found in meditation. Back then, it was my way of calming the chaos and battling insomnia. But since discovering this new world, I've abandoned it, letting my emotions run unchecked. Now, Ezra's advice feels more like a reprimand, and I realize how foolish I've been to neglect such a vital tool for self-control.

Meditation could be the key—*the* key to mastering my abilities. I close my eyes, forcing my breath to slow, making a silent vow to return to the practice. Starting now.

I start by pulling the clock off the wall, its persistent ticking gnawing at my concentration. I carry it into another room and shut the door, leaving the ticking behind. Returning to my space, I ease into a comfortable position.

Closing my eyes, I focus on my breath. Inhale deeply, exhale slowly. The rise and fall of my chest, the steady rhythm of air flowing in and out, becomes my anchor. But as always, my mind begins to wander, pulling me away.

1...2...3...

Ben.

4...5...6...

Ben's hands.

7...8...9...

Bens kiss. No, focus.

I pull myself back, reminding myself that all that exists in this moment is the breath and the numbers. Nothing more. I start again.

10...1...2...3...4...5...6...7...8...9...10... and again.

Gradually, the pull of my thoughts weakens, the chaos in my mind quiets, and the world narrows to the simple rhythm of my breath.

After half an hour, I lie back down, a sense of serenity washing over me. The control I've been searching for feels within reach, as if the stillness I've found lingers, whispering a quiet promise as I drift back into sleep.

When I wake the next morning, I'm relieved to find no trace of bizarre dreams, no lingering sense of having crossed into someone else's subconscious. Maybe I succeeded in keeping the boundaries intact.

My hand instinctively reaches for my phone, and Ben's messages blink up at me, waiting.

I quickly respond, and his reply comes almost immediately: "I dreamt about you again last night." My fingers pause over the keyboard, a flicker of hesitation. Of course, I already knew. But I feign ignorance, typing a casual reply as if I hadn't been there, hovering at the edge of his dreams. Explaining how I can slip into someone's mind would be tricky—actually it would be impossible with the Spell in place.

"You disappeared before anything good happened," his message reads.

A smirk crosses my lips as I type back, savoring the playfulness, "I can assure you that when we actually meet, I won't disappear. By the way, do you dream about other girls, too? Or just about me?" I toss in a sticking-out-tongue emoji for good measure. As curious as I am about the woman from his dream, I can't exactly ask about her.

"Can't wait. Not in that sense," he responds, adding a winking emoji.

I narrow my eyes at the screen, the answer playful but vague. No denial, no real answer. At least he's not lying. I remind myself that it's none of my business anyway. Unless, of course, he is married. *That* would certainly concern me. But delving into his mind to find out isn't an option—I must respect his privacy. My focus has to be on control—on resisting the temptation to slip back into his subconscious.

chapter 9

MATTERS OF THE HEART

My days have fallen into a rhythm, each one blending seamlessly into the next. Every morning begins the same: deep breaths, centering my thoughts, and mentally listing the tasks ahead—training during the day, and in the evenings, reading the Bible, like a good girl.

Training with Ethan is brutal. His methods push me to the brink, my muscles screaming in protest, my body aching in places I didn't know could ache. He's relentless, never giving me an inch of reprieve, but I know he means well.

Despite the rigorous schedule, my mind often drifts to Ben.

He's preoccupied with changing jobs and moving, which means we haven't seen each other in what feels like forever. I know I'll have to wait until his housewarming party at the new apartment. Oddly, I don't mind. The distance stings, but the truth weighs heavier. Being with him, knowing we could never have a real relationship—it feels like leading him on. It's cruel and selfish, and that's not who I want to be.

One afternoon, after an exhausting round of training, I find my opportunity. While Ethan and Ezra spar together, I slip away to where Marve is quietly making drinks. I've been waiting for a moment like this, a chance to ask her about something that's been keeping me awake at night.

Marve's movements are slow and deliberate, her fingers trailing along the edges of the glasses with a precision that hints at something deeper—a quiet sadness. I've never seen her just watch the guys without keeping herself busy. There's an ache in her silence that I can't quite shake.

For a moment, I feel sorry for her. An eternity to live, and yet she's unable to do what she's passionate about. The thought is as bittersweet as her favorite drink.

But today, I'm actually relieved she's not training with them. I need to talk to someone who understands immortality, someone who can see the bigger picture. For some reason, I don't feel comfortable discussing this with the guys. Maybe because they're men, or maybe because of their age, though I'm sure Marve is ancient too. Or maybe it's because Ethan is supposed to be something like a father to me. Either way, I know Marve will get it.

I hesitate, unsure of where to begin. It feels almost ridiculous—worrying about something as trivial as boys when I've been thrust into a world full of power and danger, of ancient figures and destiny. The last thing I want is to seem pathetic.

Without even lifting her gaze, Marve senses my inner turmoil. "Go on," she encourages me.

I swallow and start tentatively, "I'd like to know your thoughts on... dating." The words feel strange, almost out of place given everything else happening in my life. "Now that I'm immortal, I'm scared of falling in love with someone who isn't. Of getting hurt. And what kind of relationship could we even have if I can't be honest about who I am?"

"It's always better to be with someone who shares our immortality," Marve states plainly. "But matters of the heart are rarely logical. The heart wants what it wants. Being logical doesn't always mean happiness, anyway. Follow your heart. If you get hurt, at least you'll know you've lived."

I frown, her answer too simple, too neat. "But wouldn't it be too hard? Hiding my true identity, what I do, my connection to Ethan... It feels like a recipe for disaster. And the thought of losing him forever..." my voice falters at the thought.

Marve sighs, her eyes reflecting centuries of wisdom. "I've lived for so long that I can tell you only this: never choose the easy way. It's boring, anyway. Just because something may be hard or complicated doesn't mean it won't be worth it. Embrace every moment, and remember, you never know what the future holds. Nephilim tend to find each other, after all. Hope for the best and prepare for the worst."

Her unexpected response catches me off guard. A demon speaking of following the heart—it's certainly not what I anticipated. I half expected her to knock some sense into me, to remind me of the harsh realities. Maybe that's exactly why I chose to talk to her of all people. Instead, her words stir something softer inside me, a flicker of hope I wasn't sure I had.

Hope for the best—hope he is Nephilim too, just unaware of that part of himself. It's possible, after all—each of us, children of fallen angels, has to open ourselves enough to see beyond the veil, to break through and recognize the angels walking among us. No one else can do that for him.

But I brace for the worst. He might not be Nephilim. And even if he is, he may never awake to it, or he might not choose to accept his immortality.

With a reassuring pat on my hand, Marve places another drink in front of me and lifts her own glass. "Cheers," she says with a soft warm smile.

I raise my glass in response, taking a deep breath. "Thanks," I murmur, managing a small smile. "That actually helps."

"So, how did you know he's the one?"

"I don't know." I search my mind for something specific, but only the memory of our first meeting comes to mind. "It was just this feeling when I first saw him, when he smiled at me." A soft laugh escapes me, my lips curling up as the image of his smile flickers in my mind. "My knees went weak."

When I glance at Marve, I see only a polite smile in return, her lips barely lifting. "Oh," is the only sound that escapes her.

"Was it like that for you and Ezra?"

"Love at first sight? No." She chuckles, a mischievous glint in her eyes. "When we first met, we wanted to kill each other."

I nearly spit out my drink, choking on laughter. But as the sound subsides, I can't help but let my curiosity get the better of me. There's too much mystery in her past to leave it alone. "Have you ever fallen in love with a human? And how long have you been with Ezra, anyway?"

"Ugh. I've never been in love with a human," she replies, her nose wrinkling. "Honestly, if someone's soul is pure, not only do I lose it to the desire to consume it, but I can't see us as a good match—I'm still a demon, after all, not an angel. And if their soul isn't pure, I feel an irresistible urge to punish them. It's a strange concept, I know. I guess humans are more like... food to me. There's no attraction there. But fallen angels... they're a different story entirely."

Her gaze shifts to Ezra, and for a moment, her eyes soften, sparkling with something unmistakable. Love. Genuine, fierce, and surprisingly tender. In that moment, her demonic nature seems to slip away, revealing a layer of vulnerability I hadn't expected.

"You know, fallen angels may be essentially good, but they have minds of their own," she muses. "As for your second question, I've been with Ezra for the past two hundred years—not very long, really."

"Wow... not very long indeed," I reply sarcastically, shaking my head with a smirk.

"In our world, two hundred years is hardly a blink. But it's been... fulfilling. You shouldn't worry, Dora. Live your life. Love is more important than hunting dark creatures," Marve reassures me with a comforting smile, though the comment seems a bit forced.

I don't respond. It's clear Marve sees love and hunting as opposing forces, as if one cancels out the other. And she's not entirely wrong. If I were with Ben, he'd become a target, always at risk in a world he doesn't even know exists. Most of the people in my life are immortal now, untouchable. But Ben—his fragility would be a constant threat. I can't stomach the thought of dragging him into danger.

But my purpose, the reason I accepted these powers in the first place, is already clear to me. I know what I'm here to do—protect the innocent and fight the darkness. That's my path. And Ben would be a distraction, a liability I couldn't afford.

As I study Marve, something odd flickers through my mind. Am I really bonding with a demon?

chapter 10

CROSSING LINES

Ben's apartment is already buzzing with energy by the time I arrive, the sound of music and laughter drifting down the hallway. I'm surprised by how quickly he managed to unpack and throw together a housewarming party. It feels almost too fast, as if he rushed the whole thing just to see me. Maybe that's wishful thinking, but with how distant we've been lately, I can't help but wonder if this is his cautious way of closing the gap between us.

I deliberately arrive late, unsure if I'm ready to be alone with him until I decide whether to pursue this, or fully embrace my new life. I hope to blend into the crowd without drawing too much attention. Crowded places always make me anxious—I dread being in the spotlight, yet I fear fading into the background with no one to talk to. It's a balancing act I've never quite mastered.

I smooth down the red dress Marve loaned me, its soft fabric hugging my curves with a confidence I don't quite feel yet. She offered to help with my makeup too, but I declined. Tonight, I need to feel like myself, not some version of me hiding behind layers of powder and mascara.

As I approach the door, a wave of nerves hits me. But I remind myself—*I'm Nephilim now. What's a party compared to immortality?* In a hundred years, this night will be nothing more than a distant memory, barely worth recalling. I take a deep breath, steadying myself, feeling the power that hums beneath my skin. Tonight, I can handle anything.

I ring the bell, and within seconds, the door swings open, revealing Ben's face, his smile so bright it nearly takes me off guard. *Oh God—he looks too eager, too happy to see me. Was he waiting by the door just for me?* That familiar pang stirs in my chest, the quiet warning not to lead him on, even though I like him more than I'm willing to admit. One of us is bound to get hurt.

But as our eyes meet, his warm energy washes over me, and for a moment, I let myself get lost in it. In that brief connection, the world around us feels simpler, safer. He wears his joy like a mask for everyone to see, radiating through his smile and pulling me in, making it all too easy to forget why I've been keeping my distance. For just a heartbeat, all the doubts, all the complications, melt away—leaving only the pull of his presence.

"Welcome to my castle." He gestures grandly for me to enter.

As I step past him, he moves aside with a small, courteous bow, then quietly closes the door behind me, sealing us off from the outside world.

Navigating the narrow hallway cluttered with shoes, I barely make it past the bathroom when I feel his hand close around mine. He pulls me back, and before I can react, I'm spun into him, the suddenness making my breath catch. Startled, I instinctively step away, but he mirrors my movement, turning it into a playful dance that ends with my back pressed against the bathroom door.

Trapped, with nowhere left to go, he closes the space between us, our bodies pressing together as his lips capture mine in a fierce, urgent kiss. For a heartbeat, I hesitate, but the intensity of it sweeps through me like a wave, pulling me under. My resistance falters, and I find myself giving in, lost in the heat of the moment. His urgency is palpable, his kiss heady and breathless—he must already be drunk. He's never this bold when he's sober.

"I'm glad you came today," Ben whispers in my ear before disappearing into the other room.

I follow him, stepping into a space that's trying to be everything at once—a kitchen, dining area, and living room all crammed into one. A small sofa tucked against the wall solidifies the attempt at a living room, but with the crowd pressing in from every angle, it feels more like a packed hallway. Despite there being only about twenty people, maybe a few more, the apartment feels like it's bursting at the seams.

Among the faces, I spot Asher, Clay, and Robert, whom I first met at that beach party at the start of summer, back when Ben and I were just beginning to orbit each other. My focus had been so singular back then—so completely on Ben—that I barely gave the others a second glance. Now, as I stand amidst unfamiliar faces, I regret not making more of an effort.

Ben weaves through the room, introducing me to a handful of boys and girls. Five boys, three girls. He skips over a few others who seem to be on the fringes of conversation, unnoticed by everyone else. I suspect they're guardian angels assigned to some of the guests, their presence adding to the crowded atmosphere, but invisible to most. I keep my distance, making a mental note of those Ben hasn't introduced me to. The last thing I need is to accidentally strike up a conversation with a guardian and end up looking like I'm talking to myself.

Feeling the need to occupy myself, I gravitate toward the drinks table. It's almost funny—alcohol used to be my go-to for moments like this, something to help me loosen up, to take the edge off my social anxiety. But now, no matter how many glasses I pour, the liquid does nothing for me. I'm left to work through the awkwardness and nerves on my own, feeling them more acutely than ever.

"Nice dress," a voice breaks through my thoughts. I look up to see a guy everyone calls Mariah or Merry—I can't remember which, though I'm pretty sure neither is his first name. His eyes sweep over me, lingering just a little too long, and I feel the unease settle in.

I wish I were better at names, but this one stuck because he stands out, his resemblance to an angel too striking to ignore. Tall, dark brown hair, piercing eyes, and a physique that looks like it was carved from marble. There's something ethereal about him—

his chiseled jaw, high cheekbones—it all gives him a kind of otherworldly quality, almost elven. Of course, not all guardian angels look like this, but based on the few I've seen, he fits the mold. I have to remind myself that this one's human.

"Uh, thanks, I guess," I respond, the words stumbling out awkwardly. He probably doesn't know I'm here with Ben—or at least, sort of with him, whatever we are right now. If he *does* know and still acts like this, then he's either clueless or an idiot. As he takes a step closer, I instinctively step back, maintaining the sliver of space between us.

"Can I get you a drink?" Mariah asks, his eyes flicking to my empty hands as he edges even closer, seemingly oblivious to the discomfort radiating off me.

My gaze flickers to the drink table beside me, and before I can muster a response, Ben appears at my side, slipping a drink into my hand and draping his arm around me in a way that feels protective, maybe even possessive. "I've got it covered," he says, his voice calm but his expression far more serious than the situation calls for.

I glance up at Ben, offering him a small, grateful smile—my silent thanks for stepping in when things were getting awkward.

"Sorry, man," Mariah mutters, backing off with a clumsy sway. His drink sloshes over the edge of his cup as he stumbles toward a group of guys, who had been mocking him earlier. He nearly topples over, his drunken exit as ungraceful as the encounter itself.

As someone pulls Ben away, claiming his attention, I'm left stranded in a sea of unfamiliar faces once more. I make an effort to mingle, exchanging polite smiles and engaging in small talk with the guests, but every time Mariah drifts too close, Ben somehow reappears at my side like clockwork.

I let my gaze wander across the room, and my attention lands on two angels deep in conversation. One has a dark complexion, matching his deep black hair, but his eyes are a striking, unnatural blue. The other, pale with golden hair and amber eyes, represents a contrasting lightness. Their expressions sour the moment they realize I'm watching, as if my gaze has crossed some invisible boundary I shouldn't have breached.

My attention shifts to the third angel, standing apart from the others. His skin is a warm tan, sun-kissed and healthy, with short brown hair and sharp, chiseled features that seem almost too perfect. His pistachio-green eyes glint with quiet amusement as he catches my gaze. He smiles warmly, and before I can react, he crosses the room toward me.

"You look bored," he says with an easy confidence.

I clear my throat, hesitant to respond, and manage a feeble, "Uh-huh" in agreement.

"I'm feeling rather bored myself," he continues. "I wish we could chat, but it seems you'd attract some unwanted attention from the other humans."

He looks at the drunken crowd, but I steal a glance at the other angels. Theis disapproving stares speak volumes.

"She's the Nephilim we've heard about," one of them declares, loud enough to make me flinch. *I'm right here!* "The one who has just accepted her powers."

The angel beside me barely reacts, offering only a nonchalant shrug.

I glance around the room, noticing that, amidst the drunken laughter and conversation, no one else seems to be paying us much attention. Leaning in slightly, I lower my voice. "Is it... okay for you to talk to me?"

He shrugs again, effortlessly casual. "Sure. I'm not breaking any rules." His smile returns, and I can't tell if he's genuinely unconcerned or just pretending to be.

"But ever since I accepted my powers, angels avoid me. Why do they seem to hate me so much? And how do they even know I'm Nephilim?" I nod toward the two angels on the other side of the room, their hostility clear in their cold stares.

"They're a bit uptight," he replies. "As for how they know, word tends to get around. Maybe your father let it slip to a few angelic friends."

I watch him closely as he speaks, fascinated. He comes across as nothing like Yabbashael, my former guardian angel—no sternness, no cryptic words of wisdom. He's laid-back, more like Ethan, carefree in a way that draws me in. Even Ezra has seems more uptight than this guy. I kind of like him.

"What's your name?" I ask, meeting his gaze.

"Tubiel," he replies with a grin, a dimple appearing on his left cheek, giving him a boyish charm. "And yours?"

Before I can answer, Ben interrupts, oblivious to our conversation. "What are you looking at?" he asks, following my gaze into what seems like nothingness.

I scramble for an excuse, unable to reveal the truth. "Oh, just lost in thought." This lie was so easy I'm afraid I'm getting better at it.

Ben leans a bit closer to me, his eyes glinting with a flirtatious challenge. "What are you thinking about?"

But before I can respond, Tubiel jumps in with an unexpected joke. "Hey, do you know why Donald Trump has his Christmas dinner on a plastic plate?" He pauses and I wait, as if Ben wasn't already the one waiting for my answer. "Because he doesn't get on with China."

I can't help it—I burst into laughter, not so much at the joke, which isn't even that funny, but at the sheer absurdity of the situation. Here I am, standing between two worlds: Ben, who has no idea what's really going on, and Tubiel, an invisible angel cracking jokes that only I can hear. The chaos of it all is almost too much to handle.

I turn back to Ben, a smile still tugging at my lips. "Sorry about that. What were you saying?"

He gives me a curious look, his brow furrowing slightly as he studies my expression. "Are you okay?"

"I think I'm feeling a bit tipsy," I lie once more.

Tubiel waves his hand in front of Ben's face, as if testing the limits of his own invisibility. "Must be tough, huh? Not being able to explain things to him," he teases, his tone light but the words cutting deeper than he probably intends.

I shoot Tubiel a sharp look, my eyes silently pleading for him to stop. It's already hard enough knowing Ben can't see this other world, can't understand the half of what's really happening. I don't need the reminder, especially not like this. I know Tubiel isn't trying to be cruel—his humor is just misplaced—but still, it stings.

Ben, completely unaware, looks at me with concern etched on his face. "I don't think I can let you go home alone in this state," he says, his voice laced with worry. But there's something else beneath the surface, a subtle undercurrent telling me he has other reasons why he wants me not to leave alone or leave at all.

"Besides, everyone's leaving. Am I supposed to clean this all by myself?" he adds, gesturing to the mess scattered around us.

Cups and bowls, half-empty bags of chips, and crumpled napkins litter the space. The mere thought of leaving him to handle it all makes me feel guilty, even though cleaning is the last thing I want to do.

"Alright, I'm heading out. Hope to see you again soon, Trouble," Tubiel says with a wink, turning toward Mariah. As he walks away, he playfully mimes scratching Mariah's head like a monkey, his mischievous personality shining through. He's well suited for Mariah, I think, shaking my head with a small smile.

"See ya," I murmur, almost to myself.

"You're leaving, too?"

I pause, meeting Ben's gaze, and shake my head. "No, I'll help you clean up."

At my words, I could swear Ben's eyes sparkle, his lips curving up instantly in the most infectious way. The energy emanating from him seem to light up the room, making the looming task of cleaning up feel almost bearable.

As the last of the guests filter out, I start gathering the plastic cups scattered around, a small pang of irritation tugging at me. Ben has always talked about his concern for the environment, yet here he is with disposable cups. It's a small thing, but it doesn't go unnoticed.

The door clicks shut, and the sudden shift in atmosphere is palpable. Ben switches the music from upbeat party tracks to something slower, more intimate. I recognize the song playing— *Caught on Fire* by Holmes.

I'm scrubbing plates at the sink when I feel his presence behind me, the gentle pressure of his hands moving from my shoulders to my hips. His lips brush along my back, each soft kiss sending a shiver up my spine. It's the spot that always gets to me. How did he know? My legs tremble under the sensation, struggling to keep me upright.

Before I can catch my breath, he turns me to face him, the world narrowing down to just us and the soft music in the background.

His eyes lock onto mine, and I'm melting under the intensity. The warmth of his touch, the tenderness in his gaze—it all feels disarmingly perfect. In this moment, all my worries about keeping my distance melt away.

"I don't need you to clean up for me," he whispers, his breath teasing my ear.

I swallow, fighting the urge to chuckle—a reflex I can never quite control in moments like this, whether serious or sexy. It's like my brain short-circuits. "What do you *need* me to do?"

A faint smile plays on his lips, a silent promise in the air. I can almost sense his intentions, especially with our bodies so close. Our legs brush together, entwining naturally, and he leans in, brushing his lips against mine—just enough to take my breath away, leaving me longing for more.

Then, with surprising ease, he lifts me into his arms. I instinctively wrap my legs around him as he carries me to his bed. Given his height and size, I wouldn't have expected him to carry me with such grace and strength.

As he lays me gently onto the bed, the look in his eyes tells me everything I need to know. In this moment, nothing else matters but the connection between us, a connection that feels both inevitable and intoxicating.

chapter 11

FIGHT OR FLIGHT

As the weeks blur by, my fighting skills sharpen, pushing me to new heights of strength and agility. Every movement feels sharper, faster, as if my body has outgrown its former limits. Being Nephilim is exhilarating—what would have taken months for my human form to master now comes effortlessly in mere weeks. Strength, speed, reflexes—everything has clicked into place.

If only I could read faster. Marve keeps feeding me book after book about creatures that seem plucked from nightmares. Shape-shifters of every kind, except for cats. There are no were-cats, something about their angelic origin, as Yabbashael once cryptically hinted. Then there are horrors like the Jubokko tree, which haunts old battlefields, drinking the blood of the fallen, but able to ensnare anyone with its branches. And of course, there are the classics: vampires and wraiths, predators that feed off the life force of others. Thankfully, these creatures are becoming rare, as their creation depends on higher demons, many of whom were vanquished long ago or have shifted their cruel amusements elsewhere.

Demons themselves remain a mystery. Marve insists they're too dangerous, urging me to stay focused on my training. "Understand the creatures you can fight," she says, "leave the demons alone." But it feels like a mistake to ignore the threat entirely. What if they find me first? Shouldn't I at least know what I'm up against?

Despite my frustration, I can't bring myself to argue with Marve. She's been more than kind. She doesn't just hand me a pile of books and leave me to it—she sits with me, discussing every creature I read about as if their stories matter to her personally. And maybe they do. For her, it's not just about the facts; it's about showing me that some creatures have found a way to live differently, even if that path is often short-lived.

I've toyed with the idea of seeking out such creatures to help or protect them, or to unite for mutual protection. However, Marve is resolute about not risking their safety by gathering in one place and making themselves easy targets, and she's probably right.

I'm still thinking about the creatures when Ethan picks me up from the university, where I'd dropped off some paperwork. My mind drifts as we walk down the sidewalk. How have I not met any of those creatures yet, if there are so many? What if I have and just didn't realize it?

"Sorry!" I mutter automatically, narrowly avoiding bumping into someone.

Ethan's laughter bursts out beside me. "Why apologize? They don't care."

I throw him a sideways glare. "Maybe it's because I was raised to be polite? Would you just walk into someone without apologizing? Good thing you weren't the one raising me."

My words come out sharper than intended, but his teasing grates on me. Ethan's laid-back, careless attitude about everything, especially things like common courtesy, pushes all the wrong buttons.

"People walk right through them all the time," he says, shrugging like it's no big deal. "They don't care if you do the same."

"What?"

His expression mirrors my question.

"Hold on a second." Ethan halts, turning to face me with a look of disbelief. I hate when people do this—stop mid-walk to make a point. Why can't they just keep moving? "Can you *not* recognize angels from humans?"

"Well, I can if their wings are out or if I see that no one else notices them," I mutter, feeling a bit foolish now.

"We've got a lot of work to do. And here I thought you were all powerful with the force. You can't even recognize an angel. What a joke!" Once again, he mocks me, his laughter echoing in the crowded street—or maybe not so crowded after all. Who knows how many of these people are actually angels who occupy none of our physical space.

By the time we park near his house, Ethan's still chuckling to himself, and I'm wondering how much longer I can tolerate his endless teasing.

"Stop it," I snap. "It's your fault anyway. You only enjoy teaching me to fight, but you don't teach me *anything* else."

Ethan's laughter fades instantly, his eyes widening with surprise. "My fault?" he shoots back. "I thought you'd train your mind on your own. Instead, you spend all your time with your little boyfriend."

"Hey!" I shout, anger rising in my chest. "Don't call him 'little' like he's insignificant. I'm not ready to throw away my normal life! You wouldn't understand—you're not human. You can't feel this way about someone."

His expression shifts, just for a moment, the briefest flicker of something I can't quite place—hurt, maybe? Perhaps my words were too careless, especially considering everything he's told me about his fall, about grappling with human emotions after being so detached from them. He may not be human, but he's closer than I'd care to admit—closer than *he'd* care to admit.

Ethan doesn't respond right away. Instead, he looks past me, locking the car with a distant expression. When he finally speaks, his voice is quiet, almost detached. "But you're not human anymore... not really."

"I still am... in a way. And I always will be," I assert, though a pinch of doubt creeps into my mind. There are parts of me I never want to lose, but I can't predict what I'll be like in a hundred years. "And for the record, I am training. I'm trying to gain control over my ability to enter dreams, but it's hard without guidance."

"Why don't you read a book on the Nephilim?" he suggests, as if that were the obvious solution.

I huff. "There isn't one in your library."

"There isn't?" Ethan's lips press into a thin line. He glances away for a moment, as if searching his memory for something he missed. His fingers absentmindedly tap against the car roof before he lets out a quiet, puzzled sound. "Huh." Without another word, he pushes himself off the car and starts walking toward the front door.

"Have you even read any of those books in your library?" I ask, following close behind.

"A few," he says nonchalantly, but his lackluster response only adds to my disappointment. "But Ezra has read most of them. He even wrote some of them. He'll be a better teacher than me."

I sigh. "Is Ezra home?"

"You mean *my* home?" Ethan corrects.

"Yes, *your* home." I roll my eyes. It's like he's getting on my nerves on purpose. "Like it matters. Ezra and Marve live there too."

"Still, it's *my* house. But... you could call it home." His voice suddenly softens. "You are my daughter, after all."

My eyes widen involuntarily, though I try to keep my reaction in check. Ethan bugs me, but I don't want to hurt his feelings again. "No, thanks," I reply simply.

I prefer my own space, away from all of them. Even though I like the group of dark creatures that's now part of my life, there's something unnerving about how they seem to hear and see everything. I crave privacy, something I feel is slipping away whenever I'm in their presence.

As we reach the house, Ethan pauses on the porch steps, his head tilting slightly, like he's listening for something beyond my perception. "He's home," he finally says, answering my earlier question.

Without another word, he heads straight for the gym-bar, not even glancing at Ezra, who's already perched at the bar, as usual. Ethan seems eager to dive into our routine, already in his element.

Before I can even put my bag down, he tosses a stick at me—a weapon I've never tried to handle before. It flies toward me, and I can't tell if he's testing my reflexes, trying to push my buttons, or genuinely thinks I'm ready for a new challenge.

I catch it, but instead of engaging, I place it down on the bench beside me. My gaze locks onto his, watching sharply for any more surprises. As I unzip my bag and pull out my gym clothes, I catch the exaggerated roll of his eyes. He doesn't get it—not everyone can afford to ruin their clothes during these little 'sessions.' My casual wear won't survive another round.

My shirt clings to my skin, drenched in sweat, each drop trickling down my forehead in slow, relentless streams. There's nothing dry left on me to even wipe it away. My arms feel like lead, my legs trembling from the intensity of the session. I pull in deep breaths, but it feels like the air is too thick, not filling my lungs fast enough.

Ethan, on the other hand, seems unaffected. He leans against the bar, casual and relaxed, like we hadn't just spent the last hour locked in combat.

"Did you know?" he says, his voice light and easy, as if the training meant nothing to him. "We've been teaching her to fight, but she can't even recognize an angel. Can you believe it?"

Ethan throws the comment at Ezra, clearly expecting backup. Ezra takes a slow sip from his glass, eyes flicking between the two of us. His expression remains neutral, but there's a glint of amusement in his eyes.

I grit my teeth, fighting the urge to snap back at Ethan. I'd love to put him in his place, but my body is spent, and my brain is unable to summon enough energy for my brain to come up with a sharp comment.

Ezra sets his glass down with a quiet clink, the faintest trace of a smile tugging at his lips. "I can believe it," he says, his tone smug. "You haven't taught her anything but fighting."

I give Ethan a pointed look, my lips curving into a satisfied half-smile. His laughter falters, the sound dying in his throat.

"I'd really like to work on my other powers, too." I say, turning toward Ezra. "Will you help me, please?"

Ezra leans back, his gaze settling on me, unreadable. There's a pause, long enough for doubt to creep in. His eyes narrow slightly, as if weighing an invisible burden.

I hold my breath, waiting. He owes me nothing, I know that. But surely, with eternity at his disposal, he can spare some time from drinking.

Finally, Ezra exhales, his shoulders loosening just a little. "Alright," he says, almost reluctantly.

Relief surges through me—until his next words hit.

"But first, you'll have to fight me," Ezra adds, his eyes gleaming like a kid who's just spotted Santa. "Then I'll help you."

My shoulders slump, and I bury my face in my hands with a heavy sigh. My muscles are still screaming from the last session, the burn radiating through my limbs, and now he expects me to fight? "Fight you? But I've never actually fought anyone. I've only practiced the moves."

It makes no sense—one moment, he's suggesting I need more than just combat training, and the next, he wants me to fight him before he'll even consider teaching me anything else. Is this some sort of twisted initiation, or do they just get a kick out of it? Maybe fighting is the only currency that matters in this house.

Laughter erupts. Rich, mocking, and completely in sync as Ezra and Ethan feed off each other's amusement. Ethan's grin widens as he leans against the bar, thoroughly enjoying my discomfort.

"To get better, you need to spar with someone," Ethan chimes in.

Ezra smirks, a taunting glint in his eyes. "Plus, at least it's fun—for me, that is." His grin stretches wider.

I open my mouth to protest, to say something—anything—but Ezra cuts me off with a sharp wave of his hand. "Do you want me to teach you or not?"

I straighten up, ignoring the exhaustion pulling at me. "Yes," I say, locking eyes with him, though my nerves continue to churn.

"Then a fight is the price."

To my surprise, he's not a complete monster about it. He gives me half an hour to refresh, handing me a drink and a power bar. Apparently, for a Nephilim, this should be sufficient. And just as I can feel some of my energy trickling back, they nudge me back onto the field.

Ezra waits for me in the center of the room, standing still, perfectly composed. *Of course he is.* I approach slowly, my legs stiff with nerves, stopping about three meters away from him.

I glance at the distance between us. It always looks so easy when they fight, but I'm not them. My body isn't fast enough to match their speed, not yet. What if he breaks my jaw? My spine? I know it wouldn't kill me, but I bet it would hurt (if stubbing my toe on the bed frame still feels like hell, I can't imagine what a real injury would do).

Despite the seriousness of it all, there's an air of casual amusement in the room. For them, this is all just fun. No pressure. No stakes.

Ezra's hand rises, finger pointed directly at me, beckoning me closer. I force myself to take two hesitant steps, then a third, each one feeling heavier than the last. His lips curl into a sly smile, and with a mocking tilt of his head, he offers a small, theatrical bow.

"Cut the charades," I say, trying to inject confidence into my voice, but I'm not fooling anyone. As soon as the words leave my mouth, I regret them—charades would be a mercy compared to what's coming.

Ezra straightens, the playful glint in his eyes vanishing. "As you wish," he replies, his tone turning sharp and serious. He moves—too fast. My mind barely registers the shift before I feel his foot connect with the side of my head.

Pain erupts, blinding and sudden, as I'm sent crashing to the floor. The world tilts, spinning wildly as I try to push myself up. My vision blurs, and every nerve in my body screams in protest.

"You have to dodge it!" Ethan's shouts, laughter bubbling in his throat as he calls out.

No kidding.

"On your feet," Ezra commands, circling around me like a predator assessing its prey.

"Is it not over yet?" I ask, though I already know the answer.

No one bothers to respond as I struggle back to my feet, keeping a cautious distance from Ezra. Every muscle aches, and I know I'm in no shape to go on the offensive; even my defense feels shaky at best.

Ezra's eyes never leave me. Even as I steady myself and stand a little taller, trying to project confidence, he's watching, waiting. Then, without warning, he lunges at me again. My body moves instinctively, dodging and weaving just fast enough to avoid his blows. We dance like this for a few minutes, though it feels like an eternity.

At first, he's toying with me, allowing me to dance on his terms. We all know he could end this at any moment. We both know it's just a game of how long he'll let me play.

But then, the look in his eyes changes. The playful glint fades, replaced by something darker, more determined. His eyes harden, and suddenly, he's not sparring anymore—he's coming for me. There's a sharpness to his movements now, a raw intensity that wasn't there before.

Before I can react, Ezra shoves me backward with surprising

force. My feet skid against the floor as I scramble to stay upright, but he's relentless, driving me toward the section of the gym where the sand gives way to solid ground. My back brushes against the wall where weapons hang in neat rows.

Ezra reaches for a sword without breaking stride. The faint metallic ring as he unsheathes it makes me shudder. It looks too sharp, too dangerous.

He tosses another sword at me, the heavy steel hurling through the air. I fumble, barely catching it before it clatters to the floor. The weight is all wrong—too heavy and unfamiliar. My grip slips as I adjust my hold, and panic rises like bile in my throat.

Ezra is already advancing, his strikes coming fast, relentless. Each swing of his blade pushes me back, forcing me to retreat. My heart pounds in my chest, my breath ragged and uneven. I move to evade him, stepping from side to side, but the sword drags at me, slowing me down. Every step feels clumsy, precarious.

Ezra's strikes grow fiercer, his eyes locked onto mine. He's not just testing my skills, but my will to keep fighting.

Suddenly, his blade comes straight for my face. I throw my sword up in desperation, but my fingers slip. The blade tumbles from my hand, crashing to the ground with a deafening screech of metal on concrete. The sound is so sharp it pierces through me, making my already concussed head throb.

Disoriented, I try to back away, but my foot catches on something, and I stumble hard. The world spins as I hit the ground. Before I can fully process what happened, Ezra looms over me, his sword tip pressed cold against my throat.

"How do you expect to fight a demon—or anything, for that

matter—if you can't even fight me?" he growls, his voice rough, full of fury.

"I don't want to fight anyone yet. I know I'm far from ready." My hands tremble as I brace myself to rise, but before I can even gain my footing, Ezra's hilt slams into my side. My body collapses back to the floor, pain exploding through my ribs.

"That's enough," Ethan's voice cuts through the room, low and calm but edged with authority. The kind of authority that commands attention without raising a single octave.

Ezra's jaw clenches, his grip tightening around the sword hilt. "What do you mean, 'enough'? Can't you see she needs more practice?" His voice rises. "You go on about how she wants to face these creatures one day, but she can't even defend herself. She's going to get us all killed if she doesn't toughen up." His eyes narrow, and for a moment, there's an almost cruel glint in them. "She needs to feel pain. It's the only way she'll push herself."

I can't help but mutter, "Geez, what's his problem?" under my breath.

But, of course, Ezra hears me, snapping his gaze toward me. "This world is not for you," he spits out. Slowly, he withdraws the blade from my neck, stepping back, but the intensity of the moment remains.

Ethan steps in closer, putting one hand on Ezra's shoulder. "Ezra, take a breath. Get a drink." He turns to me. "Pan—ehm, Dora—go get some rest, take a shower, and then come down. We'll focus on your mental training."

Ezra's gaze lingers on me a beat longer, his jaw still clenched, before he throws away the sword and storms off toward the bar.

I exhale, shaky but grateful, and head to the bathroom, following Ethan's orders.

chapter 12

TRUE FACE

After the brutal session with Ezra, I head straight for the shower, hoping the scalding water can wash away not only the sweat but the sting of his words. I stand under the stream longer than necessary, letting the heat relax my aching muscles while trying to clear my mind.

Every time I close my eyes, I hear his voice, sharp and unforgiving: *This world is not for you.* Even if that were true, I'm part of this world now, and there's nothing anyone can do about it. I shouldn't let Ezra get to me. One day, I'll prove him wrong. Maybe if I stay a few minutes longer, he'll have time to cool down.

Eventually, I shut off the water and wrap myself in a towel, taking my time as I change into fresh clothes. I draw out each moment, hesitant to face him again, though I know I can't avoid it forever.

Finally, with a deep breath, I head back downstairs, bracing myself for whatever mood Ezra might be in.

To my surprise, the gym feels lighter, almost like the tension from earlier has evaporated. Maybe it's the drinks they've had while I was upstairs, though I know better than to think alcohol works on them like it does on humans. Or maybe it's Marve—she must have arrived while I was in the shower. He's always in a better mood when she's around, like she changes him somehow.

I settle onto a stool farthest from Ezra, eyes down, not ready to test the waters just yet.

"Come, sit next to me if you want me to teach you anything," Ezra says unexpectedly, his voice soft, almost pleasant.

I glance up, caught off guard by the shift in his tone. For a moment, I wonder if I misheard, but when I look over, he's actually smiling at me. Not the smug grin I was expecting, but something almost warm.

I hesitate, unsure if the earlier tension has really dissipated or if this is just the calm before another storm. Still, there's no mistaking the invitation in his eyes. Could fallen angels suffer from bipolar disorder?

I take a breath and stand, slowly making my way over.

"Alright, first things first. You need to understand that all your powers come from within. Self-awareness is key to controlling your abilities. And second... well, you'll never be as strong with the force as Yoda." Ezra's grin widens, clearly enjoying his own joke.

I roll my eyes so hard it's a wonder they don't stick. Jedi powers again? Really? I had mentioned it once, trying to make a point, a sensible comparison as a person who knows nothing of their world, and now I'll never hear the end of it. Maybe alcohol does affect them after all—no one could make such idiotic jokes sober.

"Great. Can we just start already?" I huff.

Without a word, Ezra flicks off the music that's been playing in the background. The sudden quiet feels too intimate, too heavy. He shifts his stool in front of me, closing the distance between us. I stiffen, instinctively leaning back. He's way too close—closer than I'm comfortable with. My pulse quickens, but not in a good way.

His voice is steady, every word calm and deliberate, drawing me into the exercise as if there's no world beyond this moment. "Close your eyes," he begins softly, his tone soothing yet firm. "Breathe deeply into your stomach. Slowly in and out."

I follow his instructions, feeling the rise and fall of my chest and stomach as the air moves through me, though my pulse still races from the closeness of him.

"Clear your mind. Focus on your breath. Let it center you," he continues. "Now," he says, his voice dipping lower, drawing me deeper into focus, "imagine this room. Picture yourself in it. Feel the physical sensations around you—the weight of the air, the coolness of the ground under your feet, the smell, the stillness."

I shift slightly on the stool, feeling the firmness beneath me, trying to center myself in the room as he instructs.

"And now," he adds, the words almost a whisper, "think about how you feel in my presence. What color would you attach to me?"

His proximity makes it hard to focus. I feel his presence like a pulse, strong and steady, but unsettling. *What color would I attach to him? Purple? Green? Dark gray?* I'm grateful he doesn't demand an answer, because I'm not sure I'd like to give it.

"You see, to recognize angels from humans, you need to learn to see auras. It's hard at first, but with practice, it becomes second nature. Angels' auras are strong—hard to miss, really. Humans' auras, on the other hand, are much more... complicated," he pauses, as if searching for the right words. "Learning to see theirs will take more time, but for now, we'll focus on angels."

"What does your aura look like?" I ask, my eyes snapping open before I even realize it. I'm too impatient, I want to know now, not when I master this ability.

His answer is as swift as it is dispassionate. "Plain black."

The words hit me harder than I expected, like a sudden chill in the room. *Black?* I hope an aura doesn't reflect one's personality. Ezra, with his fierce temper and sharp edges, surrounded by darkness—it seems too fitting, and the thought makes my stomach twist. Maybe it's not just his aura that's dark.

"Close your eyes again. Take a long, deep breath. Clear your mind and relax. Breathe slowly—in and out," he repeats the same mantra. "Then, when you're ready, open your eyes and look at me. But don't focus directly on me. Look just to the side, beyond me. You may not see anything yet, but it's good practice."

I count each breath slowly, steadying myself like I would in meditation. *In... one, two, three... out... four, five, six.* My thoughts gradually quiet as I focus on his presence, visualizing

Ezra standing before me.

When I finally open my eyes, I follow his instructions, my gaze shifting off-center, blurring the edges of his figure. The room seems to stretch out around us, and even though I try not to focus on anything specific, I do notice something—someone—behind him.

Marve.

I fight the urge to fixate on her, keeping Marve in the blur of my peripheral vision, where something seems to shift and pulse. Her form is no longer solid; it's as if the air around her is rippling, an undulating haze of black and gray, like smoke twisting through the ether. There's a weight to the space she occupies—something darker, more shadowed, something that feels *other*.

The murky blur intensifies, growing thicker, denser, moving with her every subtle motion. I blink, trying to steady my breath, wondering if this is what Ezra meant by seeing auras. *Is this her aura?*

I turn my gaze toward Marve, focusing directly on her for the first time—and freeze.

Deep yellow eyes lock onto mine, glowing with an eerie, almost predatory intensity. Her head is bare, but not smooth; jagged gray horns curve upward, angling away from her face. Her nose is faint, almost non-existent, and her skin... it's not just dark, it glows, an inky black radiance that highlights every sinew, every muscle beneath the surface.

A shiver runs down my spine, the kind I can't suppress no matter how hard I try. It's not just her terrifying appearance—it's the grotesque detail of her sinews, halfway between flesh and shadow, that turns my stomach, almost making me want to vomit. It's the cold, death-like energy emanating from her, suffocating and inescapable. It's the hunger in her eyes that feels like it could strip the flesh from my bones just by looking at me. Though she eats souls, not flesh.

But then, something else catches my eye: despite the monstrous transformation, she's still wearing her clothes. A blue skirt and tank top cling to her demonic form, the glowing black of her skin clashing absurdly with the casual fabric.

A bubble of laughter rises in my throat, absurdity hitting me like a punch. But I swallow it back, my lips twitching as I fight the urge to giggle.

"What do you see?" Ezra asks.

"I'm... not entirely sure," I say, hesitating as I struggle to put the sight into words. "Black skin, fire... yellow eyes." I don't see any colors around her, though. Anything I'd describe as an aura.

Ezra's brow furrows. "You can actually see that?" There's something like awe in his voice, though it's quickly masked by his usual teasing tone. "Well, maybe there's hope for you yet. A potential Jedi master in the making."

Before I can respond, Marve's voice slices through the tension, sharp and almost a hiss. "Guys." She's staring at her own hands, fingers trembling slightly, her nails—sharp as razors—catching the light, gleaming like blades.

Both Ethan and Ezra snap their attention toward her. Ezra's playful tone drops as he murmurs, "Or maybe not." His expression hardens as realization sets in—this wasn't my powers that allowed me to see Marve's true form. She actually changed.

"I guess it's time to eat," Ethan declares, his tone much lighter than Ezra's.

In a heartbeat, Marve shifts back to her human form, and it's only then that I notice the toll it takes. Her face, once smooth and youthful, now looks drained—her skin dull and dry, fine lines tracing exhaustion across her features.

"Why didn't you tell me you were getting so weak?" Ezra asks her gently, as if his voice were a caress on her wrinkled skin.

Marve glances away, not meeting Ezra's eyes. "I don't know. It felt strange with someone new here. I didn't want to go hunting souls right away and risk scaring her off." She turns to me. "I'm sorry, Dora."

"I get it," I reply quickly, hoping to reassure her. "You've been clear—you only go after murderers. It's fine. I'm on board."

"Thanks," Marve murmurs, a soft smile gracing her lips.

In an instant, Ezra's softness evaporates. He lets out a sharp snort, his hand gripping the bar table so tightly that his knuckles turn white. His disapproval radiates from him like heat, and I can practically feel the weight of his frustration. I don't even have to look at him to know what's going through his mind. Marve, clearly suffering, is the one apologizing—and to me, of all people. In his eyes, I'm the bad guy. If I hadn't been here, Marve wouldn't be starving.

After a brief pause of silence, I press on, "So, what's our next move?"

Ethan's response is almost too casual for the gravity of the situation. "Now we look for our adept."

"Can I help?" The words slip out before I can stop them, my

excitement barely contained. Part of me knows this is a bit twisted—it feels uncomfortably close to helping with a murder. But the excitement of being involved in something supernatural pulls me in.

And then there's Marve. Seeing her like this, knowing I'm part of why she's holding back, leaves me restless. I can't just stand by and do nothing. Right or wrong, the need to help her pushes aside everything else. She's a friend.

"Are you sure you want to be a part of this?" Marve asks, her gaze searching mine for any sign of hesitation. "You realize that by eating the person's soul, I will... kill them."

Our eyes lock, and I don't blink, holding her stare, my shoulders squaring. "If someone murders another human being, then that person has no right to keep their own life."

Ezra strikes one hand sharply into the palm of the other as if to cut off the conversation. His eyes narrow, jaw tightening as he speaks, each word clipped. "We must leave now. Marve won't be able to stay in this form, let alone take on an unknown one, for much longer. We've waited long enough." He gives me one final look before striding off toward the stairs. Yes, we've waited long enough because of *me*. If anything goes wrong, it'll be all on *me*. That's what the look said.

chapter 13

FEEDING THE DARKNESS WITHIN

Ezra and Ethan disappear into the distance, their pizza delivery uniforms a perfect cover as they head toward the prison's entrance. From where I sit with Marve in the car, parked in the shadow of a nearly empty mall parking lot, the scene feels surreal. The golden afternoon light bathes everything in a calm that's too serene for what's about to happen.

It's impossible not to imagine the worst. What if we can't find a murderer for Marve to feed on? Will she stay trapped in her demonic form, growing weaker, maybe even dying? Or worse, what if she loses control and turns on someone innocent? The thought twists my stomach, and I know I'd be the one to be blamed for it.

Marve remains in her true form beside me, conserving every ounce of her strength. Her presence chills the air, seeping through my skin like a slow, creeping frost. It's suffocating, this sense of death lurking just beneath the surface, sinking into my bones.

I can't take it anymore. I throw the car door open and step into the fresh air, desperate for a reprieve. The quiet parking lot feels like a false refuge, but it's better than being trapped inside, throttled by the weight of it all.

To distract myself, I focus on practicing my aura-seeing ability. I fix my gaze on a spot on the wall ahead, steady my breath, and let my vision blur. I scan the few shoppers passing by, hoping to catch a glimpse of the auras I've been learning to see.

Dozens of people walk by, but it takes me nearly forty minutes before I finally spot one—a man bathed in soft, light blue flames. For a moment, the sight calms me, unexpectedly beautiful and almost comforting.

Then he notices me watching. He stops, a slow grin spreading across his face as he strides over. My heart skips when I recognize him—Tubiel, the guardian angel from Ben's party.

"So, running with the bad guys now, huh? Didn't think you had it in you," Tubiel says, his tone light, though his words carry an edge.

"She's not bad, and she doesn't pose any threat," I reply defensively. I don't trust the way Tubiel's watching her—like he's weighing whether to strike. They are, after all, the most natural enemies.

Tubiel tilts his head, amused. "Is that so?"

Before I can respond, another voice cuts in, catching me off guard. "What's that?" A guy steps out from behind Tubiel—Mariah from Ben's party. Of all people, why him again?

I force a smile, scrambling to play it off. "Oh, just... talking to myself." My voice feels thin, barely steady. Will I ever get used to seeing what others can't? Probably not.

Mariah squints at me. "Wait... I know you, right? From somewhere, but I can't remember where."

I nod, the false cheer in my voice as awkward as I feel. "Yeah, Ben's housewarming party."

"Oh, right, I remember now," he says, scratching the back of his neck, eyes darting briefly before landing back on me. "Hey, I've been meaning to apologize if I came on too strong that night. I was... well, pretty hammered."

An apology? From him? That's not what I expected. He might not as bad as I thought.

"Sooo... things with Ben are good?"

"Things with Ben are great, actually." I break into a grin, the truth tasting sweet on my tongue and impossible to hide.

"Pity. I mean—good for you guys," he adds quickly, flashing a smile. "But, you know, if you ever break up... give me a call." He winks, completely unbothered by his boldness.

My lips twist into a sardonic expression at his audacity. "Yeah, I'll keep that in mind."

"Don't worry, Trouble, you're not his type," Tubiel comments, watching our little exchange with interest. But with Mariah still here, I can't ask what he means by that.

Mariah's gaze flicks toward the car behind me just as Marve shifts inside, drawing his attention like a magnet. My heart freezes, dread rising in my throat.

But Tubiel acts fast. He steps forward, placing a firm hand on Mariah's head, his voice steady and commanding. "Leave."

Without missing a beat, Mariah blinks, his curiosity fading in an instant. "Alright. I've gotta run. See you around," he says, his tone eerily casual as he turns on his heel and walks away.

As soon as Mariah is far enough, I shoot a sharp glance at Tubiel. "I told you, she's not dangerous."

Tubiel's eyes harden as he folds his arms across his chest. "First of all, I'll never trust a demon. I can see she's weak and starving—the worst combination for any soul nearby. And second," his gaze sharpens, "I don't know you well enough to trust you either."

His bluntness hits me like a slap, and defensiveness surges up in my chest. It shouldn't matter what he thinks, or what any of them think. But Tubiel was the only angel who spoke to me like I was just... another being, not some outcast like the others seem to think. I find myself wanting him to see me for who I really am, not whatever label the others have slapped on me. "Can't you tell I'm not like her? That I'm... good?"

Tubiel raises an eyebrow, unphased. "It's not like I can read your soul."

"But you *have* to be able to sense it," I insist, unsure why I'm pressing the point so hard.

Tubiel's eyes flicker, studying me with an intensity that makes my pulse quicken. For a brief moment, it feels like the world narrows to just the two of us. His expression softens, just for a moment, as if he wants to believe me. It's subtle—almost imperceptible—but it's there.

Then, without a word, his gaze slips from mine, scanning the surroundings. I catch the slight twitch in his jaw as his attention shifts, something clicking into place behind his eyes.

Slowly, his eyes lock onto the distant silhouette of the prison. The air around us seems to thicken, heavy with the weight of understanding. His shoulders stiffen.

"Listen," he says, his tone serious. "You might think you're doing the right thing, but destroying a soul, even a bad one, is the worst thing that can happen. No one—no matter how righteous they believe themselves to be—should take on God's role. None of us have the understanding to judge and punish a soul. Demons... they're an abomination." His voice drips with disgust, each word a stab to my resolve.

I flinch inwardly but try to shake off his words. I can't let them tarnish how I see Marve, not after everything she's been through. She can't change her nature, and I refuse to condemn her for it. I take a breath, steadying myself, and redirect the conversation, clinging to the nagging thought that refuses to let go.

"How did you make him leave?" I challenge, narrowing my eyes. "Isn't it against the rules to invade someone's mind?" I refuse to be lectured by a hypocrite.

His expression hardens, the softness from earlier gone now completely, replaced by something fierce. "I'd rather fall," he declares, his voice low and steady, "than allow my charge's soul to be consumed by a demon."

Before I can respond, he turns on his heel and darts off, disappearing into the distance to rejoin Mariah

Judging by how our conversation ended, I guess my only chance at having an angel friend is slipping away. At least he didn't judge me simply because I accepted immortality, though it seems like the survival of a soul is the most important thing to him too.

I let out a breath and turn to check on Marve, but a subtle prickle at the back of my neck stops me in my tracks. Instinctively, I whirl around and nearly jump when I see Tubiel standing there again.

A boyish grin spreads across his face, disarming me before I can react.

"I just realized you never gave me your name."

It takes me a moment to process his words, to remember. The last time we met—our first meeting—Ben had interrupted just as Tubiel had asked me the same question.

"It's Dora," I say, still trying to catch up to the sudden shift in his mood. I thought he might be angry with me, or at least wary, but now he stands there, looking like he's having the time of his life. There's a playful spark in his pistachio-green eyes, a far cry from the seriousness I've come to expect from angels.

His grin doesn't falter as he takes a few casual steps backward, watching me with that same playful glint. Then, with an effortless turn, he heads off to catch up with Mariah.

If he wasn't an angel, I might've thought he was flirting with me.

Ezra hands me the list, his expression hard as stone. Two names are underlined, their fates hanging in the balance. Without a word, I pull out my phone and search them online.

The first is a woman who slaughtered her entire family on Christmas Eve. Abandoned by what little remained of her extended relatives, she now rots in isolation, forgotten by the world.

The second name is an elderly man, convicted for murdering his closest friend after discovering an affair with his wife. He still has a family—two daughters and a brood of grandchildren who visit him, clinging to whatever remains of their father's memory.

Before I can fully process the gravity of what's ahead, Ezra's voice cuts through the quiet. "The guy's the easier mark," he says with the same cold certainty that matches his hardened features. "You go in as his daughter. He won't question it for a second."

With that, he opens the car door for Marve, the task already decided. There's no debate, no hesitation in his tone. The burden is clear; I'm merely along for the ride. Yet, I can't seem to hold my tongue.

"But what about the woman? She's worse. You could take the form of any human, pretend to be a lawyer, and offer her a way out—suggest new evidence could set her free," I interject.

Ezra pauses for a second, just long enough to make me think I've crossed a line. But then, Ethan's voice breaks the tension. "She's got a point."

Thank God for his support. I thought Ezra was about to burn me with his stare.

Marve and Ezra exchange a glance, a silent understanding

passing between them, though a flicker of desperation dances in their eyes. Their reluctant nods seal the plan, and in an instant, Marve's transformation begins.

Her shift is swift, seamless. In the blink of an eye, she morphs into a sharp-looking woman in her forties, short brown hair framing her face. From her purse, she pulls out a pair of glasses, and puts them on. But that's not all—she's come prepared. From the depths of her bag emerge a myriad of accessories: a scarf here, jewelry there, a pullover casually draped over her arm. In no time, she's no longer Marve but a convincing attorney, ready for the role.

"Let's go," she says, already striding toward the prison.

Ethan and I stand back, watching as Marve and Ezra head out. Ezra's role is simple but crucial—he'll protect her, should the woman's guardian angel intervene. Utilizing his deceptive abilities, he cloaks his presence, making it seem as though Marve is alone to the guards.

No need for disguises this time. Unlike earlier, Ezra doesn't have to play the part of a pizza delivery guy; no doors need to be forced open. The guards will open them willingly for Marve.

An hour later, they finally return, and I know instantly that something's off. "What's wrong?"

"We're running out of time," Ezra snaps, his tone sharp. "Visiting hours end in thirty-five minutes. Show Marve the photos of one of the man's daughters. Quick."

I fumble for my phone, scrolling through the images I'd found earlier, and hand it over with a knot of unease twisting in my gut. I really thought this would be over by now. But with them returning with this sense of urgency, I worry it might lead to my biggest fear: not succeeding.

"What happened?" Ethan probes, his concern mirroring mine.

Ezra sighs, unwilling to delve into it at the moment. All he wants is to go back and complete this mission. "She's innocent."

"What? She didn't kill those people?" I blurt out in disbelief.

"She did, but she was under the influence of a demon."

My heart sinks. "Oh my God. Poor girl... what do we do? She shouldn't spend all her life in prison if she's innocent."

"There's nothing we can do," Ethan responds, his voice too calm for the storm raging inside me.

"But it's so unfair!"

"Life ain't all rainbows and sunshine, honey," Ezra remarks.

I whip my head toward him, fury igniting in my chest. I'm tired of being treated like a naive child who doesn't understand the world's cruelty. "I *know* that." I'm just not yet resigned to it.

Ethan leans casually against the side of the car, his fingers idly tapping on the metal, while Marve rummages through the trunk, her movements frantic as she searches for something. "Don't worry. If she's a good person, she'll be rewarded after her judgment by God," he says, his tone as calm and detached as if discussing a grocery list.

I whirl around to face him, digging my nails into my palms. "Is that supposed to make me feel better?" I snap.

Ethan shrugs, barely glancing my way. "Yes, actually."

"But I believe in *this* life, Ethan. I want *this* life to be good, to be just for everyone. I don't care about what happens much later, after all the suffering." The passion in my voice contrasts sharply with his indifference.

Ethan's gaze finally meets mine, lingering for a moment longer than usual, as though he's weighing something, searching for an answer in my expression. His eyes narrow slightly, as if assessing how much I can truly understand—how much I've seen of this world. "You'll understand one day."

It looks like Marve finally found what she was searching for. With a relieved sigh, she pulls out a second set of clothes. She slips behind the car, her form already shifting seamlessly into that of the murderer's daughter as she quickly changes.

Dressed in the new clothes, she steps forward, her transformation complete. "Let's give it another try," she says, her voice steady with resolve. She shoots a glance at Ezra, who nods in silent agreement.

Together, they stride off once more, vanishing into the distance toward the prison, while Ethan and I remain behind, standing in silence—though I want to do anything but that. I want to slap him for not caring, I want to storm off, I want to rant, to pour out my frustration. But what's the point? Ethan's already made it clear where he stands, and I doubt he's willing to revisit the topic.

When Marve and Ezra return, I watch as Marve transforms back to her usual form. Her skin now glows with a healthier sheen, and her hair shines with renewed life—it's as if a layer of exhaustion has been stripped away. The change is striking.

"I take it you were successful?" I ask.

Marve beams, flashing a victorious grin. "We were," she replies, her voice brimming with satisfaction. "Now, let's get home. I need a good fight."

chapter 14

NATURAL INSTINCTS

The scent of sweat hits me the moment we push through the door to Ethan's gym. I don't understand why we spend so much time here, as if the rest of the house doesn't even exist. The sprawling halls and countless rooms upstairs go unnoticed, except when I sneak off to the library for some peace and quiet. Even that feels rare.

But this space, with its battered equipment and worn floors, seems to be where we all belong—a place to burn off whatever's weighing us down. I wrinkle my nose. Someone should at least air this place out every now and then.

I follow Ethan down the stairs, but something pulls at me to glance back. That's when I notice Ezra and Marve lingering at the top, their heads close together in hushed conversation.

A flicker of suspicion coils tight in my gut.

Without thinking, I slow my steps, just enough to keep out of sight. I shouldn't care what they're talking about, but a nagging thought roots itself in my mind: Are they talking about me?

I press myself against the cool wall, holding my breath and straining to hear. Ezra's voice cuts through the air, sharp and low. "You seem to feel... exceptionally well." There's something in his tone, something accusatory.

Marve's laugh is brittle, more of a noise than any real humor. "Is that a bad thing?"

A pause follows, long enough to feel like the air itself is holding its breath. I hear Ezra take in a slow, deliberate inhale, the kind that's weighed down with judgment. "The soul... it wasn't irredeemable, was it?"

"He did it, alright? He murdered the other guy out of jealousy." Marve's tone is clipped, defensive, like she's ready for a fight.

"But?"

Marve hesitates, her words slower this time. "...but he regretted it. His soul wasn't purely evil, but it wasn't good either." She almost swallows the last words but I can still hear them. Ezra can still hear them.

He doesn't wait for more. The fury surges through him, and suddenly he's gone, his footsteps crashing like thunder as he storms out of the house. The door slams shut behind him, reverberating through the house.

Before Marve moves, I slip away, careful not to let anyone

catch me eavesdropping. I dart down the rest of the stairs on my toes, moving quickly to catch up with Ethan, who's already made his way to the bar.

By the time I reach him, trying to act like I wasn't just creeping around, he's already pouring himself a drink. I slide onto a stool beside him, forcing myself to stay casual despite the nervous energy buzzing through me.

"Where's Ezra?" he asks, glancing over his shoulder, but Ezra doesn't show, only Marve with her usual calm mask firmly in place, as if the tension from upstairs had never happened.

"He had some errands to take care of," she says smoothly, her expression unwavering, the lie rolling off her tongue without a hitch.

"His loss. At least now I don't have to wait my turn," Ethan grins, eager, his eyes sparkling like a child's on Christmas morning. Marve mirrors his excitement, her smile sharp and eager.

"You're on," she says, then turns to me with a playful twitch of her lips. "Brace yourself. You're about to witness a real showdown."

Fights don't usually captivate me; they're more like endurance tests, just waiting to see who comes out on top. But this time is different. The way they talk about demons, the raw power they wield—it has my curiosity hooked. As soon as they begin, their movements blur together, a rapid exchange of strikes and parries that crack through the air.

It's not just a fight—it's a spectacle. Ethan's eyes glint with feral joy, every punch and dodge sending his adrenaline spiking.

Marve, though, moves with something darker, more predatory. Her grin is sharp, teeth flashing, and every strike she lands seems to fuel her even more.

Then, in one fluid motion, Marve sweeps Ethan's legs from under him, sending him crashing to the floor. She's on him in a heartbeat, her foot pinning him down. Her grin is triumphant, fierce. A conqueror in every sense.

"I forgot how good you are... compared to Ezra," Ethan quips, grabbing her ankle and yanking her off balance. She crashes to the floor, but in a split second, they're both on their feet again, the intensity ramping up as their struggle escalates.

It's clear Ethan is starting to gain ground, his movements faster, more precise, pushing Marve toward the edge of the sandy area. But then something shifts.

A ripple runs through her skin, bones cracking with a sickening sound as her form changes. A faint seam appears down her neck and along her back, vanishing beneath her clothes, and from her skull, thorns—or horns—elongate, twisting upward like jagged blades. That familiar chill creeps into my bones, making my hair stand on end.

The shift turns the tide instantly. Marve launches herself at Ethan, her strikes coming faster and harder, forcing him on the defensive. His footing falters as she drives him back, blow after blow landing with bone-jarring force. I can see him beginning to buckle, his breath coming in sharp bursts, eyes narrowing as he's pushed to his limit.

Just when it seems like Marve's about to land the final strike, Ethan dodges at the last second. In one fluid motion, he twists around, grabbing her arm and using her momentum against her, flipping her to the ground. Before she can recover, he's got his knee pressed into her neck, his hand pinned against her chest right over her heart.

"You're dead," Ethan growls, triumph lighting up his eyes.

Marve's response is a snake-like hiss, her yellow eyes narrowing into fierce amber slits. The ridges around her eyes deepen, her features sharpening into something more angular and predatory. In one swift, fluid motion, she drives a vicious kick into Ethan's gut. The dull thud reverberates through the room, and he doubles over, clutching his stomach.

"What the hell? We were done!" he shouts.

Marve takes a deep breath, her form slowly shifting back to human. She looks up at Ethan, her expression softening with regret. "I'm sorry. My demon instincts took over for a moment. It's just... losing to you, again... as always."

Still crouched, Ethan waves it off with a casual shrug, though the strain is evident in his posture. "It's okay," he grunts with a playful grin, wincing slightly as he straightens. "Sorry, I can't help being this good." He pats her shoulder, and I'm surprised she doesn't kick him again. I wonder if he even realizes just how condescending he's being.

Ethan shifts his attention to me. "I hope you learned something from this, Pandora," he says, his voice heavy with authority. "Fighting a demon isn't something you'll be ready for anytime soon."

I can't help the exaggerated roll of my eyes. Of course, it's the same lecture on repeat.

"And that was after I fed on just one bad soul," Marve chimes in, almost too eagerly backing Ethan up. "Imagine the strength of other demons when they've fed properly. You might never be ready for that."

The way she says it makes my skin prickle, as though the air around her has turned colder. Before she fed, Marve seemed almost kind, far removed from the image of a typical demon. But now, something darker radiates from her, like the energy she absorbed is twisting her from the inside out. It's subtle, but undeniable—the brightness in her eyes is just a little too sharp, and every now and then, a flicker of yellow breaks through her human gaze.

Maybe I was naive to believe demons could change, that not all of them had to be evil. Tubiel's warning echoes in my mind, louder now than before. Maybe he was right.

I try to push the thought away, reminding myself why I liked her in the first place—the moments she spent with me. It was Marve, after all, who gave me so much of her time to introduce me to this world, who first guided me through my reading list, handing me the Bible and telling me to share my thoughts on God when I finished. But despite having completed it some time ago, we never circled back to that conversation, and I've been hesitant to form any conclusions without discussing it with someone.

"What can you tell me about God?" I ask Ethan, no doubt surprising him with the question as he nearly spits out the drink he's been sipping. He coughs, catching himself, while Marve arches an eyebrow, her lips curving into a half-smile. She leans over the bar, watching him with amused curiosity.

Ethan lets out a dry, ironic laugh. "Nothing, really," he says, his tone more flippant than I expected. "I've never met God."

"You haven't?" My voice jumps an octave.

Ethan shakes his head, lips curling into a smirk, as if the idea of meeting God is some far-off joke. But he was an angel, how is that possible?

"Then what *do* you know about him?"

"Not much," he admits, leaning back and crossing his arms, his tone slipping into that condescending edge I should be used to by now. "Information is power, Dora. Each angel gets only what they need to do their job. No more, no less."

"But from what you've heard or seen, tell me, do you think he's a good guy? Do you think he is perfect?"

I've never truly believed in God—or rather, I was never sure he existed. I wasn't an unbeliever, but I wasn't a believer either. I had no proof, one way or the other. But I always assumed that if God did exist, he must be perfect. He must care about what's in our hearts, not just about blind faith. The idea of a God who demanded belief seemed too self-centered, too... human. But after reading just the first two books of the Bible, I couldn't shake the feeling that the God described there might be more villain than savior.

"God is definitely good, maybe not perfect. Like any being, I believe even God evolves and learns from mistakes," Ethan says shortly, barely scratching the surface of my curiosity.

"...learns from His mistakes," I repeat, skepticism coloring my words. "Like when he wiped out nearly all life except Noah, his family, and pairs of each animal? And then he said he'd never do that again. You mean *that* kind of learning?"

Marve's laughter cuts through the air, rich with satisfaction, her amusement unmistakable. She watches me with a glint in her eyes, as if pleased by the doubt seeping into my words. It's clear she's no worshiper of God. I guess it wouldn't make sense if she were.

Ethan rolls his eyes but takes a deep breath, his demeanor shifting as he leans forward slightly. "Pandora," he begins, his tone softening into something more serious, as if's finally realizing I won't understand his world just by reading the books in his library. "God didn't kill anyone. God cherishes all life. God couldn't even kill Cain for his crime; why would God slaughter so many creatures? God was disappointed and, for a while, thought it would be better to focus on Noah's family, to try a different way, see if they could do better this time. It's obvious from all the sacred books that God tried different approaches with different people at different times. Noah's story was told that way to instill fear of disobeying God. To instill some order."

Ethan pauses, roaming my face. "What's with the look?" he asks.

I frown. "You called me Pandora."

He waves it off with an exaggerated sigh, shaking his head. "The point is, you have to read between the lines. The Bible was written by humans—people who didn't always understand the full picture of what they were being told. It's complicated. Even those who think they get it might be way off. Only God, and maybe a few others, really knew the reason behind those actions. So yeah, it's easy to look at something God did and think it's bad, but it might have been for a greater good, something you can't see or understand."

I open my mouth to respond, but Ethan's not done. With a raised finger, he says, "One thing is for sure—God is good. That much you have to trust." Then, with a shrug and a casual smirk, he adds, "Why do you even care? It's not like you're ever going to meet."

chapter 15

TRICKS OF THE MIND

The next day, after wrapping up work, I head to Ethan's place, as usual. Stepping inside, the air feels thicker, more oppressive than normal. Something's off. I glance around and immediately sense it—Ezra and Marve are still not on good terms.

Marve sits perched at the bar, her back straight, chin lifted in a posture that speaks of quiet defiance. Ezra barely spares her a glance, his focus narrowing in on me the moment I step inside.

"Are you up for a lesson?" he asks, his voice cool and edged with challenge.

I straighten instinctively. "I don't have to fight you for it this time, right?" The memory of our last session still lingers, and I have no desire to repeat that particular ordeal.

Ezra shakes his head. "You can spar with your father. I'm in no mood for that today." He pauses, his eyes narrowing slightly. "You mentioned entering someone's dreams while you sleep?"

He waits as I nod, then continues. "I've been thinking about it and I believe it's something similar to our power of deception, except you don't need to be physically near the person whose mind you're entering."

He lifts a finger, his expression suddenly taking on that of a stern professor about to deliver a crucial lecture. "While we're on the subject, you must learn to protect your mind against intrusion. It's natural to protect your mind, even humans do it, though breaching their minds is not a problem. Given your increased perceptiveness, it's harder to intrude into the mind of a Nephilim, but it's still possible. That is why it's imperative that you learn how to defend your mind. The best way to learn is the real deal. I'll enter your mind, and you, knowing it, will try to search for what is different, what feels off, and you will push it out."

"But someone could still invade my mind while I'm asleep?"

"No, it'll become second nature, an instinctive defense for your mind. It's true infiltrating someone's mind during sleep is always easier. But with practice, you should be able to prevent that."

"Alright, let's give it a shot," I reply, eager to learn and master a new skill. *Finally*!

"Alright. I'm in your head. Find me," Ezra announces.

Oh. That was fast. He sure doesn't need time to prepare to do his thing. But I expected to have some time, a heartbeat at least, to brace myself before he—

"Dora, stop focusing on not being prepared and find me," he cuts in, reading my mind and reminding me of the task at hand.

A wave of dizziness hits me, the world tilting slightly as if something is deeply wrong. My chest tightens, and I struggle for air, my heartbeat pounding in my ears like it's on the verge of giving out. Panic flares, but I force myself to meet Ezra's gaze. His eyes are steady, calm, as if he's seen this all before. He's not hurting me, I remind myself—it's only the power of suggestion.

"The power of suggestion, indeed," he echoes, reading my mind again. "You're not dizzy. You're absolutely fine. You're just nervous. Now, find me in your head."

I try, but every thought I reach for slips away, lost in the labyrinth of my own mind. It's like searching in a fog, and the more I chase him, the more scattered my thoughts become. "I don't know how. I can't feel you," I blurt out.

Ezra's expression doesn't change, he's far more patient than I am. "I'll push harder. I'll put an image in your head. Remember, it's just an illusion."

In an instant, Cerberus materializes at my feet, his familiar, shaggy form so vivid it makes me smile and reach down to pet him, the softness of his fur already stirring in my memory.

"Dora," Ezra snarls, his expression hardening.

Right. It's not real. Berry isn't really here. I blink, shaking off the comforting warmth of the illusion, and close my eyes, focusing on my breath. In and out. Slowly, I try to clear my mind, pushing past the lingering distraction.

And then, I feel it—like a shadow creeping along the edges of my consciousness. It's subtle but unmistakably foreign, an unnatural presence. I latch onto it, imagining myself catching hold of the intrusion and forcing it out like pulling a thorn from my skin.

"Great job, Dora," Ezra says, his voice softer now, almost... impressed? "Let's give it another try."

I barely have time to revel in the small victory before a sudden, urgent need to use the bathroom grips me, as if my body can't wait another second. Confused, I glance at Ezra, and there it is—a faint, amused smile tugging at the corners of his mouth. No, I don't actually need to go. He's tampering with my thoughts, manipulating not just what I see but what I feel.

"Exactly, it's actually very hard to understand when a feeling is not really yours," Ezra confirms, effortlessly reading my mind again.

It's only now that I grasp how much he can see if he probes further. This training is stripping away every layer of privacy I thought I had. Panic flares in my chest, sudden and wild. He's in my head, and I need to get him out—now.

With newfound awareness, I push back hard, focusing all my willpower on expelling him from my mind, like slamming a door in someone's face. The pressure in my mind shifts, buckles, and then, all at once, it's gone. The intrusion vanishes, and a strange sense of relief floods over me. I'm whole again—no foreign presence, no lingering touch of him in my thoughts, just *me*.

"Ouch," he winces, fingers grazing his forehead. "How did you do that?"

"I just did what you said."

"You didn't just push me away," Ezra says, still staring at me like I've done something impossible. His eyes are wide, disbelief etched in every line of his face. "You pushed back into *my* mind... with force. How did you do that?"

But the question doesn't seem directed at me. It's as though he's asking himself, as if he can't believe what just happened.

I shrug. "I don't know," I admit, a hint of frustration creeping into my voice. If I've done something remarkable, I want to understand how—so I can do it again, if necessary.

Ezra and Ethan exchange a look, something unspoken passing between them. Their silent communication sets me on edge. As Ezra's presence flickers in my mind once more, I steel myself, focusing hard on pushing him out—this time without overstepping into his own mind. But there's something else, another presence, subtle yet distinct. My instincts kick in, and I shove it away too.

"You're good," Ethan says, a grin spreading across his face. "But not good enough. You didn't push me out fast enough. If I'd wanted to, I could've done some real damage."

I frown, not even registering the compliment. "I didn't expect both of you to attack me," I retort, my voice rising. How could he possibly expect me to fend off both of them at once, and quickly, when just three minutes ago, I couldn't even find or push away a single intruder?

"That's the point," Ezra says. "No one's going to warn you before they invade your mind. You need to be ready. We'll be doing this a lot more from now on, until you learn to protect your mind automatically—no matter the situation."

I nod, acknowledging they're right, even if it feels a little unfair to criticize my speed when this is my first lesson. But I push the frustration aside. "Now, how do I stop intruding into someone's mind while I sleep?" I need something practical. I don't exactly expect people on the street jumping into my head. I need something I can use *now*, not in some far-off future. I want to stop invading my boyfriend's privacy.

"If you learn to control your power, you'll likely stop using it accidentally in your dreams," Ezra says.

"Great," I mutter. "So how do I *control* it?"

"Start by focusing on me. Tell me something telepathically," Ezra instructs. "Close your eyes. Concentrate."

The familiar wave of self-consciousness washes over me, heat creeping up my neck and into my cheeks. I close my eyes, feeling the weight of Ezra's silent expectation pressing down on me. Despite my best efforts, I have no idea what I'm supposed to be doing. How do you even send a thought telepathically?

I strain, trying to reach out with my mind, but it feels like grasping at smoke—empty, elusive. My thoughts scatter, directionless.

"Nothing," I mutter. My shoulders sag as I open my eyes, the sting of failure sharp in my chest. I'd hoped—really hoped—I was more talented than this, that I'd learn to control the power I've been using by accident much faster. A sinking doubt creeps in. What if I never learn it?

"Maybe you should try it with someone you have stronger feelings for," Ezra suggests, his eyes searching mine. "You mentioned entering your boyfriend's dreams, didn't you?"

I glance away, fiddling with a loose thread on my sleeve. I nod slightly, a barely perceptible movement, hoping to keep the focus off my personal life.

Ezra notices but presses on gently. "Close your eyes," he instructs again. "Picture him. Imagine stepping into his shoes, feeling what he feels, seeing through his eyes."

I swallow hard but do as he says, letting my eyelids drift shut. The world fades, and I summon Ben's image—the curve of his smile, the warmth of his hand in mine, the way he sticks out his tongue when he's concentrating.

"Now, reach out," Ezra murmurs. "Can you see where he is?"

I focus harder, diving deep into the memory of Ben. The faint scent of his cologne lingers at the edge of my awareness, teasing my senses. For a moment, his presence feels real—tangible, yet just out of reach. I push deeper, imagining what it would be like to slip into his skin, to breathe through his lungs, to see through his eyes. Slowly, the image sharpens: his hands, steady and familiar, holding a spoon over a bowl of cereal in his apartment.

But just as quickly as the vision forms, I feel a sudden resistance, like hitting a wall. The scene shatters in a heartbeat, slipping through my grasp, and I blink back to reality—Ezra standing in front of me, his dark brown eyes steady, radiating a calm but slightly menacing energy, just like Ethan's.

"He's at home, having breakfast," I murmur, still a bit dazed. "But... he pushed me away."

Ezra's brow arches in surprise. "He pushed you away? How old is he?"

"My age."

"Strange. It's not usual for a mere human your age to be able to push someone out of their mind," he says, getting my hopes up once again. I thought I was certainly dating an ordinary human, but now there's a flicker of real hope. Hope he might be a Nephilim too.

"Anyway, is there someone else you feel strongly about?"

"My parents," I answer without hesitation.

"Well then, let's try this," he doesn't waste a moment, moving to the next step. "We'll start with the people you're closest to—the ones you feel the most attachment to—and gradually work up to using this power on anyone. You'll build control that way, step by step.."

I stiffen, my moral compass fighting me. "I don't want to use this power on anyone. That's why I'm learning to control it in the first place. It's abusive."

Ezra's expression doesn't falter. "You never know when you'll find yourself in a situation where you need to use it. Learning control doesn't mean you have to wield it recklessly. Think of it as a tool, one you keep in your back pocket, ready for emergencies."

I chew on his words, the logic undeniable, though the idea still churns uncomfortably in my gut. "Alright," I say finally, my shoulders loosening. "You make a valid point."

I just hope I don't stumble upon anything in their minds I wouldn't wish to see, anything that might haunt me for the rest of my eternal life—like my parents having sex. All the hairs on my arm rise, but I quickly push the thought away.

This is so not a good idea.

We spend the rest of the morning practicing my powers.

I manage to slip into the minds of my parents and my best friend, Raya, gently nudging them to call me. And they do, just as I'd suggested. Thankfully, I manage to keep it light, not slipping deeper into their thoughts.

But no matter how hard I push, I can't break through the mental walls of Ethan or Ezra. My emotions create an invisible barrier, blocking my way, making it impossible to even find the door—no matter how wide they leave it open.

chapter 16

WHEN DANGER HEALS

The engine hums softly as we head toward the beach, but the air inside the car feels anything but calm. Ethan's suggestion to go to the beach together, *as a family*, might have sounded innocent enough, but it's obvious his real motive is to force Ezra and Marve into the same space, hoping a change of scenery will somehow close the chasm between them.

Though the beach is only a short drive away, the ride feels interminable. The silence is thick, suffocating, curling around us like an unseen force, squeezing tighter with each mile. Tension pulses in the air, like the coiled body of a snake, ready to strike.

Every glance exchanged is a silent hiss, promising a storm on the horizon.

Ezra sits rigid in the passenger seat, and I can feel the pressure radiating off him from the backseat, where I'm wedged between the window and Marve. The fact that they refused to sit next to each other speaks volumes.

I can only hope Ethan knows what he's doing because the last thing any of us needs is for this quiet tension to erupt into a full-blown argument—especially not in the cramped confines of the car. The thought of it makes my skin crawl. *At least wait until we get out*, I silently beg, *just until we have room to breathe.*

After parking the car, we set off on foot toward the beach. The sun beats down, warm and relentless, and with every step, the scent of saltwater intensifies, cutting through the weight of the day.

I love the beach. I love the sea. The moment that salty air hits my lungs, it's like something in me awakens, an excited flutter of anticipation. It's as if the ocean itself calls to me, promising freedom, adventure—*an escape.* For a brief moment, I allow myself to imagine that this could be just another peaceful day by the shore.

But that fleeting peace is shattered in an instant.

Out of nowhere, Ezra moves, his body tensing as he steps in front of Marve, gesturing for her to stay behind him. His movements are sharp, instinctive, like a predator sensing danger before it fully materializes.

My breath catches, and I blink, confusion knitting my brows. What's happening? I glance around, my heart picking up pace, scanning the street for whatever caused the abrupt shift. That's when I see someone approaching, their figure cutting through the sunlit haze like a shadow against the brightness.

Focusing harder, I see an aura unlike anything I've ever encountered. Where the guardian angels I've seen, like Tubiel, carried a serene, soothing light blue energy, this person's presence feels entirely different. The air around them vibrates with heat, like a scorching fire, intense and consuming. It rolls off them in waves, thick and suffocating, making the hairs on the back of my neck stand on end.

As the figure draws closer, details begin to sharpen. Blond hair catches the sun's rays, shimmering like gold against the backdrop of the beach. The intense blue of his eyes feels like it could pierce straight through me, locking onto something deeper, something hidden. A sharp chin and strong jawline complete his striking appearance. Handsome yet fearsome, there's an unmistakable mix of allure and danger about him, like a predator cloaked in beauty.

The air crackles with his energy, charged and electric, and I can't shake the growing sense that we've just crossed paths with someone extraordinary—someone not to be underestimated.

"Abaddon, hello," Ezra says, his voice taking on a strained, almost forced cheerfulness. A smile—too tight to be genuine—stretches across his face as he reaches out to shake the newcomer's hand, giving him an awkward pat on the shoulder.

"Hello, old friend," Abaddon replies smoothly, his voice dripping with an unsettling familiarity. He reciprocates Ezra's awkward gesture with a firm handshake and a thin smile that doesn't quite reach his eyes. "I see you still keep company with the low ranks..." His gaze shifts pointedly toward Ethan, lingering just a moment too long. "Peliel," he adds, extending his hand.

For a few seconds, Ethan doesn't move anything but the muscle in his jaw. Abaddon's words hang in the air, a subtle insult veiled in politeness. Reluctantly, Ethan takes his hand, but his grip is firm, an unspoken defiance in the shake.

"It's Ethan," he corrects, his tone edged with irritation.

Abaddon barely acknowledges the correction, his eyes already sliding past Ethan and landing on me. His gaze sharpens, taking me in with a slow, deliberate once-over. The scrutiny feels invasive, as if he's assessing more than just my appearance.

"And who might this be?"

"This is Dora, my daughter."

Abaddon's gaze flickers, but his expression remains frustratingly neutral. "Hmm, a *Nephilim*," he mutters, as if the word itself leaves a bitter taste on his tongue.

He might as well have called me an abomination—his tone made what he thinks of me clear enough. It's as though, in his eyes, my very existence is an insult.

I wonder what's fueling his contempt. Has he heard rumors about me, or does he simply assume I've embraced my powers and forsaken the afterlife because of the company I keep? Or could he actually sense it somehow? My thoughts flash to Yabbashael's words—that there's no way to distinguish a Nephilim from a human. But the way Abaddon's eyes linger on me makes me question whether that's really true.

"So, taking a little family trip, are we?" Abaddon's tone drips with condescension, his smirk barely hidden behind the false pleasantries.

"Exactly. And what brings you to this area?" Ezra responds, his voice calm, polite, effortlessly brushing off Abaddon's disdain. It's a practiced deflection, one he's clearly used to employing when dealing with the likes of him.

"Work. Always work," Abaddon replies, with an air of superiority so thick it nearly suffocates. The way he says it, you'd think none of us could possibly grasp the burden of such responsibilities. "I have to go now; it was nice seeing you all. I hope we can catch up soon," he adds, his insincerity palpable. His hand lands on Ezra's shoulder again, a gesture laced with dominance rather than camaraderie.

As his gaze shifts toward Marve, the atmosphere changes. Ezra's muscles tense, his body stiffening as if ready to spring at any moment. Abaddon and Marve share a brief but charged look, one so intense it sends a ripple of unease through the air.

"She's not—" Ezra begins, his voice tight, stepping slightly forward in defense, but Abaddon's hand rises, cutting him off before the words can fully form.

"I know. Don't worry," Abaddon says smoothly, a faint, knowing smile curving his lips. There's something unsettling in his reassurance. Without another word, he turns and walks away, leaving the street in a heavy, eerie silence that seems to cling to the air long after he's gone.

"What was all *that* about?" I ask the second he's out of sight.

Ezra's attention shifts immediately to Marve, his hard exterior softening into concern. "Are you alright?" he asks, his voice gentle, as though speaking to something fragile, like Marve might shatter under the lingering shadow of Abaddon's presence.

"Yeah," she replies, her voice steady, but I can hear the heaviness in her breath. It's as if a colossal weight has just been lifted from her, though the traces of fear still cling to her. Only now, in the absence of danger, does she seem to realize how close the edge was.

But angels are bound by strict rules: they can only confront demons if there's a direct threat to their charge. They can't harm her if she's just minding her own business. Guardian angels protect, not provoke. Starting a war with the underworld isn't an option for them. Which is exactly why I thought we should step in—to carry the weight they couldn't.

Ezra steps closer to Marve, his movements deliberate, careful, as if trying not to overwhelm her. Something about the way they look at each other makes me feel like I'm intruding on something private, something unspoken. Sensing they need space to process whatever just happened, I decide to catch up with Ethan, who's already making his way toward the beach, his pace unhurried, almost detached.

As I follow him, I can't help but hope this might be a turning point for Marve and Ezra—a chance for them to reconnect, to bridge the rift between them. But deep down, I know it's more than just a minor disagreement. She consumed a soul, one that could've been saved. That's not something easily forgiven. Yet, a part of me can't blame her. Sometimes, there's no choice left.

And if Ezra truly loves her, forgiveness might come more easily than I expect.

When I finally reach Ethan, the flood of questions I've been holding back rushes out before I can stop myself. "Who was that? And why was his aura so different? So... potent?"

"That's because he's an archangel," Ethan says casually, as if he's just dropped a mundane piece of trivia, not something that makes my mind reel.

An archangel. I can hardly believe it. Until now, I've only encountered guardian angels—beautiful, kind beings dedicated to watching over us. But what exactly does an archangel do? What did Abaddon mean by 'work'?

It's maddening how no one ever seems willing to talk to me about angels or heaven. Especially Ethan. He's always tight-lipped about it, probably still bitter about being kicked out—or pushed down—from that world. That must be why angelic stories are so scarce in his house. Maybe if I meet Tubiel again, I can finally get some real answers.

Ethan, no doubt noticing the excitement sparking in my eyes, gives me a look and cuts through my thoughts with a blunt remark, his words laced with bitterness. "That's nothing to get excited about. Most archangels are jerks."

The sting of his words lands, but I push past it, curiosity gnawing at me. "How does Ezra come to call an archangel a friend, anyway?" I muse aloud. "I thought guardian angels pretty much only interacted with their own kind."

"He ran in different circles," he says dismissively, then adds, "Why do you think Ezra was a guardian angel?"

I falter, my thoughts tripping over themselves as I try to make sense of my assumption. "I don't know, I guess... I just thought...

since you were... and I've never met any other type of angel before now," I stammer when it hits me—I had no real reason to believe Ezra was like the others.

Ethan raises an eyebrow, waiting for me to catch up. "Then what *was* he?" I finally ask.

"He was a very special angel with a higher rank—not an archangel, but close. He was above the common guardian angels. Ezra was the keeper of souls whose bodies were never born," Ethan explains, his voice taking on a rare note of respect. "He guarded them, watching over those souls while they waited for another suitable body. Sometimes, that wait took centuries."

"I didn't realize such a position existed. Why did he fall?" I glance back, instinctively checking the distance between us and the others. Not that it matters—with their enhanced hearing, they could probably catch every word if they wanted to. Still, I lower my voice a bit. The fall of an angel is no small thing.

"He fell because he couldn't bear it any longer. Souls that were created to walk the Earth, prove themselves, and then have their happy ending in the afterlife—or, of course, spend eternity in hell if that's what they deserve—were staying in heaven waiting for a body, which was just delaying their destiny. He even told me about souls that haven't left heaven yet—souls he was guarding for millennia. He's never told me what he did to fall, but I know he did it on purpose. For him, the most important thing in the world is to see a soul fulfilling its destiny—getting judged. He couldn't watch when this wasn't happening with all the souls," Ethan explains.

My skepticism slips into my voice as I ask, "Then how can he be with a demon, knowing she's interfering with souls' destinies?"

"Living among humans can change how you see things. He knows Marve only takes what she needs to survive, and those souls... they would've ended up in hell anyway. I think he's more concerned about the ones with potential for good."

I catch the subtle shift in his tone—defensive, as though guarding Ezra's decisions. But there's no need for it; I wasn't judging, just trying to make sense of the man who seems to carry the weight of the world on his shoulders. I'm fond of Marve, and I hope Ethan knows that. This isn't about blame.

Ethan's eyes flick to my face, reading the unspoken thought with ease. His expression softens, a faint smile tugging at the corner of his mouth. He winks at me and says, "And also, love changes everything."

Before I can ask another question, the sound of footsteps in the sand draws my attention. Marve and Ezra catch up to us just as we reach the edge of the beach. The transformation in their mood is striking—they're holding hands, smiling, as if yesterday's tension had never existed. The dark cloud that hovered over them seems to have lifted, at least for now.

For a moment, it feels almost normal, like we're just a group of friends enjoying a sunny day at the coast, instead of a bunch of supernatural beings balancing between worlds.

Maybe the beach wasn't such a terrible idea after all.

chapter 17

CHECK THE DICTIONARY, DARLING

Ethan inhales deeply, a grin spreading across his face as though he's letting go of something heavier than just the day's tension.

"Who's up for the water?" he calls out, already yanking off his shirt and tossing it carelessly to the ground along with his towel and car keys, like they were nothing more than an afterthought.

Before anyone can answer, he's off, sprinting toward the waves with a kind of childlike enthusiasm I haven't seen in him before. In just his swim shorts, he dives headfirst into the ocean, his body cutting through the water like he was made for it.

I try not to stare at his well-defined physique, reminding myself that he's my biological father. Sometimes, it's hard to reconcile that fact when he looks too young to be my dad, and especially since he's been absent for most of my life.

The rest of the group isn't far behind, shedding their outer layers and heading toward the water. As they pass by, Ezra catches my eye, and the look he gives me is dark and piercing, like he's warning me without saying a word. The silent message is clear—don't pry into his affairs.

It's obvious now he overheard my conversation with Ethan. Maybe he thinks I insulted Marve, or maybe he's just remembering why he resents me in the first place—for renouncing my afterlife. Whatever it is, the weight of his stare lingers longer than I'd like, but I decide it's time to stop worrying about him.

"Come join us," Marve calls from the water.

At least she's not holding any grudges against me. Sometimes, it feels like Marve is the only one who embraces who she truly is, without shame or hesitation. She accepts my curiosity, even welcomes it, while the others seem to take offense at every innocent question.

"Coming!" I call back, starting to make my way toward the waves.

But before I can take more than a few steps, a voice cuts through the air like a cold wind, stopping me in my tracks. "So, this is who you're hanging out with now? Two fallen angels who've turned their backs on their mission, and a demon?"

The melodious voice is unmistakable. My heart stutters, and I turn slowly, already knowing who I'll see standing there.

Yabbashael.

There she is, my former guardian angel, her posture rigid and her expression stern, her eyes sharp with judgment.

"Yabbashael!" I exclaim, surprised but—oddly—glad to see her. It's been so long. Too long have I felt the void she left. Too long have I gone without hearing her scold me for considering immortal life, or feeling her caress me just for the love of me.

She stands there like a statue, unmoved, the disappointment etched into the corners of her eyes more intense than I'd remembered.

"They're good people," I blurt out, feeling the urge to defend the ones who have become my unlikely companions. I feel the need to justify myself, the same way it did with Tubiel. I crave her approval, just like I did his, but for different reasons. With Tubiel, it's because he's the only one who's treated me like a friend since I accepted my powers. With Yabbashael, it's something deeper—like seeking a parent's approval.

Though I didn't get to spend much time with her after I gained the ability to see and speak to angels, I've always felt her presence. She's been with me since I was born, constantly watching over me, guiding me, protecting me. She's like a mother in more ways than one.

But the warmth I'm hoping for doesn't come. Instead, she snorts, the sound harsh and dismissive. "You still think that? You still believe you made the right choice?"

Her words hit me harder than I'd expect. There's no anger in them, just a raw disappointment that feels worse, like I've failed her in some irrevocable way. The sting of it makes my chest tighten, but I stand my ground, unwilling to crumble beneath her gaze.

"I do," I say, trying to keep my voice steady, though a flicker of doubt creeps in at the edges. "But yeah, sometimes I wonder..." The words slip out before I can stop them. There's something about Yabbashael that makes me want to confess—everything. Even the thoughts I don't dare admit to myself. Maybe it's the energy she exudes, the quiet authority of a guardian angel, that draws the truth out of me. But just as quickly, I pull back, catching myself before I say too much. I can already picture the smug satisfaction in her eyes if I let her know I've doubted my choice. The last thing I need is an 'I told you so.'

I give her a one-shoulder shrug. "At least I've got eternity to figure it out," I say lightly, hoping to deflect.

But her gaze darkens. "What if that eternity is cut short?"

I let out a half-amused chuckle. "But I'm immortal," I counter.

She doesn't blink. "Immortality isn't invincibility, Dora. It doesn't mean you can't be destroyed. There are forces far older and more dangerous than you can imagine—beings who wouldn't hesitate to end your eternity in the blink of an eye."

"Did you miss me already? We haven't seen each other for decades, and now I run into you twice in one summer," comes a voice from behind, startling me.

"Peliel," Yabbashael greets him, her tone cool and distant, completely ignoring his playful approach.

I turn to see Ethan strolling toward us, a light chuckle escaping his lips. "Yabbashael, you're making my daughter look crazy talking to herself."

The truth is, I was so caught off guard by Yabbashael's sudden appearance that I momentarily forgot only I could see her. But I know Ethan's concern isn't really about appearances—there's hardly anyone around anyway. We chose this secluded spot for Marve's sake, away from prying eyes. The only people nearby are two adults preoccupied with their children, entirely oblivious to anything happening outside their little world, and one other guardian close by.

Yabbashael shoots Ethan a look of disbelief, clearly unimpressed by his attempt at humor. Her eyes narrow slightly, as if to say there are far more pressing matters at hand than his playful banter. It's obvious this isn't the conversation she came here to have.

"What were you talking about?" Ethan asks, though his tone carries the weight of someone who already knows the answer. His eyes flick between us, the silence stretching out as neither Yabbashael nor I bother to respond. We both know his question is just a formality—he probably overheard everything.

"Hmm," he mutters when the silence drags on, clearly unimpressed by our refusal to engage. "So you're breaking the rules now?" His words come out sharp, a quick jab aimed at her. Ethan doesn't play well with anyone who isn't Ezra or Marve, and this feels like an attempt to drive her away, to keep her from telling me something he doesn't want me to hear.

Yabbashael remains unfazed, her calm composure intact. "I am not breaking any rules. My charge is just over there," she says smoothly, not rising to his bait.

Ethan, clearly not satisfied, presses harder, his voice rising slightly. "I meant in the cave. You came to see Dora after she accepted her powers."

A flicker of anxiety crosses Yabbashael's face as she scans the surroundings, her eyes darting for any sign of prying ears. Then, with a swift step forward, she faces Ethan directly, her voice low but sharp. "What are you trying to achieve here? Make me fall?" Disgust twists her features, and I can't help but feel like whatever remaining respect she had for him just slipped away. I've lost a bit of respect for him too.

Ethan's expression hardens, his voice taking on a snarling intensity, each word biting like an angry dog. "Stop poisoning my daughter with your words. You've already lost. Deal with it."

"You have truly changed."

Ethan's face lights up with a smug smile as he shoots back, "And you haven't changed a bit. After everything, you're still so blind."

Yabbashael's lips curve into a humorless smile, mirroring Ethan's. "Yes, I blindly follow the orders given to us by God. By the creator. By the only one who knows the purpose of all this."

She gives me a glance filled with pity before striding away toward the family enjoying a sunny day at the beach. As she moves further away, I notice the tension slowly draining from Ethan's face, his posture relaxing.

"So..." he starts, hesitating for a beat before continuing. "Are you joining us for a swim?" He's trying to act casual, as though the conversation with Yabbashael didn't just rattle the air between us.

I kneel to gather my belongings from the ground, tempted to storm off, to leave all of this behind. But the unanswered questions buzz like a swarm in my mind, refusing to let me walk away. After a moment of inner conflict, I decide to stay, to confront him.

"How can I be killed?" I don't bother explaining what she told me, I know he heard everything Yabbashael said. His eyes lock onto mine, steady, annoyingly calm.

My hands ball into fists at my sides, nails biting into my palms as I wait for his answer. I need to know the truth, and I need it now.

"Don't worry about it, Dora. It's practically impossible to kill you," Ethan says, his tone smooth and dismissive. His words should be reassuring, but they clang hollow against the irritation bubbling in my chest. Does he think I'm a child who doesn't need to know anything? To a being thousands of years old, I might be, but I deserve to know more—to understand this world, my place in it, and the dangers that now seem to lurk around every corner.

He catches the determination in my eyes and sighs. "Fine. To kill you, someone would have to pierce your heart with a weapon made from the Yubokko tree. But that's highly unlikely. The Yubokko tree is so dangerous that no one can even approach it, let alone craft a weapon from it. I doubt such a weapon even exists."

His explanation does little to ease the turmoil inside me. The way he brushes it off, as though it's nothing, only fuels my frustration. "You don't *know* that," I snap. "You should've told me."

"Don't bite my head off. I didn't think it was relevant."

I don't back down. "You didn't *think*?" Unable to suppress the flood of emotions any longer, my voice cracks. "I can't... I need to go." I turn my back on him before he can offer any more dismissive explanations and leave.

chapter 18

NO SOULS ON THE MENU

For the first time since accepting my powers, I can finally focus on the people who are truly close to me—my boyfriend and Raya, my only real friend. After everything with Ethan, I needed space, and being with Raya always brings a sense of normalcy. Her long, straight blonde hair, sparkling blue eyes, and petite frame with a model-like figure have a way of making the world feel lighter, like she's carrying sunshine wherever she goes.

Today, we head to our usual spot for drinks, falling into the familiar rhythm of our routine. The waiter doesn't even ask for our order anymore; it's automatic. "Two Cuba Libres without straws," we say in unison, our voices overlapping with practiced ease.

I feel relief the minute we settle into our favorite booth, the anticipation of our usual heart-to-heart grounding me, pulling me back to a version of myself I can recognize again.

As we sip our drinks, Raya's gaze sharpens, zeroing in on me like she can tell something's off. Normally, by now, the alcohol would've started to blur the edges, making me feel a little lighter, but tonight I'm frustratingly sober. I can feel her noticing it too. I force a smile and shrug. "I think it's because I've eaten too much," I say, blaming my unusually clear head on a full stomach, hoping she'll buy the excuse.

Fortunately, my excuse is enough to shift Raya's focus. She launches into her usual chatter about her perfect boyfriend, mixing in her signature jokes. Normally, I'd be laughing along, but tonight, something feels off. Her jokes don't land the way they used to; I can't even force a proper smile. My mind keeps drifting back to Ethan and what Yabbashael told me. I'm here, but I'm not. It's like I'm stuck between two worlds, unable to fully engage with hers.

I glance down at my empty glass and consider ordering another drink, hoping it'll help me shake off this haze. But just as I'm about to signal the waiter, I notice a figure approaching our table. I pause, the words dying on my lips. It's not the waiter. It's Tubiel, his wide grin directed right at me.

I offer him a subtle, guarded smile—after all, only I can see him—but even that slight gesture is enough to catch Raya's attention. She follows my gaze, leading to nothing in her world, and laughs, nudging me playfully. "Oh, there she goes again," she teases. "Lost in your own little world, smiling at the thought of who knows what."

I try to laugh with her, but the moment Tubiel steps into view, everything else fades. The mundane chatter, the normalcy of sitting here with my best friend—it all feels distant now. Something deeper, more real, has arrived.

And that's when it hits me. As soon as I see Tubiel—part of this new world I'm caught up in—I feel more alive, more awake. I light up in a way I don't with Raya anymore. It's becoming painfully clear that I'm no longer fully part of this normal, human life. I've desperately tried to hold onto this world, to stay connected to humanity, but I'm starting to realize I belong in the other world more than I want to admit—despite what Ezra thinks.

"So, how are things?" Tubiel asks, though he knows I can't respond with people around. "Made any new demon friends lately?" His laugh is mocking, but there's something forced about it, a tension just beneath the surface.

Everything seems like a joke to him, but I know it's not. I've seen the other side of Tubiel, the one that's dead serious when it matters.

His next question is designed to rattle me, to poke at the wounds I'm trying to bury. "How did the soul-killing go, anyway?" I tense, trying to keep my composure as the familiar sting settles in my chest.

"I hate this," he suddenly confesses. "It's not very often that I get to meet a human who can see me. I want to be able to talk to you like a normal person. Angels are so boring, always gossiping or droning on about their perfect charges."

"I am not a human," I murmur, the words slipping out before I can stop them.

"What did you say?" Raya asks, snapping me back to reality. I blink, realizing I'd completely missed whatever she was saying. She's watching me now, her brow furrowed with concern.

"I need to go to the bathroom," I lie, already shifting to the side and rising from the bench. With a subtle nod to Tubiel, I signal for him to follow. I can't have him hovering around, pulling me out of this world when I'm *trying* to savor my time with Raya.

The bathroom offers a brief escape, a quiet sanctuary where the scent of lavender lingers in the air, mingling with the soft hum of running water. A woman stands at the sink, drying her hands, and I pretend to wash mine, glancing at her in the mirror. I wait, counting the seconds as she fumbles with her bag.

Finally, she leaves, the door swinging shut behind her with a soft thud, leaving me alone with Tubiel.

I turn to face him, grateful for the chance to speak freely at last. "Should I answer your questions in order?" I ask, a touch of sarcasm in my voice. "Things are... well... strange and great at the same time. No new demon friends," I add with a fake half-smile. "And as for 'soul-killing'..." My tone hardens, the bitterness creeping through. "That's not something I want to talk about."

I expect Tubiel to push, but he surprises me, letting it go. "Okay, Trouble. Tell me why things are strange." His mocking tone dissolves, replaced by a genuine interest that catches me off guard. It's as if the air between us shifts, his teasing eyes now filled with a sincere curiosity.

"Well..." I hesitate, not wanting to dump my problems onto

him. But when Tubiel's eyes meet mine, there's a quiet calm that settles over me, like his presence alone is enough to smooth the edges of my tangled thoughts. It's strange how his angelic aura seems to ease the tension I've been carrying, like an invisible balm soothing my frayed nerves.

"I had an argument with my father. I mean, with Ethan... or Peliel... you know who I mean," I mutter, the words tumbling out in a disjointed mess.

"Aah, Peliel..." Tubiel's face shifts, his eyes widening slightly with recognition. For a split second, I catch the surprise on his face—he hadn't known who my father was until now. But something in the way his features soften tells me he's familiar with the name.

His brow furrows just slightly, as if piecing together a puzzle. "Why did you argue?" he asks, his voice softer now, the concern in his tone pulling at me like a gentle warmth, inviting me to open up, to let go of the weight I've been carrying.

With a deep breath, I continue, the words flowing more freely now that I've found someone who truly listens. "It wasn't really an argument. He just kept it from me that I can be killed, and I don't appreciate being left in the dark. I hate it when people keep things from me, and he didn't tell me the whole truth before I decided to... you know, give up the afterlife. I guess I need some space from him."

There's no one else I can talk to about any of this—certainly not Ethan or Ezra, and Marve is always with them. Yabbashael? She'd just throw an 'I told you so' in my face, or something equally useful. Plus, I don't exactly run into her too often. Ben and Raya are off-limits for this kind of conversation. But Tubiel... Tubiel gets it.

"He should have told you, but what's done is done. Besides, killing you? That's practically impossible." He leans back slightly, a hint of laughter in his tone. "Who would want to kill you, anyway?"

Little does he know, I plan on killing demons one day, potentially making a whole load of enemies. But I'm not about to delve into that, so I say a simple: "Thank you for listening," accompanied by a genuine, warm smile.

Tubiel's gaze lingers on me, a playful glint sparking in his eyes. His lips curl into a half-smile—mischievous, almost teasing—and something flutters in my chest. "I have to admit, I'm rather glad you're immortal."

My eyes widen in disbelief, *who is this guy?* "Really? I thought guardian angels were all about souls and the afterlife."

"Yes, but you see, I'm immortal too." There's something in his voice—a note that dances on the edge of flirtation, subtle but there. Or maybe I'm imagining it. He's an angel, after all. Angels don't flirt with humans. Definitely not with Nephilim.

"It's comforting to know there's someone else out there, besides angels, who can be my friend for eternity," he adds.

I arch an eyebrow, my lips curving into a teasing smile. "You're quite the special angel, aren't you?"

A soft chuckle escapes me, and I can't help but appreciate how different he is—how willing he is to break away from the mold. He doesn't follow the rigid expectations the others seem so bound to, and that's what makes him stand out. That's what makes me like him more.

"Let's head back," I suggest, tipping my head toward the door. I've probably been gone long enough for Raya to wonder if I fell in the toilet.

Tubiel gives an exaggerated sigh, lowering his head dramatically as if heartbroken by the fact we have to return—his mock sorrow drawing a small smile from me.

But as we leave the restroom, his posture straightens, the mischievous spark in his eyes dimming as he slips back into his angelic role. Without a word, he glides toward the exit, his movements smooth and purposeful. I notice his focus shift to a young girl making her way out of the pub, probably one of his charges.

But I don't stay angelless for long. Before we even order our third drink, a new presence sweeps in, shattering the moment of calm. Raya's guardian angel appears behind her, tall and imposing. With brooding eyes and a strong jawline, he carries an intensity that feels more intimidating than comforting. Though his aura is the familiar, soft glow of a guardian, his stern gaze sends a chill down my spine, making me feel just as small as I did standing in front of Abaddon.

"Hmm, Nephilim... you always bring trouble," he accuses, his deep voice slicing through the ambient chatter of the restaurant. The words are sharp, unprovoked, aimed directly at me like daggers.

With a swift, protective motion, he unfurls his wings around Raya, cocooning her. The feathers, plain and white, should make him look unremarkable—just another guardian—but something catches my eye.

Tiny red tips stain a few of his feathers, as though blood had seeped into them. They don't drip, but the faint crimson makes him look almost menacing, even for a guardian. I never considered before that an angel's wings might reflect something deeper. Now, I can't help but wonder—what does the blood on his signify?

Raya, oblivious to his presence, continues chatting, but it's hard for me to focus when her guardian's wings are practically obstructing my view. I try to act natural, nodding along, but the feathers are all I can see.

Then, over the angel's shoulder, a figure emerges—a man approaching our table with an unnerving absence of aura. It's a void I've only ever felt around Marve. Must be a demon.

Unsure of what to do, I watch the scene unfold. The waiter greets the newcomer casual indifference, and I realize everyone can see him. This shouldn't surprise me; everyone can see Marve too. But I've never met another demon besides her, and the uncertainty of what will happen next tightens my chest.

"Get out of my way, angel," the demon shouts, his voice jagged and abrasive. Yet, no one else reacts, it's as if they cannot hear him. It must be the Spell.

Raya's guardian angel doesn't flinch, standing tall and immovable, a solid beacon of protective energy behind her.

"I'm not here for your human. I want the other one," the demon hisses, his voice dripping with malice as his gaze shifts toward me, eyes gleaming with a predatory hunger. A wicked smile stretches across his face, baring sharp, not exactly white teeth.

He steps to the side, positioning himself for a better view. His eyes lock onto mine, and the intensity in his gaze feels like it could strip me bare, or skin me alive.

His grin falters. A flicker of confusion dances across his face, his eyes narrowing as if something about me doesn't quite add up. "What is this... your soul..." His voice trails off, barely a murmur. He figured it out. My soul won't be his snack for the day.

The demon doesn't get the chance to finish his sentence. In a flash of movement, Raya's guardian angel conjures a wooden stake out of thin air, the weapon appearing in his hand like magic.

For the first time, the pub falls into a stunned silence. The humans around us, who couldn't see anything moments ago, now stare, their wide eyes locked on the angel, fear and fascination playing across their faces. It's clear that he had to reveal his true, corporeal form to confront the demon, even if it means being exposed.

Without hesitation, the angel steps forward, his wings arched in readiness as he faces the demon head-on. And then the battle erupts.

Their movements are almost too fast to follow, a blur of violence and speed, each blow landing with bone-shaking force. It reminds me of the clashes between Ethan and Ezra—only more desperate, more raw. Or maybe it's more like those moments when Ethan sparred with Marve, her power surging after she regained her strength.

The room explodes with chaos—tables splinter, glasses shatter, food flies into the air as the two supernatural beings tear through the pub like a hurricane.

I want to jump in, to help in some way, but the truth is fighting isn't my thing—not yet, anyway.

Everyone else is frozen in place, trapped in a surreal disbelief, as though they've been pulled into some vivid, inescapable dream. There's no way this can be real, can it? The scene feels otherworldly, watching as the world around us is ripped apart with brutal force.

Gradually, though, Raya's angel begins to gain the upper hand. With a swift, decisive strike, he drives the wooden stake into the demon's chest. The demon's eyes widen in shock, his face contorting in disbelief as his form crumbles to ash, carried away by an unseen wind.

The angel surveys the chaos and the fear-stricken faces around him. A woman breaks the silence with a piercing scream, as if just realizing the danger. I instinctively cover my ears, the sound cutting through me like glass.

With a snap of his fingers, the angel silences her, and calm instantly washes over the room, as if nothing had ever happened.

People resume their meals and conversations, their memories of the chaos erased, not even a flicker of confusion in their eyes. Even Raya looks completely unfazed, as if she's forgotten everything that just transpired. The tables piece themselves back together, chairs slide into their rightful places, and shattered glasses reform without a trace. Now *that* is magic. I had no idea angels could do that. What else are they capable of?

Then, the angel turns his blazing eyes on me. "Stay away from Raya," he growls. It's not a demand—it's a warning, a threat.

"What are you staring at?" Raya's follows my gaze, but al she sees is the menu board hanging on the wall. "You want to eat something?"

"Yeah, *it's not my fault* I'm always hungry," I say, emphasizing the words, hoping the angels hears the jab in my voice.

"He was clearly here for you," the angel's voice drips with accusation.

Raya, oblivious to the undercurrent of the conversation, just shrugs. "Then order something."

Without thinking of Raya for the moment, I blurt out, "But why?" Why would a demon come for me? It doesn't make any sense. They can't even consume my soul.

The angel doesn't even glance my way. Instead, with a flick of his wings, he takes off, vanishing into thin air. Not even an answer. Not even a look. Not even a goodbye. This is how insignificant I am to him.

"I don't know... if you're hungry, you should eat," Raya's voice filters back in, tinged with confusion as she tries to make sense of my odd behavior.

"What?" it takes me a moment to remember I'd been having two conversations at once. "Oh. Right. Of course." I plaster on a strained smile to cover up my disorientation.

We order more French fries, and I try to push the evening's bizarre events from my mind, focusing instead on enjoying a nice evening with my best friend. But the encounter leaves a bitter taste in my mouth.

Raya's guardian angel... he's not like the others. He wasn't afraid to pick a fight with a demon, even after the demon assured him that Raya wasn't the target—just a Nephilim no one cares about. Could this be the reason for the red tips on his feathers? Does it mean he fights battles that are not his? Battles he should avoid rather than engage in?

As the night winds down, Raya and I step out of the pub and say our goodbyes. The laughter and chatter fade behind me as I inhale the cool night air. The streets are quiet and empty—a welcome contrast to the lively atmosphere I've just left, yet eerily so.

The echo of my footsteps is the only sound in the still night, amplifying the quiet tension around me. With the encounter with the demon still vivid in my mind, my heart begins to race, my thoughts spinning with the possibility of danger lurking in every shadow. I shake my head, half-laughing at myself—am I seriously still such a scared little coward? I'm Nephilim, strong and immortal, for God's sake. Yet, the lifeless bird lying on the sidewalk does nothing to ease my nerves.

I quicken my pace, the desire to reach the safety of home growing stronger with each passing moment. When I finally cross the threshold, a wave of relief washes over me. Cerberus greets me at the door, his tail wagging softly. I scoop him up and settle him on my lap. As he purrs contentedly, I watch his serene expression. The knowledge that he perceives things beyond human sight provides a comforting sense of security—if he's calm, I know I can relax too.

chapter 19

TABLE FOR TWO, TENSION FOR THREE

The evening promises romance. Ben has arranged a quiet dinner for just the two of us, and the restaurant practically whispers intimacy with its soft candlelight and rustic charm. I breathe in the scent of roasted garlic mingling with the faint aroma of wine. Ben's blue eyes catch the candlelight, a soft glimmer reflecting back at me as he reaches for my hand, his fingers warm against mine. For a brief moment, everything feels just right.

But just as I begin to relax into the moment, something shifts. Across the room, near the entrance, a familiar figure appears—one that instantly breaks the delicate spell of the evening. My eyes land on Mariah—Ben's friend. He strides in with that same casual confidence I've seen before. And just behind him, like a shadow, is Tubiel.

"Hey, there's your friend," I mutter, nodding toward Mariah.

"Huh?" Ben glances over, and just like that, his easy smile fades. His jaw tightens slightly, and I can almost hear his inner groan. "That's Merry... I mean, Brian," he mutters under his breath, clearly less than thrilled. At least now I know his first name, instead of the nickname his childish friends gave him just because of his feminine middle name. "What's he doing here?"

Before either of us can process the sudden appearance, Brian is already weaving through the tables, his voice loud enough to cut through the cozy ambiance.

"Hey, guys! How is it going?" he calls out, as if he hasn't already gotten our full attention.

Ben pulls his hand back from mine and forces a smile. "Hi, what brings you here?" His tone is polite, but I can feel the tension rolling off him. This is supposed to be our night, and now we have an uninvited guest.

Tubiel, standing beside Brian, flashes me an enthusiastic grin and waves. I smile back, just slightly, hoping no one notices the silent exchange.

"Well, I texted you about hanging out, and you mentioned you'd be here, so I figured I'd join you," Brian explains with a casual shrug, his nonchalance radiating obliviousness to the tension thickening the air.

Ben's attempt at a response falters, and his eyes dart toward me, wide and desperate, practically begging for help. It's clear Brian hasn't grasped the idea that this dinner was meant to be a private evening for just the two of us.

"We've already ordered, so—" I begin, trying to suggest, as gently as possible, that this might not be the best time for company.

But Brian waves off my words before I can finish. "Oh, no worries! I'll just grab the waitress," he says, already heading toward the bar without a second thought, leaving Ben and me staring after him, our quiet evening vanishing before our eyes.

Ben's face tightens with embarrassment, his shoulders sagging as he leans in toward me. "I'm really sorry about this. He just texted me out of the blue. I had no idea he'd show up here."

I shrug, offering a smile that I hope is reassuring. "Don't worry about it. It's actually kind of funny when you think about it." But my light-hearted attempt to salvage the mood falls flat. Ben doesn't seem to share my sense of humor. Instead, he leans forward and, with a quick puff of breath, blows out the candle at the center of our table. The flame flickers out, leaving only a wisp of smoke—a symbol of our evening's romance, now extinguished.

Brian drags a chair from the nearest table and plops down next to us, all smiles and carefree energy. "You'll never believe this party I went to last weekend!" He launches into a loud and animated story about some wild antics that seem completely out of place in the dimly lit, intimate restaurant.

Ben's strained smile barely masks his frustration. His eyes are distant, unfocused, clearly miles away from Brian's endless chatter. I nod along politely, offering a laugh here and there, but my mind is elsewhere—drifting back to the quiet, romantic evening we had hoped for.

As Brian chats mainly with Ben, I start to feel like a third wheel and resort to drinking. It doesn't even affect me like it used to, so what's the harm? Maybe I'm starting to understand Ethan and his group.

Three drinks in, and my bladder is begging for a break. "I'm just going to the restroom," I announce, sliding out from my chair. Neither of them seems to notice as I weave through the crowd toward the back of the restaurant. A part of me wishes I didn't have to return.

The so-called restroom is barely more than a cramped closet with a toilet and sink, and as I'm about to pull down my pantyhose, Tubiel phases right through the wall. I freeze mid-motion, my heart leaping into my throat as I nearly lose my balance.

"Oh my God!" I start to shout but quickly clamp a hand over my mouth, remembering where I am. The last thing I need is for someone outside to hear me and think I've lost it.

Tubiel's sudden entrance is met with a sharp whisper instead. "What are you doing here?" My voice is a bit more aggressive than I intended, but I'm too startled to care.

He tilts his head innocently, like he hasn't just violated all concepts of personal space. "I thought it was like last time... you know, when you went to the bathroom so we could talk."

I shake my head, struggling to steady my racing heart and regain my dignity. "No, I actually need to pee!" My tone softens, shifting from shock to amusement. "But I'd like to talk to you... Give me two minutes. Then come back, okay?"

He nods, completely unbothered, and just like that, he disappears again, leaving me alone in the tiny, claustrophobic space.

The whole situation is bizarre, and I can't help but shake my head as I finally get on with what I came here to do. It's only when I've flushed and washed my hands that Tubiel slips back through the wall, as casually as if we were meeting for coffee.

Though I can't touch him and he's an angel—probably thousands of years old—there's something strangely intimate about being in this tiny restroom together. Plus, he's... well, handsome. Not that it matters. I'm with Ben.

Tubiel studies my face, his eyes narrowing slightly. "What's on your mind?" he asks, his voice low and probing.

"What? Nothing. Absolutely nothing," I blurt out a little too quickly, my nerves betraying me. I try to play it cool, forcing a casual smile, but I can feel the heat rising to my cheeks. I can only hope he can't sense or hear where my thoughts were just moments ago.

His lips curl into a knowing grin. The blush creeping up my face must've given me away because he leans in slightly, teasing. "But you said you wanted to talk to me, Trouble."

There it is again—*Trouble*. He knows my name, yet he keeps calling me that. What kind of trouble does he think I'm bringing? Sure, Raya's guardian seems to believe Nephilim are magnets for chaos, but Tubiel doesn't strike me as someone who buys into that. So why does he keep calling me *Trouble*?

He raises an eyebrow, still waiting for me to respond.

"Oh, that," I laugh awkwardly, feeling a bit sheepish.

Relieved to finally have someone to share the bizarre events with, I begin recounting what happened after he left yesterday—how, not long after he disappeared with his charge, a demon appeared out of nowhere, claiming he came specifically for me, and how Raya's guardian quickly intervened, taking him down before he could act.

"Hmm, that's strange," Tubiel mutters, his brow creasing as he processes my words. "The demon said he came for you? But why? He couldn't have wanted to eat your soul, that's for sure. Someone must've sent him." He pauses, his expression darkening slightly. "If he wasn't successful, it's likely more will be sent. You should talk to your father; you'll need protection."

I bite my lip, my shoulders tensing at the mention of Ethan. "Yeah, it's weird, but... who'd want to hurt me? I'm a nobody. And I really don't want to talk to Ethan right now. What do I need protection from anyway? You said it too—hurting me is practically impossible."

Tubiel leans in, a smirk playing on his lips as his eyes lock onto mine. "If you think you're so safe, then why are you still mad at Ethan?"

"Because he should've told me everything *before* I made my decision," I snap, irritation creeping into my voice. I thought Tubiel was on my side about this. "It's not just about safety—it's about trust. The principle is what's important here."

His smirk softens as he leans back slightly. "Besides, I didn't say hurting you was practically impossible. I said *killing* you was. Anyone can hurt you. That's why you need to call your father. You'll need protection."

I groan, putting my hands firmly at my hips. "Isn't there any other option? Because I'm not calling him. Period."

Tubiel's expression flickers between exasperation and amusement. He probably sees right through my stubbornness, but I can't help it.

Deep down, I know I'll forgive Ethan eventually—I'm not one to hold grudge. But right now, I don't want to. I want him to learn that there are consequences. If I keep letting things slide, he'll never feel the need to do the right thing.

"The only other option," Tubiel says, his smirk returning, "is hanging out with Brian all the time so I can protect you. But I don't know how you'd handle that."

I sigh dramatically. "Won't I be safe at home, though? I mean, they can't go through walls like you, right?"

"They can't pass through walls, but if they're at full strength, they have other tricks up their sleeves—taking other forms, like snakes, ants, flies... you get the idea," Tubiel explains with the patience of someone trying to teach a reluctant student.

"Then is there a way to protect myself? Salt? Symbols? Anything?" I plead.

Tubiel chuckles softly, the sound almost musical. "I see someone's been watching *Supernatural*. Brian's a fan too." His laughter deepens, amused at my naïveté.

I blink, feeling slightly embarrassed. I hadn't expected him to know *exactly* where I got the idea from.

"Sorry, none of that would help," Tubiel adds with a casual shrug, his laughter fading into a thoughtful silence.

For a moment, he just looks around the cramped bathroom,

his gaze sweeping over the dim, unremarkable space as if he's seeing something more. When he turns back to me, there's a shift in his posture—a subtle straightening, a deep breath expanding his chest like he's trying to appear more... impressive.

"Are you and this Ben... a thing?" he asks, his voice dropping into something softer, almost casual, though the question itself is anything but.

The words catch me completely off guard. I feel a warmth creeping into my cheeks under his intense gaze. There's something playful in his eyes, a challenge, and it sends my heart skipping a beat before I can reel it back in.

"Yeah, we are," I reply hesitantly, trying to sound more certain than I feel. Why does an angel care about my relationship? What game is he playing?

My mind races, searching for a reason behind his sudden interest. Perhaps he's just a curious little angel, and that's it. I don't even know if angels have relationships. Maybe human dating is just some odd curiosity to him—a window into a world he can't fully understand.

But then, it hits me—how strange it is that we keep talking so often. When Yabbashael was my guardian, she barely had time for me. We hardly exchanged words, and even then, it was mostly distant advice or silent observations. But Tubiel, I see him every time I go out.

"Why is it that I seem to run into you every time I go out?"

Tubiel chuckles, the sound light and teasing. "You don't go out much, huh?" He's pointing out the obvious—that we've only crossed paths a handful of times. But still, two days in a row? That feels like more than coincidence.

I can't shake the feeling that Mariah—or Brian, as Ben called him—didn't just show up tonight by accident. Was Tubiel behind that? Could he have influenced Brian somehow, like he did when we went hunting for that poor soul with Marve? Is he subtly guiding Brian's actions, making sure we're always in the same place at the same time?

I lock eyes with Tubiel, letting the question hang there, unspoken but clear. My expression says it all—what's really going on? Why do you keep showing up wherever I am?

Tubiel's green eyes twinkle with mischief. "Brian is a good listener. He believes in God and angels, you know. Makes him really open to suggestions."

If guardians try talking to their charges, influencing them, nudging them, I bet Raya's angel was screaming at her not to go out with me when I called, but she didn't listen.

"Isn't that against the rules?"

Tubiel just shrugs, flashing an innocent smile that doesn't quite match the playful glint in his eyes. "It's debatable." He winks, adding a flirtatious edge to his words.

"Okay. Thanks for all the advice, but I should get back now," I say, trying to sound composed despite the pink tint on my cheeks.

As I step out of the bathroom, the sight of a line of women waiting for their turn makes my stomach twist with sudden embarrassment. I slip past them, keeping my head low and letting my hair fall across my face like a shield.

God, I hope they didn't overhear anything. To them, it would have sounded like I'd been having an intense conversation with thin air—definitely not the kind of impression I want to leave. But hey, who cares. It's not like I'm going to see any of them again.

As I settle back into my seat, Tubiel reappears, hovering near the table in his incorporeal form. It's strange to see him there, neither sitting nor standing, his feet seemingly touching the ground, while Ben and Brian are completely absorbed in their discussion about tennis players. I've never cared much for sports, especially not as a spectator, so their conversation is nothing more than background noise to me.

With a bored sigh, I take a sip from my glass, the idea hitting me just as I set it down. I pull out my phone, open the Notes app, and quickly type out a message: "You can talk, and I'll respond on my phone."

Catching Tubiel's eye, I tilt the screen towards him ever so slightly. His grin widens, clearly amused by my attempt at subtlety. For the next twenty minutes, we carry on a covert conversation—me typing away while pretending to scroll through social media, and him talking without anyone else but me and angels hearing him.

Ben glances over at me as we walk home, his eyes narrowing slightly in that way that tells me he's been holding onto something all evening. "Who were you texting so much tonight?" His voice is casual, but the way he's eyeing me says otherwise.

I hesitate, thrown off guard by the sudden interrogation. "Uh... Raya," I stammer, forcing a smile and inwardly wincing at how fake it feels. I hate lying. Lying to Ben, though? That feels even worse.

He raises an eyebrow, clearly not buying it. "Huh. I've never seen you talking to her so passionately." There's a slight edge to his words, a hint of something deeper—jealousy, maybe?

I'm tempted to tell him just how bored I was, since Brian never gave me a chance to talk or steer the conversation towards something I'm remotely interested in. But then I realize... if we stop hanging out with Brian, I won't get to see Tubiel anymore. The only angel friend I have. The only person I can confide in about this strange, hidden side of my life.

So I say nothing, hoping the silence will smooth over the tension.

"Are you angry with me?" I ask after a few minutes.

Ben shakes his head, but there's a tightness in his voice when he responds. "I'm not mad. Anger's pointless. It just makes you open to do things you'll regret later."

I nod, even though his drunken philosophical words don't fully put me at ease. My eyes wander, and that's when I spot it—another dead bird on the sidewalk, illuminated by the harsh glow of a streetlamp. My heart skips a beat. Second one this week.

By the time we reach home, my nerves are jangling. We head upstairs, and as soon as we step into the apartment, Ben collapses onto the bed with barely a word, offering me a half-hearted kiss on the cheek before rolling away.

"Well, isn't this just the cherry on top of a thrilling evening?" I mutter under my breath, shaking my head as I pick up Cerberus. His warm body is always a comfort after a long, strange day.

I hold him close, expecting him to curl up like he usually does—

but instead, he stiffens. His eyes go wide, staring me in the eyes, as though he's looking at a ghost.

Then, with a sudden burst of energy, he wriggles out of my arms, scratching me in the process, and bolts under the couch.

What the hell was that about?

I glance around, searching the room for anything out of place. There's nothing. Ben is already snoring softly, completely oblivious to my rising anxiety.

But what if Berry sensed something? Something I can't see? But he looked directly at me, as if he were afraid of *me*. It doesn't make any sense.

For a brief moment, I consider calling Ethan. My hand hovers over my phone, but I can't bring myself to do it. Not after I've been avoiding him. But the longer Cerberus stays hidden, the more frayed my nerves become.

Just as I'm about to dial, Berry pokes his head out from under the couch, his usual self again. He blinks at me innocently, as if nothing happened, and nuzzles against my hand.

I exhale a shaky breath, setting the phone back down. *He's just a coward*. Probably heard something outside.

I crawl into bed, exhaustion finally pulling me under. Hours later, I wake up with Berry sprawled on my chest, his weight making it hard to breathe. His soft purring lulls me back into a calmer state, even though the night's unease still lingers, woven into my dreams of dead birds.

chapter 20

EYES ROLLING, DEMONS CALLING

Morning breaks with golden sunlight pouring into the room, casting a soft glow that feels like a fresh start. The air seems lighter, as if it's swept away the weight of yesterday, promising a new day free of awkward interruptions and unexpected encounters.

I turn to see Ben lying beside me, still wrapped in sleep, his breathing soft and steady. A quiet smile pulls at my lips as I watch him. There's something about the way the light touches his face, smoothing out every sharp line, that makes him seem almost... otherworldly. Could someone this perfect really just be a mortal?

Surely, God wouldn't craft something so flawless only for him to live just one lifetime.

I find myself hoping—no, wishing—that maybe he's a Nephilim too. That one day, he'll wake up, discover the truth about himself, and we'll face eternity together.

When Ben finally wakes up, we both feel refreshed and full of energy. We decide not to waste any time and make the most of the day. I suggest we invite Brian, Asher, and potentially other of his friends on a trip to the beach, an idea met with enthusiastic approval.

After a quick breakfast and some half-hearted packing, the four of us (and Tubiel, of course) head into the city. The streets are buzzing with life—cafes brimming with laughter, the smell of fresh coffee lingering in the air, the occasional strum of a street musician's guitar floating in the background, kids running with ice-creams in their dirty little hands. It feels like summer itself has wrapped us in a warm, carefree blanket.

I let myself relax, imagining what a normal day like this would be if I didn't have to think about Nephilim, angels, or demons. Just an ordinary girl, hanging out with her boyfriend and friends on a sunny day.

But of course, peace never lasts.

Out of nowhere, I catch sight of Ethan near one of the cafes. His tall figure is unmistakable, even with his back turned. How does this always happen? The one day I try to leave my supernatural trouble behind, I run straight into it.

It's almost as if he senses me. Within seconds, Ethan turns, his piercing eyes finding mine as though he'd been looking for me all along.

He strides toward me, his face set in that familiar serious expression, and I already know—there's no escaping this conversation.

As I start walking toward Ethan, I throw Ben a quick glance, muttering something about spotting my cousin. It's the easiest excuse, and he doesn't question it. As I close the gap between us, the light, carefree atmosphere of the streets fades, replaced by the heavy tension Ethan created between us with his lies and deceptions.

While the others continue towards the beach, Tubiel stays with us.

From the corner of my eye, I spot Ezra and Marve standing at a distance, not even looking our way. Perhaps they're giving us space for a private conversation, or they are simply trying to avoid Tubiel due to Marve's previous encounter with him. Tubiel had made it clear how he feels about all demons, regardless of their daily menu.

As I approach, I can see the strain in Ethan's face. "Dora," he begins, voice heavy with hesitation. "I... I'm really sorry..." His words falter, and he rakes a hand through his hair. He seems lost for a moment, searching the ground as if it might offer him the right words.

Ethan's expression tightens as he glances at Tubiel, his lips pressing into a thin line. His jaw clenches, the muscles in his face taut with restrained frustration. "Do you mind?" His words come out clipped, the forced calm barely hiding the annoyance beneath. "I'd like to talk to my daughter alone."

Despite Ethan's aggressive tone, Tubiel responds calmly, "I'm sorry, Peliel. I need to talk to you, and time is running out. My charge is moving away."

A cold wave of panic sweeps through me. My heart hammers as I shoot Tubiel a pleading look, silently begging him to keep quiet about our recent conversations.

Ethan's sharp gaze darts between us, catching the silent exchange. His brows knit together, his eyes narrowing with suspicion. "What's going on?"

"I think Dora's in danger," Tubiel says.

"Don't—" I start, panic rising in my throat, but Ethan's already stepping in, cutting me off with a firm gesture.

"Let him speak," he commands, his tone paternal. It's clear that, despite everything, my safety is Ethan's priority, regardless of my feelings towards him and his lies.

"Dora's been targeted by a demon in a pub full of people. It doesn't add up," Tubiel explains, his green eyes steady on Ethan. "Why go after her when her soul's untouchable? This couldn't have been a coincidence."

"Thanks a lot," I mutter, piercing Tubiel with my eyes.

"No, really—thank you for telling me," Ethan says, his tone softening with genuine appreciation. "I'll take care of it."

Tubiel gives a subtle nod, his eyes meeting mine briefly. There's a flicker of hope in that look, as if he's silently pleading for me to understand. Without another word, he turns and heads off to catch up with Brian.

"I need to go," I say, my voice sharp as I turn on my heel, already trying to put distance between us. But before I can take a step, Ethan's hand clamps around my arm, pulling me back like an anchor.

"Not so fast," he says, his tone firm, commanding. His grip isn't painful, but it holds me in place, making it clear I'm not going anywhere until he's done talking. The frustration in my chest tightens, but his presence looms larger, more imposing, like he's somehow grown taller.

"We need to figure this out. You can't be alone," he insists.

"Why?" I snap back, trying to shake him off. "Who'd want to hurt me? It was probably just a coincidence—a demon choosing me as prey."

"I don't know who would want to hurt you or why, but something doesn't add up. I don't believe in coincidences." He steps closer, his voice lower now. "A demon attacking you in a place like that? With so many humans around? So many angels? It doesn't make sense. Whatever he wanted—it had to be worth the risk of his life."

I can't help but roll my eyes forcing out a dismissive laugh. "You're overreacting." The words feel hollow as they leave my lips, and deep down, I know it. I try to brush it off, but there's a tightness building in my chest, a nagging doubt creeping in.

This hasn't been my world for long, and I have no idea if there's real danger lurking around the corner. I should trust Ethan—he knows more about this than I ever could—but I can't bring myself to admit that. Not yet.

I'm angry. At him, at the situation, at everything. I don't want to agree with him, I don't want to admit that I'm scared, and most of all, I don't want to accept his protection. I'm not ready to let go of the anger I've been holding onto, the hurt and frustration that's been cooking inside me since he lied to me.

I cross my arms. "I'm fine. I don't need you babysitting me."

But even as I say it, I know it's not entirely true.

Ethan's face tightens as I brush him off, his jaw clenching, eyes darkening like storm clouds. "I leave you alone for two days—*two days*—and this happens," he snaps, the anger barely restrained. "From now on, you're staying at my place." It's not a suggestion, not even close to a request—it's a command, absolute and final. There's no room for negotiation in his tone, no hint of softness or compromise. He's made up his mind, and he's not backing down.

"What?" I yank my arm back, glaring at him. "Have you lost your mind? And what am I supposed to tell Ben?"

He waves my concerns off with a flick of his hand, like they're trivial. "I don't care. Figure something out."

His dismissiveness makes my blood boil. I want to scream at him, tell him he's being unreasonable, but before I can get a word in, he steps even closer, his voice dropping into a dangerous whisper. "Just to be clear—I'll take you by force if I have to." His eyes lock onto mine, and the threat is real, simmering just beneath the surface. "I'm going to stick around until you decide to go home. I'll be watching you every second, making sure you don't get any ideas. Then, I'll walk you to your place, you'll grab your things, and I'll take you back to where you'll be safe. With us."

I just stand there, staring at him, my mind stumbling over his words. I can't even speak, my mouth hanging open, frozen in disbelief. Did he really just lay down that ultimatum?

Ethan doesn't wait for me to process it. With deliberate,

measured steps, he moves back, his eyes locking onto mine for one last moment, their intensity leaving no room for doubt. He means every word.

Then, without saying another thing, he turns on his heel and heads toward Ezra and Marve, who are waiting a little farther off, both pretending not to be listening but I'm sure they are aware of the entire conversation.

I watch his retreating figure, my thoughts racing but jumbled. How does he think he can just dictate my life like that?

I catch up with Ben, Brian, and the others, but it's hard to enjoy myself when Ethan's words keep replaying in my mind, weighing heavily on my mood.

We reach the beach, finding a decent spot to lay out our blankets, and everyone heads into the water, eager to shake off the summer heat.

But I hang back for a moment, finding Tubiel and shooting him another piercing glare, making it painfully clear I'm not happy with him for spilling everything to Ethan. He catches my gaze, looking slightly taken aback, his innocent expression almost comical. "Dora, I had to..."

Great. Just what I needed—angels meddling in my life decisions. I know he acted out of concern for my safety, and it's not entirely fair to blame him for circumstances beyond his control, but I'm not ready to let him off the hook just yet. I thought I could tell him anything—no, I thought I'd finally found someone I could trust with everything. But he broke that trust, even if it was for my own good.

I offer no response, just one last hard look before turning back toward the water. The cool breeze brushes against my skin, offering a momentary reprieve from the swirl of emotions inside me. As the sound of crashing waves fills the air, I let the rhythmic pull of the sea soothe my concerns. I chose this life. There's no sense in stressing about things I can't control now.

Ben waves me over, a playful smile on his face as he splashes in the water. For a moment, I push everything aside and join him, the memory of the conversation with Ethan and Tubiel sinking into the background as we laugh and tumble through the waves.

But as soon as we return to the shore, reality creeps back in. While the others chat, my mind drifts, trying to piece together the best way to explain my sudden need to stay with Ethan. It takes twenty minutes before I finally settle on something simple. Repairs at my apartment—water's out for the next few days.

Ben looks concerned when I mention it, and part of me wonders if he can see through the lie. "You can stay with me," he offers, his voice tinged with hope.

I shake my head gently. "There's not enough room for me, Cerberus, and all his things. It'd be too cramped." The excuse rolls off my tongue more naturally than expected, and though I see the disappointment flicker across his face, he doesn't press. He nods, understanding but still slightly distant.

As the sun dips lower on the horizon and people start packing up, Ben and I gather our things and head towards Ethan. He's been keeping an eye on us all day, first from a nearby coffee shop, then casually relocating to a bar across the street as soon as it opened. Watching us like a hawk—just with better beverage options. Ezra and Marve have long since disappeared, leaving Ethan as my sole escort.

I officially introduce Ben and Ethan—boyfriend meets *cousin*—as the lie slips out with ease. Ben, ever the considerate one, smiles warmly, giving me a gentle kiss and reminding me to call him, especially if those creepy bird dreams bother me again. I watch him walk away, my hope for a second chance at a romantic evening fading with each step he takes.

Ethan breaks the silence before I can stew in my disappointment for long. "You're having nightmares?"

"Not really," I reply quickly, trying to shut down the conversation as I begin walking toward the parking lot. "I just saw some dead birds on the street, and now it's stuck in my head."

I don't want to talk about it. I don't want to talk about anything with him right now. But of course, Ethan isn't letting it go.

Ethan halts suddenly, mid-step, his brow creasing as concern etches itself across his features. "Wait," he says, his voice tense. "You've been seeing dead birds and had a nightmare about it too?"

I sigh but nod, hoping it gets the message across that I'm not interested in this conversation. I really don't have the energy for this level of drama. We're talking about dreams, for God's sake.

"Did you see anything else in the dream?" he presses, and I can tell from the look in his eyes that this isn't just small talk. He thinks something serious is going on.

"Like what?"

"I don't know," he sighs, visibly annoyed that I'm not reading his mind. "A face, maybe? Someone approaching you or appearing building. "Oh, I'm sorry for not keeping up with the *feline demon defense manual*," I shoot back sarcastically. But then it clicks. Yabbashael had told me about this before, something about cats and their origins being similar to angels. That's exactly why I feel safe when Berry seems peaceful.

I pause, my tone calming down as the realization dawns. "Wait... You think someone got into my head while I was sleeping? Made me dream about this?"

He nods, not even sparing a glance in my direction. "Sometimes you're slow to catch on."

Before I can respond, he's already walking ahead. *Finally.*

"So, someone could've been in my house? In my room?"

"Not necessarily. There are demons who can mess with your thoughts from a distance, like you can." His attempt to sound reassuring falls flat, as though this should calm me.

Oh great, so I have a demonic power. That's just fantastic.

"Don't overthink every little thing," I tell him, trying to convince myself that he's overreacting. Or maybe I'm just desperately hoping he is.

He stops in his tracks again and shoots me a cold, irritated look. "Pandora, I've been around much longer than you. Don't act like you know it all."

"It's *Dora*," I remind him, the sting of his condescension still fresh, but unable to come up with a better retort.

He rolls his eyes dramatically, clearly fed up. "Maybe I should just let them have you."

out of nowhere? Someone who felt like a threat? Who scared you?"

I shrug, trying to recall the details. "Can't say. Just dead birds everywhere, then I woke up. Or, actually, Berry woke me up," I rattle off in one breath, hoping it'll be enough to end this conversation.

Ethan's eyes widen, as if my revelation holds some profound significance. "Your cat woke you up?" he repeats, this time with an urgency that makes me question if we're even talking about the same thing.

"Yes," I reply, my voice louder than intended. *Wasn't that clear the first time I mentioned it?*

"Hmm."

"What? Why is it so important?" I demand, growing more irritated by his cryptic response.

"You know about the thing with cats, right?"

"What thing?" I snap, my annoyance sharpening.

"What thing?" he mimics, his voice adopting a childish, mocking edge, like a brother trying to push your buttons. It's clear my irritation is getting to him too.

I roll my eyes, feeling the conversation slipping into ridiculous territory.

"What else could I mean in this context? The thing with cats and their nature... how they're here to protect humans from demons, blah blah." His tone shifts into something bordering on patronizing. "I'm surprised that you, such a cat lover, and with all the time you've spent in my library, couldn't figure this out on your own."

His words hit a nerve, and I feel the familiar heat of frustration

chapter 21

HOME SWEET DRAMA

We load Ethan's car in silence, the trunk sagging under the weight of my belongings. Berry, curled up in his carrier, lets out a soft, annoyed meow. I'm feeling the same—displaced. The engine hums to life, the only sound breaking the stillness as the city blurs by in a haze of streetlights and passing cars, neither of us saying a word, lost in our own thoughts.

When we finally arrive at Ethan's house, he grabs my bags without a word and guides me to my new room on the second floor, then leaves me alone.

The room is beautiful, spacious, and utterly unfamiliar. The king-sized bed looks too pristine, the room too perfect. It's like a five star hotel. Not home.

I sigh, setting Berry's carrier down. Slowly, cautiously, he darts out, sniffing the air and investigating the unfamiliar surroundings.

I start unpacking, pulling out clothes, toiletries, and Berry's meat—meat that needs to go in the freezer. As I clutch the cold package in my hand, I realize I have no idea where the kitchen is.

Wandering through the hallways, the house feels like a maze. I've only seen a few rooms, so I have no idea where to go. As I turn a corner, raised voices catch my ear, stopping me in my tracks.

"You can't be serious. Her being here puts Marve in danger," Ezra's voice slices through the house, sharp and angry. "If someone's after Pandora and follows her here, they'll learn about Marve. Anyone would go straight to Baal with that info."

"Then she stays hidden inside," Ethan says, his tone brooking no argument. "We have no other option but to protect them both here."

"It's too risky. And if Andras is involved..." Ezra's voice trails off, but the concern is clear.

"What do you want me to do? She's my daughter!" Ethan's voice hardens, but there's a tremor of desperation behind it.

"She has a human boyfriend, friends with guardian angels. She'll be safe with them," Ezra presses.

"And if not? Not every guardian angel is strong enough," Ethan snaps back. "They might let a demon take her if it shows no interest in their charge. I can't risk that."

"You're being unreasonable!" Ezra fires back, his patience

fraying.

"Am I?" Ethan lets out a bitter laugh. "You're the one blinded by emotions."

Without waiting for a response, Ethan storms off, his footsteps fading into the house. I guess staying here with Ezra... it's going to be harder than I thought. I can only hope Marve will stand by me, even if Ezra doesn't. Having at least one ally in this house would be a relief.

I retreat to my room, hoping not to bump into anyone until the mood lightens. But pacing around the room does little to settle my nerves, and I find myself unpacking aimlessly—clothes half-folded, toiletries scattered, none of it really sinking in. After a few restless minutes, I realize I can't stay here, trapped in this whirlpool of uncertainty. I need to find Ethan, and I really need to put that meet in the freezer.

Following the faint sounds of movement, I step cautiously through the halls, hoping it's Ethan and not Ezra I'm about to run into. My heart quickens at every creak in the floorboards, each noise making me second-guess my decision. Finally, I reach the kitchen, where the low hum of activity guides me.

The kitchen, at least, is a welcome sight: sleek, modern, with cool gray counters and a large island in the center. The space feels calm, orderly—something I could use right now. Ethan stands by the counter, thankfully alone, crunching on a bag of chips.

"I need to store Berry's food," I say quietly, holding up the package of meat.

He glances over, his expression softening just a bit as he gestures toward the freezer. "Here," he says, opening it for me.

"You can put his stuff here. Everything in the kitchen is shared, so don't hesitate to take what you want."

"Thanks," I murmur, sliding the package into the cold drawer.

As I open the fridge and scan the near-empty shelves, I frown. "Is this all you have?"

Ethan lazily holds out the bag of chips, crumbs clinging to his fingers. "Want some?" he offers, though I can tell he's not thrilled to share.

"No, thanks." My stomach growls in protest, reminding me that all I've had today are pancakes and a few fries. I'm starving.

"We'll order some food—it's what we always do."

Just as I'm about to respond, explaining I can't afford to order food every time, I feel a subtle pressure in my mind—Ethan, trying to slip into my thoughts. "Hey!" I cry out, jerking back, startled. "What do you think you're doing?"

"Sorry, it's an old habit. But don't worry, I'll pay for everything. You're my guest. And... my daughter, after all."

"You think it's okay to read my mind? It's not. Don't do it again," I snap. I know he can't actually read my thoughts if I stay guarded, but I hate that he tried.

"I wasn't reading your mind, just sensing your emotions. It was instinct of—" He cuts himself off.

An instinct of a guardian angel. I know.

"I apologized, and it won't happen again."

I glare at him for a second longer before deciding to let it go. Right now, all I care about is food. "What are we ordering?"

"Whatever you want."

"How about Indian?" I suggest, throwing out my favorite

option.

Ethan nods. "Indian it is," he agrees, though his lack of enthusiasm makes it clear he's just trying to keep the peace.

As we settle on our order, Ethan makes the call, handing me my own bag of chips while we wait. Without much thought, we both end up sitting on the island in the middle of the kitchen, despite the perfectly good chairs just beneath our feet.

I nibble on the chips absently, my feet swinging lightly beneath, while my mind drifts back to the conversation I overheard earlier.

"Who's Andras?" I ask, curiosity getting the better of me.

Ethan sighs, rubbing his face with both hands, as if trying to erase the question itself. It's clear he didn't want me to know about Andras.

He lowers his hands, studying me closely, his brown eyes searching mine. This time, instead of trying to sneak into my thoughts, he's reading me through my expression.

"I don't want you to worry or be scared," he says softly, like he's talking to a fragile child.

But I'm not a child. I can handle whatever this is. "Who is he?" I press, keeping my gaze as sturdy as possible.

Ethan hesitates for a second before finally giving in. "A demon," he says, his tone flat, almost as if he's resigned to me knowing.

"A very dangerous and powerful demon. One of those that's really hard to defeat," Ezra's voice cuts through the room as he and Marve enter the kitchen.

"How do you know he's involved?" I ask, trying to piece

everything together.

"We're not entirely sure," Ethan says, shooting Ezra a warning look, but Ezra, ever blunt, doesn't hold back.

"It's the birds. It's his thing. He uses them to scare his victims first, creating fear and paranoia."

Birds? Seriously? I think back to the dead ones I saw. Sure, they were unsettling, but they didn't exactly send me spiraling into fear or paranoia—yet. Though, I guess if it kept happening, I might lose it after a while.

"How can we kill him?" I ask the obvious question.

"We?" Ezra laughs while Ethan rolls his shoulders. "It's our job to kill him, not yours. You're too weak."

"It's not my fault, you know?" I say, trying to stand my ground.

Ezra doesn't even bother to acknowledge my defense, just waves me off like I'm nothing more than a child interrupting the grown-ups, before leaving the kitchen.

Marve stays behind, her presence quiet but somehow comforting. She doesn't say anything, just watches the space where Ezra was, unfazed by the tension or the sharp words exchanged.

"We ordered Indian food. Should I call to add something for you?" Ethan offers, trying to lighten up the mood in the room.

Marve shakes her head gently. "No, thanks," she replies, her voice soft but distant.

Without another word, she quietly exits the room, her footsteps barely audible against the tile. Whether she's upset, sad, or simply caught in the crossfire between Ethan and Ezra, I can't quite tell.

I don't waste much time once we're alone again. "So?"

Ethan glances up at me, acting confused. "So what? The food will be here soon."

I narrow my eyes. "You know that's not what I meant. How can Andras be killed?"

Ethan sighs, his shoulders slumping slightly. "You never give me a rest," he mutters, but he gives in. "With a weapon made of Wootz steel, which is nearly impossible to find. The method of making it was lost ages ago. It was originally made in ancient India, and the technique for producing it became a closely guarded secret before it was forgotten. The process involved preparing porous iron, hammering it while—"

I cut him off, my patience thinning. "Sorry, I don't really care about that," I blurt out, not bothering to hide the edge in my voice. Normally, I hate interrupting people, especially when they're passionate about something, but I can't focus on a history lesson right now. Not when I'm still upset with him.

Ethan chuckles softly, seemingly unbothered by my rudeness. "Sorry, weapons and fighting are my passion." His grin fades. "But even with that steel, Andras is too fast and too strong. Even for me. Getting close enough to kill him, even with the right weapon... well, let's just say it's no easy task."

First, we need a weapon; then we can worry about our abilities. "Where do we find a weapon made from this steel?"

Ethan grins, his eyes gleaming with a flash of pride. "In my safe."

I shake my head, exasperated. For someone who doesn't like talking and explaining, he's really dragging this out. "Why didn't you say that right away?"

"I have a Damascus blade," he says, leaning in a little closer. "But I only have one, and I'd prefer to keep that a secret. I will keep it close, and if I need to, I will use it, but until then, you can't tell no one—I mean absolutely anyone. Agreed?" His voice drops to a whisper.

"Okay."

Now comes the hard part. If Andras is so fast and powerful, even someone like Ethan can't match him, how do we kill him?

"So...what's the plan?" I whisper back, automatically mirroring his tone.

"Leave that to me."

"What do you mean? I need to know what's going on," I argue.

"Just trust me with this, okay? Do what I tell you."

I grit my teeth, trying to keep my temper in check. "Whatever," I mutter, pushing away from the counter and leaving the kitchen.

I know arguing with him would be pointless. It always is. He gives me scraps of information and expects me to blindly follow. It's frustrating, the way he keeps me in the dark, like I'm not capable of handling the truth. But I guess I have no choice. I'll have to get over it—for now.

I make my way to the library, determined to find out more about Andras and this mysterious steel. After scanning the shelves, my eyes land on *Wootz Steel: The Lost Weapon*. The title feels like a key to unlocking some part of this puzzle.

Flipping through the pages, I find confirmation of what Ethan mentioned—Wootz steel was indeed forged in ancient India, known for its ability to harm high-ranking demons. But the book dives deeper, revealing a chilling history.

The method of crafting Wootz steel was shrouded in secrecy, passed down only to select individuals deemed worthy. Despite efforts to keep it secret, demons eventually discovered the method and ruthlessly eliminated anyone with knowledge of it.

I read on, my fingers tracing the lines about modern attempts to recreate the steel, but they've all fallen short. Without the original technique, no one has managed to replicate its full power. No wonder Ethan wants to keep his blade a secret.

One detail stands out—a key ingredient: oak wood. Oak symbolizes strength and resilience, the very qualities needed to defeat demons. I wonder if that's what makes it so deadly to them.

Before I can dwell on it further, the smell of food drifts through the house. Dinner has arrived. I close the book and head back to the kitchen, where Ethan's already unpacking the takeout.

We sit in silence, the tension between us thick as ever, a shadow looming over what's supposed to be our first *family* meal.

chapter 22

FALLEN GUARDIAN

Two weeks unfold in a slow, predictable dance, each day blending seamlessly into the next. My fighting skills inch forward, but the progress feels hollow against the backdrop of monotony. The only spark of excitement comes from finally being allowed access to the demon texts, though even the thrill of new knowledge can't fill the growing emptiness inside me.

With every page I turn, I feel the ache in my chest grow sharper. I miss Ben. I miss Raya. Even Tubiel's teasing presence has become something I long for. Each dawn, the sun's rays feel colder, each twilight a little more lonesome, until I reach the breaking point. I could not, would not, spend another day without them. Especially not without Ben.

"It's not up for debate. I'm going out tonight," I declare, my voice steady, every muscle coiled with determination.

Ethan's face contorts with fury, nostrils flaring, brows knitting into a dark line. His jaw clenches so hard I can see the tension in his neck. For a moment, he's silent, clearly thrown by my defiance. I doubt he's used to being opposed, certainly not like this, and certainly not by a girl in her mid-twenties.

"You can't keep me here by force," I continue, sensing the battle in his mind.

"I can," he argues, his voice low and menacing. His eyes bore into mine, dark and intense, leaving no doubt he means it.

"But you can't keep me locked up forever," I say, my tone deliberately light, hoping to soften him up.

Ethan raises an eyebrow, the challenge clear in his eyes. We both know he could. He could lock me away in this house without a second thought, but what would be the point?

Andras, or whoever's after me, isn't going to storm in through the front door. But I can't live like this, hiding in the shadows forever. Sooner or later, I'll step outside, and when I do, the danger will be waiting. We need a plan to reclaim my life.

His gaze softens, just a fraction, as if he's weighing the truth of my words. Then, after a short pause, Ethan exhales, the rigid set of his shoulders easing ever so slightly.

"Alright," he finally concedes, his voice gruff with reluctant acceptance.

I blink, caught off guard by his sudden surrender. But this is

Ethan—there's always a catch. I brace myself, feeling like a rebellious teenager standing before a strict parent, waiting for the inevitable conditions to be laid out, curfew included.

"You can go out, but not alone."

There we go.

"What do you mean?" I ask, silently praying he doesn't intend to be my personal bodyguard... my fallen guardian angel.

"You can go out with Ben, but only in the presence of the guy that Tubiel guards and your best friend... that girl—what's her name again?"

"Raya," I correct, frowning. The casual dismissal in his tone stings. I've told him about her countless times. A caring father would remember her name.

"I trust Tubiel. He'll protect you, and the girl's guardian angel will be watching too, if she's there," he adds, not bothering to correct himself. "From what you've said, her angel really doesn't trust you."

"He doesn't. I wonder why..." I mutter, more to myself than him.

Ethan laughs—a sharp, ironic sound. "Well, he's afraid you might bring demons to his charge, which is exactly what you're doing, so... cut him some slack."

I open my mouth to argue, but he has a point, and I can't deny it.

"How do you even know Tubiel will be there? He's a guardian angel—he must have more people to protect, more places to be..."

Ethan's lips curl into an amused smile. It's like he's sitting on some big secret he's too smug to share.

"What?"

Ethan doesn't answer. Instead, he gives me a grin, boyish and teasing, like he's enjoying this far more than he should. "I just know," he says, with a conspiratorial wink.

I bite back a sigh of frustration, realizing I won't get any more answers out of him. He's enjoying this game too much. "If you want to go out, get the whole group together," he repeats, his tone leaving no room for negotiation.

I don't waste any time. With newfound energy, I dash to my room, grab my phone, and call the group. They all agree to meet.

Ben, however, sounds puzzled, wondering why, after a week apart, I've arranged to meet him only to have others tag along.

Inside, I ache for his company, craving to be alone with him—to feel his touch again, his kisses. But at least I get to see him tonight, even if we won't have the intimacy I crave. I have to take the win, even if it's small.

Restless and anxious, with hours still left before the evening, I slump onto my bed, trying to pass the time. A soft knock on the door pulls me from my thoughts. "Come in," I call out, and the door slowly creaks open. As Ethan steps into the room, Berry immediately reacts. Hissing and arching his back, fur bristling like needles, he darts under the bed, clearly not fond of fallen angels.

"Do you want to go for a run?" Ethan's unexpected offer catches me off guard. He hasn't let me step outside, not even for a breath of fresh air, in the entire two weeks I've been here. I hesitate for a moment, wondering what brought on this sudden change, but I'm not about to question my luck.

Before I can respond, he adds, "I'll meet you downstairs in

five."

Excited to go out again, even for a run, I leap off the bed and dig through my drawer, pulling out my running clothes without wasting a second.

When I dash downstairs, Ethan's already there, pacing back and forth. He looks out of place, tense, like this is more than just a casual run.

"Why do you want to go running?" I ask, raising an eyebrow. We've never done this before. Ethan, with his obsession for martial arts and weapons, doesn't exactly strike me as someone who enjoys cardio.

"If we need to lure out Andras, there's no point in keeping you in here anymore."

I'm a bit disappointed. I half-expected something more personal—a desire to spend time together, maybe even bond. But this works. At least he's trying, even if in his own roundabout way.

I shrug, letting it slide, and head towards the door. Ethan follows closely, and we step outside. The fresh morning is crisp and refreshing. I take a deep breath, savoring the freedom.

Then, without another word, we start running. Each step feels like a release, the rush of adrenaline flooding my veins. For a moment, I forget everything else—the demons, the danger. It's just me, the open road, and the steady rhythm of my feet hitting the ground.

Since embracing my abilities, running has become effortless, almost automatic, like breathing. After thirty minutes of weaving along the beach, the rhythmic pounding of my feet against the sand turns meditative.

We eventually veer off, leaving behind the familiar stretch of coastline and heading toward the quieter outskirts of town, into a small forest. The shift in terrain injects some excitement into the otherwise steady pace—dodging ditches, leaping over narrow streams, weaving around the occasional rock or tree branch. It feels more like an obstacle course than a simple run.

But then, suddenly, my lungs burn, a sharp wave of dizziness hitting me out of nowhere. I slow down, trying to catch my breath, but something else catches my eye—Ethan speeding up. He's not just running—he's chasing something.

Or some*one*.

My pulse quickens. I glance around and spot it—movement flickering between the trees. My heart thuds harder, this time not from the run, but from the thrill of the unknown.

"What's happening?" I call out, struggling to keep up. But before I can even finish my sentence, Ethan spins around and presses a finger to my lips. His eyes are sharp, serious, filled with a warning I can't ignore.

He touches my arm and says quietly, "Open your mind to me."

With slight hesitation, I do as he says. I focus, unsure of what exactly he's expecting. I relax, allowing whatever barrier I normally keep up to fade.

Slowly, I feel it—our minds connect, like a thin thread linking us together. The forest around us sharpens. Trees, bushes, and meadows I've never seen before appear vivid and clear. It's as if we're not standing still but exploring them—moving through the forest with our minds.

I can hear the soft thud of rabbit paws against the earth,

darting frantically as if fleeing an unseen predator. The birds' songs overhead come to a sudden, unnatural stop, leaving behind an eerie, heavy silence.

Then the connection snaps, the vision dissolving into the real world.

I blink, disoriented, the forest now feeling smaller, quieter. I stand there, frozen, confused.

"What... was that?" I exhale, barely able to process what just happened.

Ethan scans the area with his eyes once more. "I was trying to find him."

"Who?"

"The vampire," he replies as if it were obvious.

"What vampire?" I feel my frustration rising. I always have to ask him a dozen questions before I get a clear answer.

Ethan sighs and turns to face me. "There was a vampire. He approached us but then fled. Either it's a strange coincidence, or you were his target, and he didn't realize you had protection."

I try to wrap my head around what he's saying, but I'm still too confused. "But I didn't see anything. How did you even know he was there?"

"I sensed death."

It suddenly clicks. The dizziness, the shortness of breath—it wasn't just the run. It was that thing. A *vampire.*

"Wow, a real vampire?" I say, excitement creeping into my voice. "Why did you have to scare him off? I've never seen a vampire before."

Ethan looks at me, his eyes cold as ice. "Trust me, some things are better left unseen. And for the record, I wasn't trying to scare him off. I was trying to catch him. And kill him."

"Oh, I'm shocked he ran away then."

"We need to kill him before he comes back, so that he doesn't get another chance to come after you," he says, his voice low and firm. "In times like these, you never know."

I stifle the urge to roll my eyes, keeping my annoyance in check. The vampire didn't even get close to me. For all I know, it could've been a coincidence. Maybe not every supernatural creature is gunning for me. But Ethan knows better, right? He always does.

Ethan's gaze sweeps the area again, but it's clear he's found nothing. He glances back at me with a sudden spark in his eyes. "I'm surprised you're not peppering me with questions. You usually do."

"Like what?" I ask, tilting my head.

"Like if he changed into a bat," he says with a smirk.

"I've already consulted your library on this topic," I reply smugly, enjoying the brief flicker of surprise that crosses his face.

"Oh, really? My apologies for doubting your expertise," he says, still holding that mocking edge in his voice.

I cross my arms, shaking my head, unimpressed by his response. "Marve's shared many stories about vampires. They're fascinating creatures, and not all of them are bad, you know?" I counter, meeting his skeptical gaze head-on. "You shouldn't be so quick to judge and want to kill him without knowing his story."

He bursts into laughter, loud and disbelieving. "Not all bad?" he echoes between chuckles. "I'll believe that when I see it."

I lift my chin, feeling proud of my next retort. "How will you ever *see* if you kill every vampire you meet?" I raise an eyebrow, daring him to prove me wrong.

Ethan's face tightens, his stance shifting defensively. "Watch your tone, young lady. What happened to your *I-want-to-kill-all-the-monsters* attitude?"

A chuckle slips out of me. He's scrambling for a solid argument.

"I still do," I say with a shrug. "But I also want to give them the benefit of the doubt first."

"With that attitude, you're just going to get yourself killed," he growls. Without waiting for a response, he turns and stalks off.

Oh, he's a sore loser.

I watch him for a moment, not convinced by his reasoning. After all, didn't he say killing me was practically impossible?

Sensing my doubt, he stops again and turns, his eyes locking onto mine. "You know what I mean—captured, hurt..."

"If you don't believe in giving someone the benefit of the doubt, then what about Marve?" I ask, tilting my head to the side, a small smile playing at my lips.

Ethan's face hardens instantly, and I can tell he's biting his cheek from the inside. "What about her?"

"How come you haven't killed her? How come you let her into your house?"

His lips part and for a moment, I think he might snap at me. But instead, his voice comes out steady, though it's clear the question stings. "I gave her the benefit of Ezra. He saved her from other demons. He trusted her, and I trusted him. Simple as that."

But nothing is simple. Not in this world. Not in my new world.

"And you?" I hold his gaze, studying every flicker of emotion in his eyes. "Do *you* trust her?"

His eyes narrow, as if searching mine for any hint of a trap. "Of course. I thought you liked her."

Turning this against me, how clever.

"I do. It's Ezra I have doubts about, but they're together after all," I say, my voice quieter now, as if confessing a secret I'm not sure how he'll take.

Ethan halts, tilting his head toward the sky, his lips pulling into a tight line. It's almost as if he's asking God whether he sees this madness.

I can't resist echoing his earlier words with a playful wink. "In times like these, you never know."

His gaze drops from the sky, meeting mine with a fierce focus that quickly softens. A small smile tugs at the corner of his mouth. "Don't be smug," he mutters, but there's no real bite to it. His lips quirk into a full smile before he lets out a brief, reluctant laugh, the tension between us breaking, if only for a moment.

When we get back to the house, we run into Ezra in the entry hall. He doesn't bother with the usual polite nod or muttered greeting, just strides past us like we don't exist.

Suddenly, he halts mid-step and slowly turns. His gaze lands on me, not with the usual indifference or scorn, but with something else—a thorough, almost calculated once-over that makes the hairs on the back of my neck prickle. His stare lingers, deliberate and unsettling, as if he's weighing something about me.

He doesn't speak. Just watches for a beat longer than comfortable, before finally turning away and disappearing down the hall.

My first thought is that he's surprised I made it back from the woods. Maybe he knew there was something after me, hoping it'd get me.

But then again, this is Ezra. Probably just another attempt at reminding me how much I don't belong here, how much I'm endangering his precious demon.

I shake it off, trying to ignore the cold knot that's forming in my chest, but a part of me wonders—what exactly was he looking for?

chapter 23

JUST AWKWARD

The sun sinks behind the horizon, casting the sky in a fiery blend of gold and amber, the colors deepening as twilight takes over. In the quiet of my room, I stand before the wardrobe, fingers grazing the soft fabric of each dress.

After a moment's deliberation, I settle on one of my newest—a silky number that slides over my skin like water. The moment it settles on my frame, I know it's my favorite. I use my fingers to style my hair, giving it the direction I want it to curl. A little trick to tame it to my will.

The mirror reflects my nervous smile and eyes brimming with

anticipation. I know tonight's dinner is just an excuse to lure Andras, but my heart still races at the thought of having my first official dinner with both my boyfriend and Ethan.

Though Ethan didn't raise me, and I don't consider him my real father, I still crave his approval. After all, why not? I rely on him to stay with me for eternity.

Given the likelihood (and secret hope) that we'll face another demon tonight and get this over with, Ethan chose a restaurant in a quieter, more secluded part of the city. Raya seemed uneasy at first, but Ethan had me put her at ease by mentioning their famous Hong Kong-style waffles—a distraction that worked like a charm. While Ethan wanted to lure her in with their steaks, I figured the desserts would be more her thing, and I was right.

As I settle into the car next to Ethan, the hum of the engine fills the silence. My thoughts, however, are far louder, and the quiet car ride seems like the perfect moment to pry some answers out of him.

"Why would Andras come after me?" I ask.

Ethan frowns, his eyes searching for answers in the emptiness before him. After a long pause, he finally shrugs. "I really don't know. It doesn't make sense. Maybe he heard about you and thought it would be a good challenge... maybe he's just doing it for fun."

"You think he'll show up tonight?"

Ethan glances at me, a faint smirk tugging at the corner of his lips before his focus shifts back to the road. "I think demons are really impatient, and we've just gifted him two weeks of pure boredom."

"But how would he or anyone else even know about me?"

A brief flick of his eyes meets mine, his fingers gripping the steering wheel a bit tighter than necessary. "I don't know," he replies quietly. "I might have mentioned you a few times."

"To demons?" I scoff. I doubt he'd tell demons about me, but who could he have told? I don't see him hanging out with anyone other than Ezra and Marve. Who else could he have been talking to? Some old angelic acquaintances maybe, but even then, I doubt they'd spill anything to a demon.

He leaves his expression flat, guarded. "No... not directly. But, you know, word gets around." His voice is emotionless, but I catch a flicker of something in his eyes—regret, maybe.

The landscape rushes by in a blur, but my thoughts are anything but fleeting. They twist and knot, tightening with every passing second. A part of me hesitates, unsure if I dare to ask the question that's been gnawing at me. My fingers clench in my lap as I take a deep breath, trying to steady the nervous energy buzzing beneath my skin.

When I finally speak, my voice comes out softer than I intended, barely more than a whisper. "Do you trust Ezra?"

Ethan's gaze snaps away from the road, his eyes locking onto mine with an intensity that makes me shudder. His grip on the wheel tightens as if he were about to crush it.

"Watch the road!" I yell, my pulse spiking as the car veers slightly before he quickly corrects it, the tires skimming the edge of the lane.

"What do you mean, *do I trust Ezra*?" he snaps, his tone laced with an anger I've never heard from him before. "Of course I trust him. He's the only person I truly trust."

I swallow hard, but I don't back down. "Look at it from my perspective. He's never seemed to like me. Remember how he spoke to me during our training? And he told you straight up that he didn't think you should protect me. I always feel like he's waiting for me to screw up. Like he's convinced I'll bring doom on Marve or something. Plus, he has connections to demons, doesn't he? He seems like someone who'd want me gone."

Ethan's jaw clenches."Enough with this nonsense," he growls, dismissing my words with a firm shake of his head.

"But he—"

"I said enough!" His voice reverberates through the car, cutting through the air like a blade. It's as if he's reached into my mind and flipped a switch, silencing me completely. I open my mouth to respond, but no words come out, as if he's stolen them before I even had the chance.

The rest of the drive passes in thick silence, tension hanging between us like a heavy curtain. I stew in my thoughts, replaying every interaction with Ezra, trying to fit the pieces together. Something doesn't add up, and I can't shake the feeling that Ezra is at the heart of it all. He knows my whereabouts, my movements, and he has more than enough reasons to want me gone. He resents me for giving up my mortality, and he's terrified I'll put Marve at risk. No wonder he's treated me like garbage most of the time.

When we finally arrive, Ethan gestures for me to head inside, assuring me he'll be right behind. As I turn to go, I catch sight of Tubiel slipping into the car beside him. Their expressions are serious, brows furrowed in conversation, though I can't hear a word. They're keeping something from me again, and I hate it.

With a reluctant sigh, I follow the others into the restaurant.

The rich scent of roasted meat and freshly baked bread flows through the room, immediately making my stomach growl. Our table, nestled by the window, offers a sweeping view of the glowing city below.

As we settle in, Ethan appears less than two minutes later, sliding into his seat. Tubiel, however, is nowhere to be seen.

I fidget in my chair, trying to ignore the hunger growling in my stomach as I flip through the menu. With my new abilities, I burn through calories like wildfire, so I don't hesitate to order enough for two. Ben, Brian, and even Raya exchange curious glances, but Ethan, as if it's the most natural thing in the world, orders food for three without batting an eye.

"Wow, you guys really know how to eat," Brian remarks, sounding half impressed, half jealous. Ethan just shrugs and nods, while I can feel my cheeks heat up. I don't want to look like a pig, but I'm starving.

As the waiter takes our orders and leaves, Ethan sets down his menu and directs his attention to the guys. His gaze lingers on Brian before he turns to me. "Is he a Nephilim?"

"I don't think so. He doesn't seem to see angels," I reply, glancing at the rest of the group to gauge their reactions, checking if the famous Spell was doing its job.

Ben seems oblivious and Raya is in the restroom, but Brian, chewing on a breadstick, looks between us with genuine curiosity. "What's a Nephilim?" he asks nonchalantly once he's swallowed.

I nearly choke on my own saliva, my eyes darting to Ethan. I shoot him a questioning look before allowing him access to my thoughts.

He heard me because the term means nothing to him. Doesn't he look rather angelic, though? Ethan's playful voice echoes in my mind, as clear as if he were speaking aloud. It feels strange, almost like someone else is narrating my own inner monologue.

"Yeah, he does," I answer automatically, forgetting for a moment that I'm not just thinking but actually speaking aloud.

Both Ben and Brian raise their eyebrows, clearly puzzled by my sudden comment. Brian looks particularly thrown off, his breadstick paused mid-air.

I catch myself too late. Their eyes are locked on me, waiting for an explanation that I haven't prepared.

"Just an inside joke," Ethan interjects smoothly, the corners of his mouth twitching with amusement before he quickly suppresses it. He seems all too familiar with these kinds of awkward moments.

My cheeks flush with embarrassment, but Brian just shrugs it off, seemingly unfazed by the odd comment.

An awkward silence falls over the table like a thick fog, stifling any chance of light conversation. Ben and I can't seem to stay still in our chairs, our legs bumping under the table, adding another layer of discomfort to the moment. I steal a quick glance at him, but he looks just as unsure as I feel.

Raya returns from the restroom, her unease apparent as she glances around. She's only met Ben once, and the rest of the group is new to her. What a mismatched group of people we are—thrown together by circumstance rather than any real bond. The strained silence highlights just how little we have in common.

Unexpectedly, it's Ethan who breaks it, even though it's obvious he couldn't care less about anyone here except me. This evening is just a means to an end for him—luring out Andras or whoever else is hunting me.

"So, Ben," Ethan begins loudly. "What are your intentions with my... cousin?"

Ben's face flushes deep red, and he opens his mouth to respond, but I jump in before he can say anything. "What... stop it!" I snap, glaring at Ethan.

"Don't answer him," I tell Ben quickly, shooting Ethan a look that I hope conveys enough threat to shut him up.

Ben gives me a nervous, sweet smile, his eyes glued to the glass of water in front of him, as if willing himself to disappear.

"I'm sorry," I whisper to Ben, sliding my hand onto his leg beneath the table. He responds with a gentle squeeze, intertwining our fingers

Ethan, completely ignoring my attempt to rein him in, switches his attention without missing a beat. "Nice watch," he says casually, his gaze landing on Brian's wrist.

Brian, eager to share, holds up his arm with a proud grin. "Yeah, it's a Patek Philippe," he says, diving headfirst into a detailed history of the brand's Swiss origins and craftsmanship.

Ethan nods along, clearly impressed. "I've always been a fan of Tag Heuer myself." They start swapping stories about their favorite models, and the technical specs of mechanical watches become the new topic of the evening.

To me, it's just noise. The technical jargon flies right over my head, and judging by the way Ben is staring blankly at the table, I'm not the only one left out.

I shoot him a small, sympathetic smile and he returns it, though there's a hint of resignation in his eyes. Ethan should be trying to connect with Ben, not swapping brand names with Brian.

But as I glance back at Ethan, it's clear that he's more invested in the booze than building bridges. He's already knocked back a few drinks, the glass refilling as quickly as it empties, the alcohol barely registering with him. No one else here knows that, though. They probably think he's just on the verge of getting hammered.

As the waitress sets yet another drink in front of Ethan, her disapproving frown doesn't go unnoticed. But before Ethan can even reach for the glass, Tubiel reappears at Brian's side. Suddenly, the room shifts.

One by one, guardian angels materialize, their faces etched with concern, all eyes drawn toward the door. Tubiel, however, seems almost... pleased, as if he's been waiting for this moment. His gaze flickers briefly to where Ben's hand rests on my thigh before locking onto Ethan, as if communicating something unspoken.

The air thickens with tension. I feel it—something dangerous is approaching. My heart pounds in my chest. We knew this was coming; we planned for it, but the nervous knot in my stomach tells me that no amount of preparation could ease the fear gripping me now. Suddenly, all thoughts of awkward conversations and bonding slip away. Survival is the only thing that matters. And in that moment, I just hope we all make it out alive—except the demon. That one, I want gone for good.

Raya's guardian angel appears as well, immediately moving closer to her, his posture tense, ready.

"Hello, Rizoel," Tubiel greets him with a calmness that feels out of place in the rising storm.

So that's Raya's guardian's name. I can't say I like it—just as much as I don't like him. The way he talks to me, the way he looks at me... even now, when he first appeared, his eyes seemed to pierce straight through me. It's a good thing he doesn't have a weapon made from the Jubokko tree. I bet he wouldn't hesitate to use it, just like he doesn't hesitate to attack demons that aren't even after his charges.

"How can you speak to this abomination?" Rizoel sneers, nodding toward me with thinly veiled disdain.

"She's not an abomination." Tubiel's voice is firm, and in a subtle move, he steps closer to me, positioning himself like a shield. His protective stance is impossible to miss.

But the conversation ends there. Tubiel's attention shifts to Ethan, and his expression darkens. "It's time."

Ethan gives a brisk, almost imperceptible nod, and without another word, Tubiel strides out of the restaurant. The other angels remain in place. Even Rizoel stays inside this time, not moving to confront whatever is coming.

Around us, the humans are blissfully unaware. Laughter rings out, glasses clink, and the rich scent of roasted meat fills the air as if nothing is amiss. The normalcy around me feels surreal—two worlds intertwined, while one remains oblivious to the other.

"I need to make a call," Ethan announces to the group, already rising from his seat and heading for the exit.

Without hesitation, I push back my chair, following after him and Tubiel. Ben and Raya are left in the dark, but I barely spare them a glance. "I think the call concerns me too. I'll be right back," I toss over my shoulder as I dash after them.

As I approach the exit, a sudden chill crawls up my spine, the once-warm air of the restaurant now weighed down by an invisible menace. The demon doesn't even need to be inside for my blood to run cold. My steps falter, and I hesitate, fingers hovering just above the door handle, my heart hammering against my ribs.

Taking a deep breath, I steel myself, push open the door, and step into whatever's waiting in the shadows beyond.

chapter 24

WHO'S HOOTING NOW?

I step out of the restaurant, scanning the area until I spot Ethan and Tubiel standing in the shadows of a nearby alley. I quickly make my way over, leaving the lively noise of the restaurant behind me.

"Why didn't you stay inside?" Ethan's voice rings out, laced with his usual frustration.

"This is about me."

Ethan sighs, a deep, dramatic sound that only fuels my resolve. "You don't know how to protect yourself in this world."

I cross my arms, stepping closer. "I'm part of your world now,

Ethan. You can't keep me away from all this," My glare should convey everything, yet I still add, "I'm staying. Deal with it."

Ethan murmurs something indistinguishable. His expression darkens, and a low, threatening sound escapes him as he steps forward, positioning himself between me and whatever danger is approaching.

Just as he moves closer to shield me, a figure emerges in the distance. Despite the darkness, my enhanced senses allow me to see him with unsettling clarity. He's tall and lean, with blond hair framing a face dominated by piercing yellow-orange eyes that remind me of an owl's predatory gaze. His sharp, birdlike features, paired with a small, flat nose, make the resemblance even more unnerving.

There's something both grotesque and frightening about him, and I can't help but wonder why anyone would choose such an unflattering form.

As he draws nearer, his lips curl into a grin, the kind that promises nothing good.

"Ah, a welcoming party, how delightful," the demon remarks, his voice a grating, dissonant blend of tones that cuts through the air. It's like the screech of metal grinding against metal layered with the piercing scrape of nails on a chalkboard, all twisted together into one unsettling voice. It's as if multiple voices are speaking at once, each more jarring than the last, resonating in a way that makes my skin crawl.

His grin widens as he surveys us. "So, what do we have here? An angel, a fallen angel, and a girl? Is this why my troops were disappearing?" He pauses expectantly, waiting for a response that never comes.

"I thought if this girl was only protected by a weak fallen angel, a demon should have no trouble reaching her. But alas, he ended up dead. It piqued my curiosity, you see. I simply had to see who was protecting her with my own eyes, though I must admit, I didn't expect this," he gestures at us with exaggerated flair, while clearly relishing the sound of his own voice. His arrogance radiance through the brief silence, as he basks in the power he believes he holds over us. Then, with a subtle shift to the side, his gaze sharpens, narrowing as he examines me more closely.

"She's a full Nephilim," he remarks calmly, though the quick flutter of his eyelid betrays him. Despite his efforts to mask it, this realization has clearly caught him off guard. The demon who discovered the truth about my soul didn't make it back to him—thanks to Rizoel, and so he was left in the dark.

"What do you want from her, Andras?" Ethan demands, his voice surprisingly steady.

So it is *him*.

Andras inhales slowly, a theatrical display as if savoring the moment, pretending to relish the tension and the looming threat of violence. But I can see through the act—it's just a ploy to buy time, to calculate his next move.

I'm certain he's scrambling for a new plan now that he's realized I've embraced my powers, and my soul is beyond his reach. His sharp gaze flickers between Tubiel and Ethan, sizing them up, weighing his options.

"To be honest..." he starts, his voice taking on a mockingly thoughtful tone, as if still toying with his decision. "This is rather amusing." He lets out a light chuckle, and I'm starting to hate the sound—grinding and hollow, like the creak of old bones, echoing unnervingly in the silence. "I expected a powerless Nephilim girl, offering up a ripe soul, and a lone angel to have some fun with." His candidness throws me off. I had fully expected him to mask his surprise, to act as if he'd known about my powers all along.

Tubiel and Ethan exchange a quick, uneasy glance, both of them clearly unsure of what Andras will do next. I can almost feel Ethan's frustration mounting with every word the demon utters. He's never had much patience for needless chatter, and Andras is spinning a web of words that lead nowhere. The muscles in his jaw are tightening as he resists the urge to cut Andras off, and I'm sure every second wasted on this monologue must be grating at him.

"It seems I have no use for her." *Yeah, tell me something I don't know.* "But I had to get up and come here—that's not something I usually do," Andras muses, as though he's weighing the inconvenience I caused him.

His gaze shifts to Ethan and Tubiel's hands, checking for the weapon—the one they need to kill him. To my surprise, they don't seem to have it on them.

How in hell do they not have the one weapon we need?

Ethan and Tubiel move with calculated precision, circling Andras like hunters, each positioning themselves strategically on either side of him, preparing for the inevitable confrontation.

"I came for a snack and a good fight. I'm not getting the snack, but fighting the two of you at once will make for a memorable moment. A short one, though," Andras says, his owl-like wings spreading wide, the leathery sound echoing in the tense air.

"Memorable, for sure. But you won't be the one to remember it," Ethan shoots back, a sly smile curling at the edge on his lips.

Is Ethan bluffing, trying to make Andras back down? Or does he have the blade hidden somewhere, and that smile is actually well-founded? I can't decide whether to hold onto doubt or hope.

Andras mirrors Ethan's smile, his eerie, birdlike face twisting into something even more unsettling. "Let's see." The two of them stand poised, their smiles mere masks for the deadly intent behind them.

Ethan lunges first, but Andras vanishes in a blur, reappearing behind him. A swift, brutal kick sends Ethan flying several meters, his body crashing against the pavement.

"You didn't see that coming, did you?" Andras taunts, his grating laughter cutting through the air, needling my nerves.

But I know Ethan expected this. He'd mentioned being too slow for Andras, which is why Tubiel is here.

Without hesitation, Tubiel charges forward, his fist arcing toward Andras. The demon dodges easily, but Tubiel isn't finished—he vanishes, only to reappear in the same spot he left. With the element of surprise on Tubiel's side, his kick slams into Andras' chest, forcing him to stagger back.

Seizing the moment, Ethan dives back into the fight, his fist connecting with Andras in a brutal strike that sends the demon crashing to his knees. Andra's sneer fades just as the Damascus blade materializes in Tubiel's hand, its gleaming tip pressed firmly against Andras' throat. Blood begins to drip from the shallow cut on the demon's skin, marking the severity of the threat.

"You didn't expect this, did you?" Tubiel taunts, throwing

Andras' earlier words back at him.

Andras examines the blade closely, his eyes tracing the intricate carvings along the steel. "I have to admit, I didn't." His lips twist, but the confidence in his voice never wavers. "Though, you've got to admit, this isn't exactly a fair fight. Two against one, and I'm a little rusty," he quips, his tone unnervingly playful.

With a violent thrust of his wings, Andras shoves Tubiel backward, knocking him off balance. In the same breath, his foot connects with Ethan's torso in a gut-wrenching kick, sending him sprawling. Before anyone can react, Andras launches himself into the air, attempting a swift escape.

"Oh, no you don't," Tubiel snarls, grabbing hold of Andras' wings mid-flight and slamming him back to the ground with a force that makes the earth shudder.

In that instant, Tubiel transforms before my eyes. He's no longer the quirky, slightly crazy, and surprisingly cute angel I've come to know—now, he's all power and precision, a warrior wrapped in terrifying grace. I never imagined him as such a fierce fighter, but it's undeniable now—he's not just good; he's better than Ethan.

As Andras crashes to the ground, he retaliates fiercely, managing to hurl both Ethan and Tubiel aside when they pounce on him.

Ethan skids across the dirt, while Tubiel flickers out of sight, only to reappear in a heartbeat. What follows is a strange, almost hypnotic dance, both of them blinking in and out of existence, striking at one another from different angles, each blow a blur.

Finally, Tubiel lands a brutal punch, his fist smashing into

Andras' face before driving straight into his chest, momentarily pinning him.

Ethan, having regained his footing, seizes the opportunity. With a sickening rip, he grabs Andras by the wings and tears them away in one vicious motion.

But Andras remains silent, his lack of reaction somehow more horrifying than any scream could be.

A wave of nausea crashes over me, and the ground beneath my feet seems to undulate like the waves of the ocean. The scene before me is the most revolting thing I've ever witnessed.

My instinct is to look away, but I force myself to keep watching—I need to know what's happening. Slowly, cautiously, I turn back to the blood-soaked ground, bracing myself to cover my eyes if it becomes too much.

A bitter taste rises in my throat, and I can feel the bile churning in my stomach, threatening to spill over. I swallow hard, but it only makes it worse; the acrid flavor fills my mouth, and I fight the urge to gag.

Andras lies on his back, drenched in a pool of his own blood. Tubiel stands like a grim executioner, the tip of the Damascus blade pressed against Andras' chest, poised right over where his heart should be.

Tubiel opens his mouth, as if to speak, but his expression shifts suddenly. His eyes flick to Ethan, and an unspoken exchange passes between them.

"Tell us who sent you and why, and we'll spare you," Ethan demands.

Andras scoffs, blood dripping from his lips as he lets out a harsh, raspy laugh. "Do you take me for a fool? I know you wield Wootz steel; you'll never release me. That's why you're making the offer, isn't it?" He spits a glob of blood onto the ground, a sneer twisting his features. "Unlike your angelic friend here, you're capable of lying."

He's not wrong. There's no way they'd let him go. If Andras were released, he'd alert the entire demon world about the blade Ethan possesses, and soon, demons would swarm like vultures. Ethan might stand strong against one, but against a horde? He wouldn't stand a chance.

"Can't blame a guy for trying." A wry smile tugs at Ethan's lips as he signals to Tubiel with a subtle nod.

Without a second thought, Tubiel drives the blade deep into Andras' chest with a wet crunch as the metal punctures flesh.

The demon smiles, as if even in death he refuses to give anyone the satisfaction of seeing his devilish spirit broken. But as the blade does its work, that defiant smile falters, and in an instant, he crumbles to ashes.

Tubiel hands the blade back to Ethan, who accepts it with a grateful nod. "Thank you for everything you've done." Ethan pats Tubiel on the shoulder, releasing a deep breath as if he's been holding it the entire time. Or maybe he's just catching his breath after the intense fight.

With Andras's ashes carried away by the wind, the chaos subsides, but in my mind, the turmoil remains. "How come you had the blade?" I turn to Tubiel. It's the first question that escapes my lips, overshadowing the gratitude I should express or the concern for their well-being. I hadn't expected Ethan to trust anyone else with such a powerful and unique weapon.

As Ethan turns to leave, he pauses mid-step and looks back. "I'll give you two some privacy," he says, gesturing toward the restaurant.

Privacy? Why? Tubiel could answer my questions with Ethan here.

"Ethan knew he couldn't handle Andras alone, so he gave me the blade earlier," Tubiel explains, watching as Ethan walks away, disappearing into the dimly lit street.

"So, you were in on it with Ethan from the beginning? But why? I'm not even your human to guard. Why do you help a fallen angel and a Nephilim whom you barely know?" I ask him, genuinely puzzled. He's risking so much by doing this, and I can't figure out why.

Tubiel glances around cautiously, ensuring we're alone. Then, in an unexpected move, he fully materializes—his form becoming solid, tangible. He steps closer, his hand gently touching my shoulder before sliding down my arm until he's holding my hand in his.

"I'm in love with you, Pandora," he whispers, and it feels like the words carry more than just sound. I can see it in his eyes now, something that's been there for some time but I'm only just noticing. It's in the warmth of the energy that surrounds him, different from any other guardian's. It's in the way his breath catches, as if he's taking me in so deeply, completely.

I open my mouth to say something, but no words come out. Nothing even comes to mind. I close it, then open it again, trying once more. "Why do you call me that?" I whisper, my voice barely audible. It's not relevant—not right now—but my mind blanks. An angel confessing his love to me is the last thing I expected. Despite the shock, I don't pull away from his touch.

"That is your true name," he says simply, though nothing about this moment feels simple.

Despite everything, an undeniable closeness forms between us. Tubiel isn't just an ally anymore—his presence gives me a sense of security I hadn't realized I was craving. His hand in mine feels reassuring, almost intimate. And there's no denying his attractiveness.

Standing here with him, holding my hand, gazing at me with such affection, I almost feel compelled to lean in and kiss him. But deep down, I know the pull isn't genuine—it's the effect of being near a guardian angel, amplified by his physical presence.

"I'm with Ben," I remind him, pulling myself back to reality, breaking free from the swirl of emotions clouding my mind. What I feel for Ben is entirely different. Just thinking about him makes my heart race in a way that's all too real.

Tubiel's expression darkens, and his voice carries a bitterness I've never heard before. "He can't even see me. You know what that means."

I understand his implication all too well. Ben may not be a Nephilim. He might not share the immortality that defines my existence. Our relationship could have an expiration date. I can't even share this side of my life with him, a barrier between us that feels more solid with each passing moment.

Tubiel's gaze softens as he catches the sadness reflected in my eyes. "But we could be together forever," he murmurs, his voice gentle, filled with a quiet yearning. Hope flickers in his eyes like distant stars, fragile yet persistent, as if he's daring to believe that what he's offering could be enough to sway me.

But this isn't a matter of persuasion or hope. A pang of guilt squeezes my chest as I meet his gaze. "I'm sorry. Truly, I am. You're wonderful, and I care for you... deeply, but as a friend." I pause, hesitating to say more, but ultimately deciding that he needs to hear the truth. It might hurt now, but it will hurt less than falling from the skies would. "It's strange, I know, but something tells me Ben might be the one. Despite everything, there's this sense... like we're meant to be. He feels perfect."

"I feel the same way about you," he confesses, his voice thick with a desperation he's trying to suppress. His fingers tighten slightly around mine, as if holding on will change the truth between us.

I hold his gaze, my lips pressed together. When the silence becomes too prolonged, I finally find my courage to speak again. "Just promise me that you won't do anything stupid you might regret later."

His eye twitches and his jaw tightens, an unreadable expression crossing his face. It's as if something just clicked for him—something that makes this all a little easier.

"I won't. Not until you're ready for me," he says, his voice firm, like an unbreakable vow. "Just be careful. Nothing in life is perfect. If something seems too good to be true, there might be a surprise waiting."

His gaze is steady, serious. Then, he leans in and presses a soft kiss to my forehead, his breath warm against my skin. As he pulls away, I catch a glimpse of his wings—majestic and radiant, each feather shifting in color, blending into a living rainbow. For the first time, I see them in all their glory. Before, he always vanished too quickly for me to fully take them in. Now, each feather seems to hold its own secret, a reflection of the depth and complexity within him. With one last look he flies away.

Taking a moment to collect myself, I head back to the restaurant where Ethan waits outside. He remains silent about my recent conversation, likely sensing my discomfort. The only thing he manages is, "I must admit, you have a much stronger stomach than I thought."

I look up at him, a half-smile breaking through as the tension eases slightly. "Yeah, well, I might've vomited a little in my mouth, so..."

"Ew, that's gross." Well, he asked for it.

We walk back inside together, but Ethan doesn't stop at our table for long. Instead, he quickly downs his untouched drink and heads toward the bathrooms, leaving me alone with the group.

"What happened to his shirt?" Brian asks, his eyes glued to Ethan's half-naked figure as he walks past. It's only now that I notice the state of Ethan's shirt, hanging in tatters with nearly half of it missing.

I shrug, trying to keep my voice steady as I struggle to come up with a reasonable excuse on the spot. "Why don't you ask him yourself when he comes back?" I say, forcing a casual tone as my fingers absentmindedly toy with the strap of my dress, betraying the calmness I'm trying to project.

"He looks like he got into a fight," Brian mutters, his brow furrowing in mild judgment as he glances toward the restroom.

Well, it's not surprising that there's a bit of judgment in the air. Ethan hasn't exactly put his best foot forward tonight—not in front of them, at least.

I shrug again, feeling drained. I've already used up all my energy today, and I don't have anything left to spare for coming up with more lies. Instead, I pick up my own drink to flush away the bile still sitting in my mouth.

"Man, that guy is crazy," Brian whispers into Ben's ear. "But he's ripped!"

Ben glances at me, a faint smile tugging at the corner of his mouth, while I silently pray they don't probe any further into the night's events.

But before they get the chance, I spot Ethan moving toward Brian with a stealth that catches him completely off guard. He stops just behind him, leans in, and with a quiet whisper of, "Thanks," surprises Brian, who jerks slightly, his cheeks flushing red.

Brian stammers, nervously laughing. "Oh, uh... Yeah, nice six-pack."

Ethan leans in even closer, now just a breath away from his ear, almost brushing against it with his lips. "I bet you've got some too," he replies, his tone playful, a sparkling smile lighting up his face.

Brian glances quickly at Ethan's muscles. "I'm trying, but my body's nowhere near as perfect."

Ethan's grin widens, his eyes twinkling with mischief as he

gives Brian an appreciative once-over. "I wouldn't say that."

Brian tries to relax, though the deep blush staining his cheeks gives him away. His fingers nervously play with the hem of his shirt, his legs shifting restlessly, but he doesn't pull away from Ethan. Despite the clear tension in his posture, there's a subtle flicker of something else—an enjoyment he's not quite ready to admit, even to himself.

As I watch their interaction, something finally clicks into place. The laughter, the playful banter—it's obvious now. How did I not see it sooner? I'm supposed to be perceptive, but I completely missed this. Tubiel's comment that 'I'm not Brian's type' makes sense now, though I hadn't thought much of it at the time.

Ben, completely focused on me and seemingly oblivious to the rest of the world, steps closer. He gently tucks a lock of my hair behind my ear. "What about that call? Is everything alright?"

It takes me a moment to pull my thoughts back to the present and force a calm smile. "Yeah, I think things will finally get back to normal."

Before any of us can say anything more, Ethan steps forward. He gives me a quick nod, his eyes flicking to the door, a silent signal that he's ready to head home and swap out his battle-worn clothes.

"I have to go now, but we'll talk tomorrow, okay?" I say to Ben.

For a brief moment, I consider asking Ethan if I can go home with Ben tonight, now that the immediate threat seems to be gone. But after my conversation with Tubiel, I know I need some time alone to process everything. I can't help but feel a twinge of guilt at the thought of spending the night with Ben while the one who saved me today just confessed his love for me.

Ben steps closer, and I can tell he's hoping for a goodbye kiss, but with Ethan watching us closely, standing there like a guardian angel who doesn't understand the word 'privacy', it's way too awkward. "Do you mind?" I throw a quick glance at Ethan, hoping he'll leave us alone for a second.

"One minute," Ethan mutters, frowning, but he steps outside. Though honestly, I probably wouldn't mind if he protested—it would've given me an excuse to keep things light, a fleeting kiss without making Ben feel like I don't care about him anymore.

Ben grins, pulling me close. "Let's make it a good one then," he teases, leaning in for what should be a passionate kiss. But the spark that usually ignites between us feels... dim. Instead, all I feel is guilt, growing with each passing second in Ben's arms.

"Goodnight," I whisper, barely managing to meet his eyes as I pull away.

Without another word, I turn and walk out.

chapter 25

OUT FOR STAKES, HOME TO STAKES

I slide into the car beside Ethan, the soft click of the door closing behind marking the end of the evening, along with the fading shadow of the threat that had loomed over us. For the first time after weeks, I can finally breath again. It's not just the relief of the immediate danger being over—it's knowing I can actually go back home, to where I belong.

As the engine purrs to life and we pull away from the restaurant, I glance over at Ethan. His fingers barely brush the steering wheel, as if he's guiding the car with just a touch. He leans back in his seat, almost as if he were lying down. The fleeting glow of streetlights dances across his face, softening his sharp features.

He looks different—lighter, like a man who has finally let go of something heavy.

"That was easy," I say, the words slipping out before I even have a chance to hear how they sound in my head.

Ethan shoots me a pointed look that says it all. Of course, it was easy for me—I didn't have to fight anyone. "Tell that to my shirt," he quips, his voice rising in pitch as he gestures to the tattered fabric hanging off him. "I wouldn't have stood a chance against him alone. Tubiel's way stronger than me, and with his wings, he was able to play Andras' game."

Wow. I never thought I'd hear Ethan admit he wasn't the strongest fighter. And lending his blade to an angel? That's a shock in itself. Turns out he's got more strategy than I gave him credit for. He knows when to drop the tough-guy act and play smart when it matters most.

"Thank you," I murmur, realizing I haven't properly shown my appreciation for *everything* he's done to keep me safe. I've just acted like a spoiled child. I had been harsh with him, angry for keeping me cooped up, for coming along tonight when I'd wanted to be with my friends, for being so protective... when in reality, he'd done it all for my own good.

I haven't really thanked Tubiel either.

Ethan's gaze warms, and for once, there's no edge to his smile. "You don't need to thank me. I'll always have your back."

"But it's not your job."

"Dora, I am your father."

We lock eyes for a moment, and then we both burst into laughter, realizing he sounded just like Darth Vader.

And in this moment, something clicks. I realize that while I've only known him—or known about him—for a few months, he's been aware of me my whole life. He's always known he had a daughter and would occasionally check up on me. Though he hadn't been present as a father, I had always been his daughter. It makes sense now, why he cares for me more than I'd realized. The depth of that connection settles into my heart, bringing with it a newfound sense of belonging.

Until this moment, I hadn't even realized how much I needed this feeling in my life. It's like a warmth spreading through me, filling spaces I didn't even know were empty. I guess I've always felt like an outsider, always on the fringes, never fully belonging. Maybe that's why I turned inward, retreating into myself because I sensed something was different about me, something that set me apart from everyone else. I used to think it was just a quirk of my personality, that maybe I was just more introverted than others. But now I see it was more than that—a quiet, persistent feeling that I didn't quite fit in, that I was somehow out of sync with the world around me, because it was not my world.

Now, the sense of being different isn't something to be ashamed of; it's the very thing that defines me. For the first time, I feel like I can truly be myself and be accepted for it—even loved.

As our laughter dies down, Ethan shifts in his seat before saying, "Honestly, I didn't expect it to be over so soon." He shrugs as if the battle with Andras had been nothing more than a slight inconvenience. "Too bad. I wouldn't mind hanging out with that Brian guy again." He pauses, glancing at me with a playful smirk. "He seemed alright."

I blink, completely thrown off. Out of everything that happened tonight, Ethan's takeaway is Brian? Does he actually *like* him? I mean, really *like* him? It's surprising, especially considering how he said he hadn't been able to control himself around my mom. I assumed she—or women—were the ones who caught his attention. "I thought you and my mom..." I start cautiously, unsure how to approach the topic.

Ethan's eyebrow arches, his voice rising in a pitch as he asks, "So I can only appreciate one sex?"

I backpedal quickly, the narrowness of my question suddenly dawning on me. "Of course not," I say, my voice coming out a little too fast. I hesitate, then venture further down the rabbit hole. "Did you ever like Ezra that way?"

His reaction is immediate—his eyes widen in genuine surprise. "What?" There's a short pause before he adds, "Just because I like both men and women, you think I'm out here trying to jump everyone I know?"

I feel the heat creeping up my neck, embarrassed by my own ignorance. "No, sorry, that was stupid," I mutter, cringing inwardly. Fortunately, he doesn't seem truly offended, his expression relaxing, like he finds my blunder more amusing than insulting.

"Plus, Ezra is a fallen angel," Ethan adds with a chuckle, shaking his head slightly "I don't like *any* kind of angels that way. I prefer them naive and innocent," he adds with a sly grin.

A flood of discomfort sweeps over me, making me squirm in my seat. The conversation suddenly feels too intimate, too weird, like I'm learning things about Ethan I'd rather not know. Without thinking, I blurt out, "Can I move back home?"

I'm desperate to steer us back into safer territory, away from the unsettling direction the conversation has taken. I guess I'm finally starting to see him as a father figure, and this is definitely not a conversation anyone wants to have with their dad.

Ethan's face shifts, the teasing look fading. His usual seriousness creeps back in as he refocuses on the bigger picture. "We still don't know why Andras came after you, or who tipped him off."

"He said he just wanted a snack, didn't he? Please, don't read too much into this. I want this to be the end," I try to deflect his concerns, eager to put the danger behind us. "He probably just heard about a Nephilim soul and thought it would taste good or something. Even the angels know I'm Nephilim; the word's out. It's a fact."

Ethan pauses, considering my words, his brow furrowing as he mulls it over. "You know what?" he finally says, his tone thoughtful but firm. "You can move back, but I'm spending the first few nights with you. I want to make sure nothing else happens, and if it does, I want to be there." His voice carries that unyielding resolve I've come to expect, making it clear there's no room for debate.

I bite my lip, weighing my options—or rather, the lack of them. Saying no isn't really on the table. Ethan's mind is made up, and I can see that nothing I say will change it.

Part of me knows he's right; having him around could provide some comfort, even if I'm not entirely thrilled about the idea of being babysat.

"Okay," I agree. This is the best compromise I'm going to get.

As we pull into the driveway and step out of the car, I expect the usual sense of familiarity to settle over me.

But as we approach the front door, something feels off, an uneasy quiet hanging in the air. I try to brush it off, attributing it to my frayed nerves from the night's events.

But at least now I know I'm safe. I just need my brain to send the message to my other organs too.

Ethan pushes open the door, and in an instant, that thin layer of reassurance crumbles. The sight before us is nothing short of a nightmare.

Marve lies on the ground, her body slowly disintegrating into ash, as if the very air around her is consuming her. Kneeling beside her, Ezra clutches the wooden stake embedded in her heart, his eyes filled with raw pain and despair. His grip is so tight it's as if he's trying to hold on to what little remains of her.

Nearby, Abaddon stands, silent and imposing, his presence like a heavy shadow that suffocates all hope, the darkness in his eyes a chilling reminder of the power he wields.

Since the last time we met, I looked up who he was supposed to be—an archangel of death and destruction. Now, seeing him here, I know he's the physical embodiment of that very title.

Ezra lifts his head at the sound of our footsteps, his eyes red from crying. His gaze locks onto Ethan's, a deep sorrow etched into his expression. "I'm sorry," he murmurs, his voice thick with regret.

Ethan freezes in place as if an invisible force is holding him back.

Before I can fully grasp the chaos around us, Abaddon acts. His wings spread wide, each feather an unsettling blend of pure white and shadowy gray. In one swift motion, he grabs Ezra, and before I can react, they vanish, leaving in their wake only a gust of wind that scatters the ashes around.

My thoughts whirl, colliding in a chaotic mess. Did Ezra betray us? Was he the one who killed Marve? And why is Abaddon here, in the middle of all this? Each question pounds in my skull, my heartbeat echoing in my ears. The room spins, and I struggle to make sense of the madness unfolding before me.

What just happened?

"Open your mind to me," Ethan commands, but I hesitate. The idea of someone entering my mind right now makes my skin crawl, but there's an urgency in his gaze that I can't ignore. "Time is running out," he adds. "I need to show you Ezra's memory."

Reluctantly, I lower my guard, creating a small door in the mental walls I've built.

chapter 26

BETRAYAL

The tumult of the present fades, and I find myself seated on a bed beside Marve in what must be her and Ezra's room. The air is unnervingly calm, almost too serene. Marve's gaze is fixed on me, her eyes brimming with admiration and affection—a look I've only ever seen her direct at Ezra.

"Want to hear a secret?" Ezra's voice echoes softly around us, though I can't see him anywhere in the room. "But remember, it's not ours to share."

I'm inside Ezra's memory. This must be the moment Ethan wanted me to witness, seen through Ezra's eyes and shared with us.

I watch the scene unfold as though through a fogged window, feeling a disconcerting detachment from the vivid details. I see Ezra's hands move, the minutiae of his gestures, but I remain a passive observer. I'm trapped in his perspective, unable to influence or alter the events as they play out before me.

Marve's face lights up with a radiant smile, her eyes sparkling. "I won't tell anyone, I promise," she says, her tone as sweet as the first bloom of spring.

Ezra shifts closer, his excitement barely contained. "Pandora is pregnant," he whispers tenderly, as if the revelation is the most precious, the sweetest secret.

Marve's smile falters, her eyes widening in surprise. "Really?" she breathes.

Ezra nods. "There's no way she knows this yet. I think biology did its job just... today."

Marve straightens up and rubs her neck. She takes a deep breath, her face growing paler by the moment. "How do you know?"

"I didn't see anything yesterday." He shrugs. It's simple as that to him.

But what does he mean by "see"? Is it some special ability of his, akin to Ethan's talent for sensing one's purpose at birth?

"That's... interesting." Marve says softly, her words not quite matching the enthusiasm Ezra seems to radiate. Her expression is gentle but subdued, a flicker of doubt hidden behind her soft smile. Her fingers toy with the edge of the blanket draped over her legs, absentmindedly tracing patterns, as if grounding herself while Ezra speaks.

Ezra leans back, his shoulders sagging as he exhales a shaky breath. He lets himself fall onto the pillow behind him with a soft thud. "It's the worst timing," he murmurs, his voice thick with despair. "Her life is in danger... our lives are in danger... I don't want anything to happen to the child."

Marve leans closer, her hand gently resting on Ezra's arm, her thumb drawing small circles. "Why don't you tell her?"

I wonder the same; why doesn't he tell Pandora?

Wait... they're talking about *me*.

My heart skips a beat, and the room seems to tilt for a moment. Could it be true? I'm on birth control; I *shouldn't* be pregnant. But what if my new abilities, my altered body, are interfering with its effectiveness? No, that can't be true. Surely, someone would have warned me.

Right?

Ezra's voice cuts through my spiraling thoughts. His gaze drops to his knees as he explains, "It's not something she should hear from me. She should discover it on her own. We haven't formed any real bond—she thinks I'm angry with her for giving up her afterlife. I don't want to ruin the moment when she finds out she's going to have a child. I've already done enough damage, just because she's a mirror of the person I used to be."

Emotions surge inside me, spinning out of control. A *child*. The idea, once a distant thought, suddenly feels like an overwhelming blessing. Ezra's excitement is so contagious that I'm almost swept away in his joy. Yet, as quickly as that rush of happiness enveloped me, my own fears surge to the forefront. Ben and I have only been together for a few months—this isn't something we're prepared for, not even close. My heart races, a confusing blend of longing and dread pulling me in different directions.

Marve forces a smile, nodding softly. "You're such a good person, always thinking of others." Her eyes linger on Ezra, filled with a deep, unspoken affection. She leans in and kisses him gently, a slow, tender touch given out of nothing but love.

As she pulls away, she rests her head in his lap, her body sinking into him, completely at ease. Ezra's hand instinctively moves to her hair, fingers threading through it with a tenderness that speaks volumes—this is more than affection; it's a quiet devotion. The love between them isn't loud or flashy, but it radiates warmth, filling the room with a steady, unspoken connection. It's a love that goes deeper than fleeting chemistry, a bond that's been nurtured over time.

Sharing Ezra's real memory, I can feel it all—the depth of his emotions, emotions I've never experienced through my own heart before. Compared to this, my relationship with Ben feels paper-thin, as if everything we share is only on the surface.

What Ezra and Marve share is solid, unshakable, while what I have with Ben is a passing thrill, a surface-level connection. The contrast hits me hard, and suddenly, the excitement I felt with Ben seems hollow, lacking the depth and security I hadn't even realized I was yearning for.

The scene shifts abruptly, as if the world around me has been rewound and replayed with a single blink. We're still in Ethan's house, but the setting has changed, perhaps to another day and a different part of the house. It's unsettling, like stepping into a dream that's almost familiar but not quite right.

Ezra descends the creaky staircase, his footsteps echoing softly in the stillness of the house. Shadows drape the room, the only light coming from the faint, silvery glow of moonlight spilling through the French window, casting a silhouette in soft focus.

In the entrance hall, Marve stands with her side against the wall, her posture rigid, arms crossed tightly over her chest.

"Is everything okay?" Ezra asks, his voice low but threaded with tension, his eyes sweeping over the room as though searching for an unseen threat.

Marve turns toward him, her brows knitting together in mild confusion. "Of course. Why?" she replies, her tone measured, though the subtle tugging of her fingers at the hem of her skirt betrays her unease.

Ezra halts, he holds her gaze before flicking back to the shadows. "I sensed something strange," he murmurs. "A powerful energy. I was afraid someone had gotten in here."

Marve lets out a dismissive laugh, light and airy. She waves her hand in a nonchalant gesture, trying to wave away Ezra's worry. "You're getting paranoid," she says with a smile that never quite reaches her eyes. Despite her effort at reassurance, her gaze flits nervously around the room.

If Marve's facade doesn't fool me, it certainly isn't fooling Ezra. "No," he says. "I know what I felt. Ethan sent me a message—another demon has found them. This isn't a coincidence; they must be tracking her, which means they're tracking us. They might already know about you. We can't stay here. We need to move somewhere far away, where we can't be found." Ezra gestures toward the staircase, clearly prepared to pack up and leave immediately.

Marve's features tighten with concern, her smile slipping away as her face turns pale. "But... our life is here. This is our home."

Ezra glances around the room, his eyes lingering on the familiar spaces and objects they've grown to cherish. Every corner holds a memory, a piece of the life they've built together, making the thought of leaving even more painful. "I know," he says quietly, his voice heavy. "I don't want to leave either. Ethan is my family. But we have to. It's the only way to keep you safe."

Marve's gaze drops to her shoes, her shoulders hunched as if the weight of her thoughts is too much to bear. Her face is a canvas of internal conflict, the subtle tremor of her lips betraying her struggle to articulate her feelings.

Ezra's concern deepens as he notices her distress, his unease matching my own. "What's going on?" he asks the question I'd ask her if I could too.

Marve shifts where she stands, clearly wrestling with her words. She meets Ezra's gaze, her voice faltering. "I... I'm not sure how to say this."

Ezra cups her face, his touch steady yet gentle. "Just tell me, Marve. Whatever it is, we'll handle it together." His hands glide down her arms until they meet hers, holding them firmly.

"They're not watching us. We don't have to leave," she says, her eyes reflecting hope.

I feel Ezra's confusion shifting into disbelief as he listens to Marve's words. "What do you mean?" He takes a step back, his grip loosening as he struggles to understand. "How can you be so sure?"

A hesitant cough escapes Marve, but she remains silent. Ezra's expression hardens, a sharp edge of urgency cutting through his concern. "Explain, now," he insists, his tone uncharacteristically fierce, revealing a side of him I've never seen before, at least not in his interactions with Marve.

Marve's voice trembles as she begins to speak, each word carefully measured as if trying to soften the blow of the truth. "I told Abaddon who Pandora is," she says slowly, her eyes darting between Ezra and the floor, clearly bracing for his reaction. "He was troubled by the implications of her name... he knew about Ethan's gift. He believed she could become the downfall of the good side. So, he decided it would be better to... end her... sooner rather than later."

Ezra's breath hitches, the shock crashing over him like a tidal wave, threatening to sweep him under. His hands ball into tight fists, his knuckles whitening as he grapples with the devastating news.

His voice turns cold as ice, as if the body in front of him doesn't belong to his loved one anymore. "When did you tell him?"

"When we met the day we spent on the beach. He invaded my mind, and I couldn't resist. He manipulated me," Marve explains in a rush, her voice fraught with plead as she tries to justify her actions.

"And you've been feeding him information about her movements and whereabouts ever since?"

"Yes," Marve admits, despair evident in every word. "I was afraid he'd harm me. He threatened to send a powerful demon after her. I feared for my life. If I didn't tell him what he wanted to know, he'd expose me to the demons. It would be my end. I had to protect myself."

"Nice story. But I taught you to protect your mind. No one can invade it without your consent." Ezra's voice starts steady, but the intensity in his voice rises with each word. "Do you think I'm stupid? Do you think I wouldn't see through this? Even if what you're saying were true, which we both know it isn't, you still continued to help him after I told you she was pregnant?"

As his emotions erupt, I can feel the blood rushing to his cheeks, his clenched fists trembling with fury. Ethan once told me about Ezra's role as a guardian of the souls of unborn children, those who never got the chance to enter the world. The burden of so many lost souls, denied the opportunity to fulfill its purpose, was what ultimately led to his fall. And Marve knows this all too well.

"What was I supposed to do?" Marve's voice cracks, her eyes welling with tears as she begs for understanding. "I didn't want to, but was I supposed to protect her child at the risk of our lives?"

"Not our lives," Ezra corrects her, unmoved by her tears. "Your life." His scowl deepens as he takes her in. "And please, just drop the act. Why did you tell Abaddon about Pandora's name? At least explain why you did what you did. You owe me that much."

Marve hesitates, her eyes flickering with uncertainty for a moment, but then something shifts. Slowly, her gaze rises, no longer pleading or fearful but filled with a new resolve. The trembling woman, once manipulated and afraid, seems to vanish, revealing someone sharper, stronger. A fire burns behind her eyes now, and with it, the mask she's been wearing begins to slip away.

"Look," she says, her voice cool and steady now, "from day one, she talked about killing demons and stirring up trouble. She was going to attract the attention we've all been avoiding just to live our peaceful lives. She was putting my life at risk."

"*She* was going to attract the attention..." Ezra's face twists in disbelief as he repeats her words, his anger simmering. "So you took matters into your own hands? You were afraid she'd bring demons into our lives, so you beat her to it?"

"I didn't bring demons into our lives. They are in her life—not mine, not yours. Abaddon is the one who got in touch with them, and they don't need to follow her around; they get all the information from me through Abaddon. No one else but him knows about me."

"Don't tell me you are that naïve," Ezra growls. "You're a demon; you know exactly how they think. What did you expect would happen? They'd capture Pandora, not being able to kill her, they'd just torture her for amusement, for any scrap of information. She'd mention a demon she knows once, and you'd be finished. We were never going to stay out of this."

"But the worst part? You kept helping Abaddon even after knowing Dora was pregnant," he adds, his tone heavy with disappointment.

Marve lifts her chin, meeting his gaze with unwavering resolve. "If my life is on the line, then I won't stop at anything."

Ezra recoils, her words hitting him like a physical blow. "I was wrong," he mutters, the quiet devastation clear in his hushed voice. "You're no better than any other demon. Your true nature is undeniable. I should never have trusted you." Each word, though softly spoken, cuts deeper than any shout. His eyes darken with a newfound resolve. "Now, either Baal will kill you, or I will."

In a heartbeat, Ezra moves. His hand slips into his back pocket, retrieving a wooden stake. The motion is smooth, practiced, the tool meant for enemies but now turned on the one he once loved. Before Marve can even take a breath, the sharp point plunges into her chest.

Her eyes widen in disbelief, her breath catching as the realization settles. She didn't think he had it in him to actually go through with it.

The defiance that once hardened her expression melts away, replaced by something softer, almost resigned, as the life slowly drains from her.

"Forgive me," she whispers, the words barely a breath as her knees buckle, her body sinking to the floor.

Ezra sinks down beside her, as if they were both defeated. Marve's body is touched by a chill that spreads like the icy hand of fate. Slowly, she closes her eyes, her last words echoing in the silence of the room, like the whisper of the wind in a deserted forest.

Ezra's breath grows ragged, the burden of guilt pressing heavily upon him, like a hurricane he can't outrun. He brought Marve into Ethan's life—and thus jeopardized his daughter.

His face contorts into a bitter smile, an attempt to mask the anguish that churns within him. Kneeling beside Marve's lifeless body, his eyes brim with a sorrow so deep it nearly consumes him.

Despite everything she's done, an insatiable yearning pulls

Ezra closer, desperate to touch her one final time before she slips away into nothingness. His hand trembles as he reaches out, gently grazing her cold cheek. The unexpected dampness beneath his fingers makes him pause, and he realizes her cheek is wet—not from her own tears, but from his. His grief, uncontainable and raw, spills out in silent rivulets, marking her skin in a final, tender farewell.

Without warning, the air beside them ripples, and Abaddon appears. His eyes gleam with malicious joy, and his mouth stretches into a wide, terrifying grin.

"What irony," Abaddon sneers, breaking into a cold, heartless laugh. "I have waited for this moment for so long, my friend. I cannot describe the pleasure it gives me to see you so broken."

But before Abaddon can continue his taunting victory speech, the heavy front door creaks open, flooding the dimly lit foyer with the glow of the porch light. It's an unexpected glimmer of hope amidst the shadows, as if fate has intervened to offer an opportunity to set things right and uncover the true mastermind behind it all.

Ethan and I step through the door, sharing a light-hearted smile, but as we cross the threshold, the sight before us steals the breath from our lungs. Our smiles vanish, replaced by expressions of sheer horror and confusion as the scene unfolds.

"I'm sorry," Ezra whispers, his voice trembling on the edge of breaking. His eyes close as he reaches out with his mind, searching for a connection with Ethan, desperate to explain, to make him understand.

And Ethan doesn't falter, his trust in Ezra is unwavering.

Without a moment's hesitation, he opens his mind, fully prepared to accept whatever truth or burden is about to be revealed, no matter how heavy.

chapter 27

PROVERBS 16:18

As I open my eyes, the world around me sharpens, pulling me back into the reality of the hall seen from my perspective. The past slips away, leaving me in the cold grasp of the present. I take in my surroundings, and everything feels different, like the very air has shifted.

The walls, once silent sentinels, now seem to echo with the weight of what has transpired. It's as if they have absorbed the tragedy, reflecting it back at me in a thousand tiny, distorted ways. Shadows that once seemed ordinary now stretch longer, darker, as if they too mourn the loss. The hall feels smaller, suffocating.

Ethan stands beside me, his eyes locked on the ashen remains of Marve, now nothing more than a faint, ghostly smear on the floor. His face is set, unreadable.

"Prepare yourself," he murmurs. I suppress a shiver, fighting to steady my breath. "We won't be alone for long."

He shifts from leg to leg, his gaze sweeping the room with sharp precision, searching for hidden threats. Every muscle in his body is tense and ready for action.

"Where did he take Ezra? And why?" My hands tremble despite my desperate attempts to control them.

Ethan stops in his tracks, his eyes locking onto mine, mirroring the same helplessness I feel. I can see in his gaze that, for once, he doesn't have any more answers than I do.

"I don't know," he mutters, jaw clenched as if holding back a flood of emotions. "He can't kill him," he reminds me, reminds himself. "He probably hid him somewhere, kept him out of the way so he couldn't help us. But we'll deal with that later. Well save Ezra later."

His words barely touch the tension coiling tighter inside me. A sharp pang twists in my chest, and I lower my head, as if the weight of my guilt is too much to hold up. "I should've trusted him." The memory Ezra shared with us plays in my mind like a haunting melody I can't escape. He was never on the other side, never a threat, never an enemy. It wasn't him, yet I blamed him, while he was willing to do anything to protect me. He even killed Marve.

Dead. She's *dead.*

And Ezra is *gone*. Taken away.

My breath quickens, each inhale too sharp, too fast. The room spins, and I clutch my chest, desperate to ground myself, to slow the frantic beating of my heart, to will it to push through the panic. But it doesn't work.

Ethan steps closer, his presence a steady anchor against the storm of panic inside me. His hands gently clasp my arms, grounding me, urging me to slow my breath, to match the calm steadiness in his own.

His gaze, softened with understanding yet sharpened by a firm resolve, locks onto mine. "We both learned something here."

In that moment, his touch, his voice, it's like he's trying to show me how to hold on—to the here, to the now.

"Trust isn't something you can hand out like a gift; it has to be earned," he continues. "I shouldn't have given mine so easily to Marve." It's as if he's compartmentalizing, focusing on the facts to keep his own world from shattering completely.

"So much for the benefit of the doubt," I murmur, tasting the bitterness on my tongue.

As if in response to my words, the room darkens, shadows stretching until they seem to pulse with power and authority.

Abaddon reappears, his presence warping the air around him, thickening it like a suffocating fog. The force of his power seems so heavy and oppressive it feels as though the walls themselves are closing in. Unlike the guardian angels, whose presence radiates calm and protection, Abaddon's brings no peace—only a cold, overwhelming dread that sinks deep into my bones.

Ethan steps in front of me, his body a shield, his stance firm and resolute. Every muscle in his frame tenses, his entire being standing between me and the suffocating darkness Abaddon carries with him. His shoulders square, feet planted as though he's ready to face whatever this monstrous being might unleash.

"Where did you take Ezra?" Ethan demands.

Abaddon's smile is chilling, his eyes gleaming with a dark intensity as he locks his gaze with Ethan's. "It doesn't matter," he replies, his words laced with cold finality. "You won't see him again."

A desperate need for answers surges within me, pushing aside my fear. No, it's not the need, it's adrenaline. "What do you want?"

Abaddon tilts his head, considering my question with a dark, almost playful pensiveness. "What do I want?" he echoes. "I want to win."

"Win what?"

"The ultimate game," Abaddon says. "Good versus evil. Angels versus demons. Soul protectors versus soul eaters."

Ethan, clearly done with the theatrics, cuts in, his patience wearing thin. "Alright, we get it."

"We're on the same side then," I say, puzzled as to why he's standing against us. If this is about good versus evil, shouldn't he be fighting with us? He's an angel, we're fighting for the same side, yet against each other.

"I doubt that," Abaddon responds coldly, his gaze fixed on me. "Your fate is clear, Pandora. You will unleash misery. I can't allow that. Your very existence brings uncertainty, and I won't tolerate anything that jeopardizes our cause. I need to ensure our victory, by any means necessary."

The accusation hits me hard, but before I can gather my thoughts to respond, to defend myself, Ethan steps forward, taking control of the conversation.

"So what's your plan?" he asks, a calculated question meant to buy us time. I sense his strategy—to play on Abaddon's arrogance, to coax him into revealing more than he intends, giving us insight into his next move. Ethan knows that Abaddon's sense of superiority might compel him to share his intentions, and in that moment, any piece of information could be our lifeline.

Abaddon's smirk widens as he responds, his gaze flickering between us as if relishing the attention. "Well, after I delved into your little demon friend's mind and learned about Pandora's name, I knew I had to take action."

"So you did invade her mind?" I blurt out.

"She willingly opened her mind to me, she was practically inviting me in." He *winks* at me. Winks! The gesture is a mockery, twisting the knife of betrayal even deeper, as if he's enjoying my misplaced trust in her.

"It was her own decision," Abaddon continues with a dismissive shrug, brushing off my question and Marve's actions as if they were insignificant—mockworthy, but irrelevant in the grand scheme. *Of course*, they don't concern him; and it's all he's about—himself. I never realized narcissism could run this deep, even among angels.

"Regardless, I had to stay in the shadows. Those guardian angels of yours are a nuisance—always poking around. My original plan was simple. Let the demons catch Pandora, give them what they needed to finish her off."

My stomach twists at his words. He planned all this, played us all. And he wanted to kill me, actually *kill* me.

"But they proved to be incompetent," he adds with a sneer. "So, I took matters into my own hands. Your house became the perfect opportunity for me. No guardians here. No one to witness what I'm about to do..."

"You have no idea what her future holds. For all you know, she could bring misery to demons, not the world," Ethan argues.

It's clear he's trying to steer Abaddon away from conflict, appealing to whatever reason the archangel might possess, hoping to plant a seed of doubt in his certainty. His eyes, though sharp, soften slightly as if urging Abaddon to pause, to think, to reconsider the path he's set on.

"No, I don't know what will happen; it might bring misery for them, but it might bring misery for us. We can't allow that. She's a threat, and I must eliminate it for the greater good," Abaddon declares. It's evident his conviction won't be shaken.

"You've been corrupted; you're talking like a demon. Do you truly believe that killing her will aid the forces of good? It only means you turned to the dark side," Ethan counters.

Despite the gravity of the situation, a flicker of amusement dances through my mind. *Turned to the dark side*? Perhaps he should cut back on the Star Wars marathons.

Abaddon's lips curl up again, a chilling display of his twisted pleasure in the chaos. Ethan's assessment is spot-on; Abaddon's motives may have been noble once, but now he revels in the pain and suffering he inflicts. He's not fighting for the right reasons; he just wants to be on the winning side, regardless of the cost to others.

Abaddon paces from side to side like a predator sizing up its prey. His eyes gleam with cruel amusement, flickering with malicious delight as he surveys us.

Two wooden stakes materialize in his hands like lethal extensions of his will. One stake is plain and rough, as though hastily carved from a tree trunk. Its surface is raw, splintering in places, exuding a crude, primal danger. The other stake, however, is something else entirely—sleek and polished, intricate carvings running along its length, faint symbols glowing as if alive with dark magic. The wood is so smooth and dark it seems to swallow the light around it. But when Abaddon shifts it in his grip, and the moonlight catches it through the window, the color becomes clearer.

Crimson.

There's something far more sinister about it, as though it holds secrets meant to stay buried, whispering of death and dark rituals.

Abaddon's presence shifts. It feels different, even more dangerous now—he must have materialized in the physical realm too, ready to take us down. "So who do I kill first? I have my oak stake, I have my Jubokko stake, and a father and a daughter."

Ethan once told me obtaining a stake from the Jubokko tree was nearly impossible. But of course, if anyone could get their hands on something that rare, it would be the archangel of death and destruction. But if Abaddon has one, what's stopping Baal from having one too?

"I wonder, does her blood have to be warm?" Abaddon taunts us, flipping the stakes in his hands with practiced moves.

"You're not getting anywhere near her," Ethan declares, his expression dead serious. There's no trace of fear in his eyes; only a quiet, unshakable confidence etched into his features.

Abaddon unfurls his massive wings, each feather humming with dark energy. "Oh, I'd love to see you try and stop me."

Ethan doesn't flinch. "There's no *try*."

Abaddon's laughter fills the room, genuine and mocking. It's more than just noise—it's a force, so loud and piercing that it reverberates through my skull, making my head throb with pain. "What are you going to do?" Abaddon sneers, his voice dripping with disdain. "You're not strong enough to fight me. You were always just a powerless little guardian."

Ethan's eyes narrow, a subtle, almost imperceptible shift crosses his features. His expression remains composed, but there's an edge now, something far more lethal beneath his calm exterior. "There's just one little fact you're forgetting. The higher the rank, the harder the fall. But my fall? Not very high, as you just mentioned."

Ethan tilts his head slightly, a mocking smile curling his lips. "It's something you should've considered before breaking the rules," he says, his tone dripping with feigned sympathy that barely hides the iron beneath. "Your fall's gonna hurt like hell."

Ethan unfurls his wings, and both Abaddon and I freeze, our jaws slack with shock. I had no idea Ethan still had his wings; he had told me they were gone, lost in his fall. But now they stretch wide, dominating the space, plain black and stripped of the radiant energy that graces other angels' wings. Yet, they radiate an entirely different kind of power—raw, unyielding, and dangerous. These wings are larger, thicker, and more imposing than any I've ever seen, like they've been forged for battle, not grace.

Abaddon's sneer falters, surprise flickering across his face. *Oh, how good this expression looks on him.*

Ethan moves in a blur, his wings snapping out like a predator's jaws, wrapping around Abaddon with precision. It's over before it even began.

Abaddon, caught completely off guard, struggles as Ethan's wings coil tightly around his own, pinning them against his body. The sickening crunch of breaking bone echoes through the room as Ethan's grip tightens, shattering Abaddon's wings as if they were nothing more than fragile twigs. Abaddon is left immobilized, his escape brutally thwarted.

"Call Tubiel with your mind," Ethan orders me.

I want to comply immediately, but uncertainty clouds my thoughts. How do I reach out to Tubiel when he's not my guardian angel? I've only ever connected with those closest to me, and I've only met Tubiel a few times.

Ethan, as if sensing my hesitation, offers reassurance. "You know how. Tubiel's open to you—his feelings make him vulnerable to your call. Reach out. Tell him we've got an angel on the brink of falling. He'll know what to do. But you have to hurry!"

I nod, trying to quiet the doubt rising in my chest.

As I focus on Ethan's words, Abaddon's voice seeps through, muffled beneath the crushing embrace of Ethan's wings. "Seems like there's more than one angel ready to fall," he chuckles darkly, his breath ragged.

I know Abaddon's words are meant to distract me, to plant seeds of doubt. But knowing doesn't make it any easier to shake off the fear curling in my chest. The thought of Tubiel getting dragged into this mess makes me sick, but I can't afford to let it cloud my mind right now.

I force the worry aside, focusing on Ethan's command. There's no room for hesitation. No time for doubt.

With a deep breath, I close my eyes and focus on summoning Tubiel's presence in my mind. I visualize him standing before me, his unique energy, his radiant wings—every detail as vivid as I can make it.

With every fiber of my being, I reach out, trying to embody his essence, to feel his emotions, his energy wrapping around me. Though I haven't practiced this skill much, I press on, desperately sending the memory of Abaddon's threat through the fragile link I hope to establish with Tubiel.

I don't know if it's working, but I pour all my will into this connection, hoping he'll hear me.

As I open my eyes again, Ethan's trembling, his once firm stance now faltering, and his breath growing shallow. "Where's Ezra?" he demands of Abaddon, but the only response is a low, mocking laughter that echoes through the room. Ethan doesn't seem surprised, but I can see the light fading from his eyes, the toll of the struggle weighing heavily on him.

"Take the stakes from him," Ethan orders me, but even his voice is losing its former strength.

With careful movements, I navigate through the feathers tightly wrapped around Abaddon's struggling form. My fingers brush against his cold hands, and I manage to retrieve the stakes. But even with Ethan's iron grip around him, Abaddon radiates a raw, menacing energy, a power that feels ready to explode the moment Ethan's strength falters. Being so near him is... it's like being near death. Death that was supposed to be out of sight, something to never claim me.

As I step back, the air around Abaddon ripples with a sudden, jarring intensity, and in the blink of an eye, three figures materialize beside him. Their arrival is like a thunderclap, the sheer intensity of their presence crackling with raw, undeniable power. There's no doubt—they are archangels.

Two of them move with blinding speed, seizing Abaddon's arms with an iron grip, holding him in place. The third angel locks eyes with Ethan. From the way they look at each other, it's clear there's a history between them, though, I can't tell whether they used to be friends or foes.

"Raguel," Ethan breathes out with a slight nod after finally releasing Abaddon from his crushing grip. His wings twitch behind him, shifting with a subtle ripple, as if shaking off the strain of holding such immense power in check. It's like the instinctive movement of someone rolling their shoulders after a long exertion, trying to relieve the tension. He stretches them out slightly before tucking them closer to his back, their dark feathers settling into place.

"Peliel. Always in trouble," Raguel responds wryly.

Ethan's lips curve into a faint smile as he rubs his palms together as if wiping off dirt. "I'm not the one in trouble this time, as you can see. In fact, I'm the one saving the day."

Raguel strides over to me, wordlessly retrieving the stakes from my hands.

"What are you going to do with those?" Ethan asks. I'm sure

he'd love to get his hands on them, especially the Jubokko stake.

Raguel remains silent, dismissing the question with a cold indifference, but one of the other archangels, standing a step behind him, answers instead. "We are going to hide them in a secure location."

"No. You need to destroy it. It's too dangerous; you've seen firsthand that we can't even trust the angels anymore," Ethan speaks angrily, surprising me with his stance. He is pragmatic, I have to give him that.

Raguel's eyes narrow. He turns to Ethan with a sneer, his voice icy and dripping with contempt, much like Abaddon's. "We don't take orders from you."

"Pride goes before destruction, and a haughty spirit before a fall," Ethan quotes, surprising me with the sudden biblical reference.

Raguel shoots a quick look at Ethan's wings, his nose wrinkling in disgust before he spits on the ground. "Keep your filthy wings out of our affairs."

"And your daughter away from our guardian angels," he adds with a scoff, casting a glance in my direction, clearly referring to Tubiel.

Without another word, they whisk Abaddon away, leaving behind only a calm silence. Just Ethan, me and the scattered ashes of Marve.

I huff, planting my hands on my hips, my arms resting at my sides. "So much for a thank you."

chapter 28

BEFORE THE DUST SETTLES

"I told you archangels were arrogant dicks," Ethan grumbles as he slowly opens his hand, revealing a small, black feather resting on his palm. With a flick of his wrist, he reaches into his pocket, fingers curling around a lighter. A smooth spark ignites, and a small flame bursts to life, casting a warm glow on his face. He holds it close to the feather, the heat licking its edges until it ignites with a quiet hiss.

"Just to make sure," he says, the flame reflecting in his eyes as a sly grin spreads across his lips. The feather curls and burns away into nothingness, vanishing in a wisp of smoke, leaving behind a faint smell of charred air.

As I silently watch the feather crumble to ash, I find my gaze drawn back to Ethan, his towering figure now accentuated by the massive black wings that spread out behind him. There's something both awe-inspiring and unsettling about the sight—those wings, full of raw, untamed power, seem to pulse with life.

Sensing my scrutiny, Ethan casts a brief glance my way, and with a flicker of movement, the wings fold, disappearing as though they were never there.

For a moment, nothing's happening. There's just the two of us and no threat, no danger, no rush. I could ask him anything I want and he'd have the time to answer, explain. But my thoughts are spinning in relentless loops, each question blurring into the next. I feel unmoored, drifting in the wake of everything that has happened. Nothing feels solid anymore—everything I thought I knew has been turned upside down.

I swallow hard, trying to calm the frantic churn of my mind. I attempt to catch hold of my racing thoughts, to focus on just one. But in the chaos, only the question tied to the last sight burned into my memory stands out.

"How... how come you have wings?"

Ethan glances at me, a faint smirk twitching the corner of his lips. "Guess I'm full of surprises," he says, his tone as casual as if I'd asked him about the weather. But the confusion I must be wearing on my face makes him realize I need more than just a quip.

"As I said, the fall didn't hit me that hard. I kept my wings hidden to avoid attracting attention. I'm of no real importance to anyone, and I'd like to keep it that way. No one knew about them—

not even Ezra," he explains, his voice calm but layered with that familiar guardedness.

I nod, piecing it together. He's said it before—information is power, and sometimes secrets are worth more than anything else.

"I understand," I murmur, but another question pushes its way to the surface. "Why did you burn that feather?"

Ethan shrugs, a casual motion that contrasts with the weight of his words. "I made sure he fell. Without wings, he can't stay an angel."

I frown. "But... wouldn't that mean anyone could fall if their feather ended up in the wrong hands?"

"In theory, yes. But it's nearly impossible. For one, no one can get close to an angel's wings. Only other angels—or fallen ones—can touch them. And even then, it's not as simple as plucking. If an angel is pure, no one can pull out one of their feathers. The fall isn't instant—it's gradual. Their wings weaken as they break rules, stray further from the order. It's a slow process. That way, even if no one notices that an angel has become evil and corrupted, the angel won't be able to stay amongst other angels."

He pauses for a second before asking, "Are you okay?"

I blink, then follow his gaze to my trembling hands. The sight surprises me—why am I shaking so much? Embarrassment creeps into my cheeks. Here I am, standing in the aftermath of a battle I didn't even fight, while everyone else risked their lives to save me. Ethan isn't trembling; why should I be?

Determined to push past this moment of weakness, I steady myself, forcing my thoughts back to what really matters—Ezra. I cross my arms, tucking my trembling hands into my armpits as I straighten my posture. When I finally speak, my voice is surprisingly steady though I feel like I'm going to break down every second now. "What are you going to do about Ezra?"

"It's simple. I'm going to search for him until I find him." Ethan's voice is resolute, as if finding Ezra will be as easy as realizing the glasses you've been looking for were sitting on your nose all along.

Simple. Right.

Find Ezra wherever Abaddon has taken him. Because of me. Because of my name. Because I endangered them all. I can't believe I asked Ethan if he trusted him. I doubted Ezra, while he'd always been looking out for all of us, even me.

I give a silent nod, not trusting myself to speak anymore, and turn toward the stairs. My thoughts drift to Berry, the only source of comfort I can cling to right now. I need him, the steady warmth of his presence. Ethan and I both could use a moment—a brief pause to gather ourselves, to gather our strength before facing the inevitable questions that will come later.

As I step into my borrowed room and scoop Berry into my arms, a wave of relief washes over me. His soft body presses against mine, and the tension begins to unravel. I sink into the bed, holding him close, my fingers absently running through his fur. His deep green eyes lock onto mine for a moment, grounding me in their quiet intensity. I bury my face in him, exhaling slowly, and just like that, the chaos of the night begins to dissolve.

With Berry in my lap, my thoughts drift. I think back to Yabbashael, her portrayal of angels as beings of pure goodness, bound by rules and deeply invested in humanity's welfare. But

Abaddon's presence lingers in my mind, shattering that idealistic image. He is proof that even angels can lose their way. His actions before his fall and his continued belief in his righteousness reveal a darker truth.

Ethan, on the other hand, challenges the idea of blind obedience to authority. He convinced me to give up my afterlife, yet kept me in the dark about the vulnerability that came with immortality. Sometimes, his actions felt selfish, driven by a deep fear of loneliness, but ultimately, he never sought to harm anyone. In fact, he's more human than most angels, swayed by his emotions and his own insecurities, letting them guide him more than rules ever could.

Then there's Ezra, dedicated to safeguarding souls, while at the same time, helping a demon consume them, even if just the worst ones. And Tubiel, who's willing to bend the rules if it serves a higher purpose. Both of them blur the lines between right and wrong, raising difficult questions about the nature of goodness.

And Marve—her constant battle to suppress her demonic instincts was a testament to the inner struggle between nature and choice. It wasn't simple for any of them, not even Abaddon. His descent from a supposedly pure being into a twisted form of righteousness shows how deeply convictions can warp, even when one believes they're still fighting for good.

All of this makes me wonder—how is one judged in their afterlife? What truly defines good or evil? Is it the way you think, the choices you make, or the motivations behind your actions? Or is it a complex web of all these factors intertwined? And is there even such a thing as pure good or pure evil?

I know I won't find all the answers right now, but with eternity ahead of me, I'll have time to unravel these mysteries—even if I don't get to be judged by God Himself or continue to the afterlife.

I shift further onto the bed, sinking into the plush pillows as Berry nestles against my chest, his tiny head tucked beneath my chin like a sleeping child. This moment—right here—feels pure. It's animals, in their innocence, that embody pure goodness.

But then, like a lightning strike, I remember something.

"Oh my God!" I gasp, my voice cutting through the quiet. Berry jumps, startled, and scrambles off the bed, leaving a sharp sting of claw marks across my thighs in his frantic escape.

And just like that, reality crashes back. In the middle of everything, I completely forgot about the bombshell that Ezra had dropped on me through his shared memory.

I forgot that I'm supposed to be pregnant.

chapter 29

PROMISE OF ETERNITY

I hurry downstairs, my steps echoing in the quiet house, until I find Ethan in the midst of carefully gathering Marve's ashes into a small glass jar. After everything, I'd have expected him to sweep the ashes away, not carefully collect them. But here he is, treating them as something worth saving.

"She made mistakes," Ethan says without even tilting his head my way as he continues the action. "I wouldn't be able to forgive her. But Ezra should be the one to decide what to do with her ashes." He pauses and shakes his head, as if trying to shake away the reality. "Not me."

His words are heavy with sorrow, yet beneath the surface, I catch a flicker of something else—a glimmer of hope, perhaps. Keeping Marve's ashes for Ezra means he's committed to finding him. It means he believes in it, believes he'll succeed, and the jar will serve as a reminder of that.

"He will," I say softly.

I hesitate, unsure whether to break the silence that follows. Ethan seems to need this moment for himself. Perhaps a minute of quiet reflection for Marve. But I can't wait. I have to get my life sorted.

"I'm going to Ben's. I need to talk to him."

For the first time since I came downstairs, Ethan's eyes lift from the floor. His gaze settles on my stomach, lingering just long enough to show that he understands exactly why I need to leave.

In that brief moment, any doubts about Ezra's powers or the possibility of pregnancy vanish. Ethan's look says it all—a silent admission of the truth I can no longer deny. He knows Ezra's abilities, and, apparently, he believes in them too.

Ethan pats his pockets, searching for the car keys. Once he finds them, he pulls them out with a soft jingle. "Alright. I'm coming with you."

I furrow my brow. "Why? The threat is over, isn't it?"

Ethan's expression softens, his gaze tracing the tension still etched in my posture. "It is, I'm sure of it. But look at yourself—you're shaking. You're not in any condition to go anywhere alone right now."

I glance down at my trembling hands, clenching them instinctively as if that would stop the shaking. "You know I can't die."

"But other people can." He sets the jar holding Marve's ashes on the nearest stool, then gestures toward the front door.

I nod.

He's right. Immortality may protect me, but I could still be a danger to others. I really shouldn't drive in this condition.

Despite Ethan's reassurances, the fear gripping me refuses to loosen its hold, gnawing at the edges of my mind like a shadow that won't fade, holding my feet in place. And for the first time, I decide to let it out. "I know it's all over, but I can't shake this feeling... of fear, of betrayal, of not understanding this world at all..." Ethan stops midway to the front door, turning to face me. His eyes search mine, scanning my expression with concern. "I don't know what to expect, and I feel like I'm putting everyone in danger," my voice breaks as I add, "I feel so lost."

The mask I've been wearing—the illusion of control—cracks and crumbles. The fear is too real, too consuming. It feels like the ground beneath me is slipping away, and I can't find anything solid to hold onto.

Ethan comes back to me and reaches out, his hand resting gently on my arm, steadying me. "I will always protect you, you know that, right?"

Without waiting for an answer, he closes the gap between us and wraps me in a comforting embrace. This time, I don't hesitate; I let myself lean into him, surrendering to the safety and solace he offers.

"Thanks. For everything."

Ben opens the door with a big smile on his face, his eyes lighting up as he discovers I was the one who rang that bell. "Dora?

Hi!" He's already leaning in for a kiss when he notices Ethan standing behind me and stops. His smile fades, his eyes narrow, and the hand that was about to touch my shoulder remains suspended in the air. "Is everything alright?"

"Can I come in?" I ask, shifting my weight from one foot to the other, the hallway suddenly feeling too big, too expansive, its open space screaming a lack of privacy.

Ben blinks, as if snapping back to reality. "Of course, sorry." He quickly steps aside, motioning for us to enter.

I brush past him and head straight for the couch. I sit, trying to find a comfortable position, but everything feels off.

Ethan, however, doesn't follow me. Instead, he stops in the small entryway, casually leaning against the doorframe with arms crossed, his face a mask of detachment. He's here only for the case I crumble.

I rub my hands together, my palms slick with sweat. "I have to tell you something," I say. My eyes flicker briefly to Ethan. Even though I know this conversation should be just between Ben and me, I can't imagine doing this without Ethan nearby. His presence is the only thing keeping me from unraveling completely.

"What is it?" Ben asks, eyes flicking anxiously between me and Ethan. When my silence stretches too long, he takes a step closer, though the clear hesitation makes all his movements too slow. Finally, without another word, he lowers himself onto the couch beside me, his body angled slightly toward mine, as if ready to offer support but unsure of what's coming. His hand brushes against mine—light, gentle, patient. He's giving me the space I need, while showing me I can go on when I feel like it.

Fear coils tightly around my heart, squeezing until my chest feels too tight, my breath shallow. It's too soon—too soon for this conversation, too soon for us. We haven't even said we loved each other yet. The last thing I want is for him to feel trapped, bound to me because of this. And I don't want to feel trapped either.

The thought spirals, tangled with the impossible explanation of how I ended up pregnant despite being on birth control. How do I even begin to explain that my new Nephilim physiology has overruled it? He's going to think I did this on purpose.

My mind races, the fear of how he'll react sinking its claws deeper. I take a shaky breath, forcing myself to speak. My eyes drop to my knees, unable to meet his gaze as the words finally spill from my lips, barely above a whisper. As if by keeping the volume low, I can pretend it's not true.

"I'm pregnant."

Ben's face lights up like the sky on New Year's Eve, a burst of joy so bright and sudden that it leaves me breathless. His excitement is so intense, as if he's been waiting for this moment, a countdown to midnight that ends in nothing but hope and new beginnings. "What?" he exclaims, his eyes wide with disbelief and a smile stretching across his face. "Is it true?"

"Yes," I stammer nervously. I don't understand why he's smiling like that—so wide, so real. Is he truly pleased? Or is this some kind of reaction he feels he's supposed to have? Maybe he's just masking his real feelings, afraid Ethan is here to play enforcer, making sure he reacts the right way.

But Ben's focus is no longer on Ethan; it's solely on us. Without hesitation, he pulls me into his arms, his embrace firm, his lips meeting mine in a kiss filled with a passion I haven't felt in what feels like forever.

"I love you," he whispers in my ear.

But despite his words, doubts still stir within me. I look away, unable to fully accept the joy in his eyes. "You don't have to pretend," I murmur. "Be honest with me. What do you really think? How do you truly feel?"

Ben cups my face in his hands, his fingers gently caressing my cheeks. He lifts my chin and when our eyes lock, I catch a glimpse of something genuine in his expression—a warmth, a spark of happiness that feels real. "I love you," he repeats, his gaze piercing, as if he's trying to imprint that thought into my mind. "I've wanted to tell you for a long time... but something always got in the way. Actually, it was mostly Brian showing up at the worst moments."

"Really?" I ask, still needing that extra reassurance. I guess I just can't believe anyone could *love* me. Truly love. Like I'm special, like I'm someone they can't be without.

"Really," he says, his eyes reflecting nothing but certainty.

I feel my heart race, my cheeks flush under his steady gaze. I lower my head slightly, feeling like it's expected of me to reciprocate his feelings, like I should say the same words to him. We're having a baby together after all.

"I... I love you too," I whisper, the words catching in my throat. But as I say them, I wonder if they're entirely true. I know I feel something—there's chemistry, an attraction that draws me to him. I'm happy when I'm with him. But *love*? Do we really know each other well enough to be sure it's this deep, soul-baring connection that everyone talks about—this kind of love that's supposed to last, where you *truly* see each other for who you are, and still feel the same way?

"Really?" he repeats my earlier question.

This time, I muster the courage to meet his gaze, forcing myself to hold it steady. "Really," I say, though the word feels fragile, slipping out as a small, hesitant smile tugs at my lips. But with that smile comes a wave of guilt, heavier than before, for lying again about being sure of the depth of my feelings.

But at least I *hope* I will grow to truly love him and give him everything he deserves.

"A child is always a blessing," he reassures me and pulls me into another tender kiss.

For a moment, the world narrows down to just the two of us. But the illusion shatters when Ethan clears his throat, a deliberate cough to remind me of his presence, bringing me sharply back to reality.

"Should I go? Do you feel better?" Ethan asks, blushing as his eyes shift uncomfortably from one place to another.

"Yeah, I think so," I decide, but then a question pops into my mind, refusing to be ignored. "Wait... before you go, I have a question. Will my child also be Nephilim? Will it be immortal?" I speak the words aloud, trusting the Spell to shield Ben from hearing them.

The shift in Ethan's eyes gives away the answer before he even says a word. "Nephilim have an angel as a father..." He pauses, searching for a gentler way to deliver the truth but ultimately failing. "I think it will be human, mortal."

His words hit me like a ton of bricks. The reality sinks in, cold and unforgiving. My child. Mortal. One day... gone. "You're saying... my child will die one day?" My voice breaks mid-sentence.

Ethan nods, his expression a solemn confirmation of my worst fear, and the world tilts beneath me. Panic claws its way back into my chest, tightening its grip with every breath. It's as if the air has thickened, becoming impossible to pull into my lungs. My heart pounds in my ears, the weight of my choices, the consequences I never fully considered, slamming into me with the force of a tidal wave.

Everything I had set into motion—this whole new life, these powers—now feels like a trap, and I can't undo any of it. I'd overlooked the most important thing: my child, my mortal child, will one day face the inevitable fate I thought I had escaped. The future I had imagined, the sense of immortality I thought I could pass on, was nothing more than a lie I'd told myself. How could I have been so stupid?

Ben, unaware of the conversation I'm having with Ethan, catches the subtle change in my expression. Without missing a beat, his smile softens, and he leans in slightly, his hand brushing against mine. "I know it's way too soon to talk about names, but if we have a daughter, I always like the name Thana," His voice is gentle, as if he's trying to ease the tension with something light, hoping to pull me back from whatever is weighing on me.

I force a smile, trying to maintain composure even though my thoughts are spiraling. "Thana is a beautiful name," I reply, my voice automatic, but my mind isn't fully processing his words.

My gaze drifts back to Ethan, who's standing quietly, but there's something off about his expression—it's harder now, even more unsettled than just moments ago. "What?"

"It's just that... Thana means death in Greek mythology."

Tears well up and spill down my cheeks, unbidden, as my chest tightens at the thought—Thana, death. The very name feels like a cruel joke from the universe. I know Ben doesn't have Ethan's gift, but in this moment, it doesn't matter. It doesn't calm me. It feels like a stab at my heart I can't dodge.

Or can I?

I wipe the tears from my face and rise to my feet as if rising against fate itself. *I won't allow this.*

"I'll do anything," I whisper into the silence. With each breath, my determination solidifies. "I'll find a way to ensure my baby's immortality." In my mind, I already see the endless path ahead, strewn with challenges and dangers, an uncertain journey with no guarantees, but it doesn't matter. I am ready to face anything, even Baal.

Ethan's eyes lock onto mine, his unreadable mask slipping just enough to show that he understands. Slowly, he nods, his eyes mirroring my determination.

Ben, blissfully unaware of our secrets, smiles as he stands up and takes my hand, sensing my resolve without fully understanding why. My heart pounds in my chest, but it's no longer fear—it's determination. I will protect my child. Whatever it takes.

chapter 30

THE LOST

"What are you doing here? Where's Ezra? Did you find him? Where have you been? Why haven't you stopped by or called?" The questions spout off of me in a rush, one after the other, as soon as I get over the shock of seeing Ethan.

It had been three weeks since I last saw Ethan; three weeks and a day since I witnessed Ezra, his best friend, bending over the lifeless body of Marve.

I just sat down to watch TV in the living room, when Ethan appeared out of nowhere. No, not appeared. Flew in. I jumped to my feet, ready to greet him, but he doesn't seem like someone who wants to be welcomed. His eyes dart around the room, refusing to meet mine. His clothes are wrinkled, and a layer of dirt clings stubbornly to his boots. "There was no reception," he mutters, his voice as distant as his gaze.

The first thing he does is head to the nearest bar. There isn't just the one in the basement/gym, but many more scattered throughout his huge house. He pours himself a whiskey, a choice that surprises me; I've never seen him opt for it before. He usually sticks to mixed drinks, something with a bit more flair.

As much as I want to cling to optimism about finding Ezra and, hopefully, rescuing him from whatever situation he's trapped in, I can't help but acknowledge the reality of the moment. The glass isn't half empty, nor is it half full. The glass is full—full of whiskey, that is. Fortunately—or unfortunately, depending on how you look at it—no amount of alcohol will affect Ethan, not with his supercharged metabolism working against him.

As usual, I'm left staring at him, unsure whether I should press for more answers to the questions he's skirted around or simply wait for him to share his thoughts when he will.

Which might never happen, I fear.

He gulps down his drink, the liquid sloshing as his throat works. Suddenly, his eyes narrow and lock onto mine, sharp as a hawk's. In that moment, I almost wish he'd kept ignoring me.

"What?!" he barks at me. A wonder he doesn't bite my head off.

I swallow hard, my response barely more than a whisper. "Nothing." My curiosity shrivels under his glare. I keep my eyes on the floor, and breathe shallowly, as if afraid of disturbing the air he breathes.

As I turn away and head back for the living room, each step feels like a retreat from a coiled predator. Suddenly, a whoosh cuts through the air, followed by the sharp sound of glass shattering against the wall. Shards fly past me, scattering across the floor.

I resist the urge to glance back at Ethan, not wanting to fuel his frustration. Navigating the debris, I leap over the glinting fragments like a startled deer and quietly settle on the sofa.

I consider tidying up the mess before Cerberus wanders in and possibly gets hurt or tries to ingest the shards. But fear paralyzes me; I dare not move or do anything that might upset Ethan further. Hopefully, Cerberus won't come around after hearing the loud noises and sensing Ethan's presence—he doesn't like Ethan anyway. Or any other fallen angels. Or any other *people* for that matter.

Meanwhile, Ethan grabs a new glass, pours himself another drink, takes a deep breath, and eventually settles beside me, ignoring the crunch of glass shards under his footsteps.

After a few minutes of sitting in silence, he mutters a simple, "Sorry."

I nod in acceptance, not daring to look up to see if he's even watching me, nor to speak yet.

"This is all my fault, you know?" he says, his voice breaking.

I finally look at him and see his eyes welling with tears. I blink, taken aback—is he about to cry? I mean, he does have a good reason—his whole world has turned upside down. His best friend's girlfriend, who was also his own friend and housemate, betrayed them, and now his best friend is gone too.

I shift uncomfortably, unsure how to handle this raw vulnerability from such a badass. I've never seen him show any real feelings, let alone weakness.

"It all fell apart because of me."

"It's not your fault," I whisper gently.

He seems not to hear me, lost in his own torment. "Because I wanted you in my life. Because I wanted a daughter. A real family. But I already had a family." He shakes his head. "I failed big time. I fell again." He pauses, his voice dropping to a whisper. "They should tear off my wings for good."

I don't know what to say. I wish someone were here who knows Ethan better, someone who could offer the wisdom and comfort I lack. What am I supposed to say? I know so little about his world. I know so little about him.

I hope he finds Ezra, but I have no idea where to start looking. And I also feel the guilt, of course—it all happened because of me. But Ethan is right; he is the one who wanted me in his life, who brought me into their world, made me a Nephilim with all these powers that feel utterly useless in this moment of need. I can't tell him that, though. The last thing I want to do is hurt him even more.

"Does this mean you're giving up?" I ask, searching his eyes for some sign of clarity. If he's giving up, then that's it—we should just accept everything as it is. But if he's not, then there's still hope, and no reason for desperation.

He tilts his head, a look that says he thinks I'm crazy to even pose that question. "Of course not," he replies, his jaw tightening. "The angels refuse to lead me to Abaddon to question him, and I have no idea where he might be, but I will not stop looking until I find Ezra, until I make it all right. I would search the whole world before giving up."

I reach out, my hand trembling slightly as I touch his arm. It's not a gesture that comes easily to me, but right now, it feels like what he needs—the warmth of human connection, a small offering of comfort to help him find the strength to keep going. "Then you have nothing to blame yourself for. Nothing fell apart. It will be okay, I *believe* it."

He remains silent, his eyes shut in an attempt to compose himself.

"And, you know, we... you got something out of all this," I add softly.

"Yeah? What is that?" He slowly opens his eyes at my words, the serenity he was seeking giving way to doubt.

"Well, at least Marve was revealed for who she really was." And you have me—I think to myself but dare not say out loud. I bet he'd take back giving me my powers if he could. Then he'd still have the rest of his family.

"Someone I should have never trusted," he mutters, his voice heavy with self-reproach.

"So what's our next step?" I ask, trying to change the subject, fully aware that my next step is sitting on this sofa, waiting for him to do all the work and find Ezra. I just want him to know he is not alone in this.

"*Our*?" He forces a bitter laugh, clearly upset by my choice of words. "There is no—" He stops mid-sentence, a flicker of realization crossing his face.

He pauses, then murmurs, "*Our* next step. That's it!"

He gazes at me as though truly seeing me for the first time in weeks, and for a fleeting moment, I catch the glimmer of hope flickering in his eyes—a spark I thought had long since burned out.

"What is?" I ask skeptically, not even daring to hope he's found a solution to finding Ezra.

"You."

"Me?" I know that if we don't eat, drink, or sleep, we won't die, but it's becoming clear that it can drive one to madness, because Ethan is clearly starting to unravel before my very eyes.

"You can try to connect with him, talk to him through your mind!" Ethan explains. He's far too enthusiastic. It's as if he doesn't realize this might *not* be the solution—especially if I'm not successful. And right now, the odds don't seem to be in my favor. "You have to try, please!"

"I will try... Of course, I will," I respond, though my voice wavers after hearing Ethan's plan. My hands fidget restlessly in my lap as doubt creeps in. "But I've only ever managed to connect with people I have a strong bond with. I never really connected with Ezra. You know how we tended to avoid each other during the little time we all had together," I remind him, hoping to temper his expectations for the outcome.

Ethan's eyes harden with resolve, as if he hasn't heard a word I've said. "You will reach out with your mind, and you will be successful. You will find out where he is."

To him, the possibility of failure doesn't exist. His unwavering belief only adds to my stress, though, making this that much harder. Maybe he's trying to instill confidence in me, but the weight of his expectations is overwhelming.

I'm still learning to use my powers, and we don't know all the powers I might have. We know I have the ability to connect with people even when they're not physically present; I can get into their heads, meet them in their dreams, and call out to them.

But how do I do it when I need to? More importantly, how do I do it with someone I don't have strong feelings for or a deep connection with? That's still a mystery.

Ezra had been teaching me to control and expand this power, but we didn't get much time before everything went sideways—before we lost him.

"It's all in your head," Ethan says. "This is Ezra's area of expertise, not mine... but I think he'd say something like—you just need to imagine what you want to do. Push your mind to give form to your thoughts."

But I remember Ezra's lessons. The problem isn't that I don't know what to do technically—it's that I can't fully control it, can't push myself through and beyond the veil of emotions.

With Ethan staring at me like I'm his only hope, I realize I can either focus on the impossibility of the task or believe in myself for once and give it a real try.

Ethan said it's all in my head, in my mind. It's a world of its own in there, and I just have to venture into it and shape whatever I want. As an introvert, I've lived in my head, through my imagination, my whole life. *I can do this.*

"You can do this," Ethan echoes my own thoughts.

"Are you reading my mind?" I ask, knowing his ability to do so, even though Ezra taught me to guard against such intrusions.

"You'd know if I were. If not, then it's pointless to even try this."

"Thanks, that really helps..."

Instead of shooting me an annoyed glance or mocking my concerns, as he usually does, he tries to boost my confidence further. "I *do* believe in you. Truly. I know Ezra would."

I brush aside the shards of glass and settle on the floor, resting my back against the sofa. Crossing my legs into a meditation stance, I draw a deep breath and close my eyes.

Exhale.

Another deep breath, then I try to visualize Ezra: his features, the energy he radiates, the way it feels to be near him. I focus on his scent and the expressions he makes. I attempt to slip into his skin, imagining how it felt in his memory, what it was like to be him, mimicking his thoughts and reactions.

But it's challenging to do so with someone I wasn't very close to. *No, don't focus on that.* I *am* Ezra. I picture myself with closed eyes, trapped somewhere, feeling uncomfortable. I immerse myself in the situation I believe he's experiencing.

Now I open Ezra's eyes and see where I am, I mentally urge, trying to see through his eyes.

But only darkness envelops me.

I repeat the process, trying to recall his scent but failing, trying to recall his energy and any moments we shared. But again, I find only darkness.

I have no problem opening my own eyes to find Ethan standing before me, quietly observing my efforts. But the feeling of his breath brushing against my skin makes me uneasy, like a pressure I can't quite escape.

"Well?" he asks way too eagerly.

"I... I'm sorry, I didn't see anything."

A surge of frustration radiates from him, hitting me like a powerful wave that nearly knocks the breath out of me. My heart rate quickens, my pulse matching the intensity of his emotions.

Though I wasn't successful in connecting with Ezra, it seems I've inadvertently opened my mind to everything around me, making me acutely sensitive to Ethan's emotions. His frustration seeps into me, amplifying my own anxieties and leaving me feeling raw and exposed.

Ethan seems to notice the change in my heart rate, realizing the impact he's having on me. We both recognize that the stress I'm feeling isn't entirely mine—after all, I had to calm myself down to reach this level of mental openness.

He bites his lip, closes his eyes, and takes a deep, mindful breath, just like I did a few minutes ago—something I rarely see him do.

"It's alright," he says, his voice softer now. "It was your first try. It'd be weird if you were successful right away. Maybe you need a break."

"Maybe I should do this alone," I suggest, trying a different approach. "It's hard to be myself and connect with someone on a deep level when I feel and hear and smell the presence of someone else who's not even calm."

Ethan nods swiftly. "Sure, makes sense."

"Do you think I could do this in his room?" I ask his permission, uneasy about invading someone's personal space, even in a situation like this.

He shrugs indifferently. "If it helps."

"I'd like to give it a try."

"You should, but take a break first. You need to get out of your head for a while, or you'll overthink it."

"You're right," I admit, the tension in my shoulders easing slightly. "I'll go for a run. I need fresh air. The air in here is too heavy, I feel like I can't breathe."

Ethan arches an eyebrow, glancing at the open windows before shaking his head.

"Ehm, yeah. Going out sounds like a good idea," he says, his tone softening. "I don't want to put any more pressure on you. If you find out something about Ezra's whereabouts, let me know."

chapter 31

NEW GUARDIAN

The grass yields under the weight of my feet, bending and folding with each step I take as I run along the river near Ethan's house, trying to drown out the noise of my thoughts. But the storm inside me refuses to calm so easily.

After a short while of no success, I pause and slump onto a stone ledge, gazing at the water beneath me. The rhythmic flow of the river soothes my mind, the gentle sound of the water clearing my thoughts. Water has always been my refuge, the yin to my fiery nature's yang.

Breathing in the fresh air, I close my eyes and picture a black void. For a moment, I need there to be nothing but the calming sound of the stream.

Just...

...nothing.

But the urgency of finding Ezra soon breaks through. How can I concentrate on nothing? How can I enjoy the run, the birds singing, or the water smoothly flowing, while Ezra is somewhere, waiting for us in misery?

I know I need to calm down, to find some inner peace to control my ability and connect with Ethan. But how can I calm down when finding him is the only thing that will ease my mind? It's a cursed loop, a never-ending cycle.

I open my eyes, the peaceful void shattered by my racing thoughts. *This is pointless.*

Rising to my feet, I prepare to sprint back to the house, but I stop abruptly.

There, seated on the ground with his back against the trunk of an old tree, is Tubiel.

"What are you doing here?" I ask, glancing around for one of his human charges. But I don't see anyone.

Tubiel smiles, his perfect white teeth gleaming, his expression suggesting he knows something I don't. Then again, that's not unusual. He always knows more than I do. Everyone does in this world.

"What is it? I can see you're eager to tell me. It must be important if you appeared here without any of your humans," I say a bit smugly, pleased with how well I think I can read him.

"And that's where you're wrong, Trouble" he says, the nickname he gave me rolling off his tongue in that charming voice of his.

"What do you mean?"

He savors the moment, watching me with a knowing smile as I try to guess.

"I *am* here with my charge."

"Where are they?" I ask, scanning the area once more to make sure I wasn't mistaken. I don't sense anyone's presence either; all I sense is the calmness of nature—the scent of fresh flowers and the cheerful songs of birds filling the air.

His smile widens, stretching his cheeks and crinkling the corners of his eyes.

"What?" I shout, my patience wearing thin. He's starting to get on my nerves, making me feel like a fool on purpose, just like Ethan used to do. Yet, despite my frustration, I can't help but smile back, caught up in the surge of joy he's radiating.

Tubiel stands up, his tall and athletic frame towering over me. He brushes his short brown hair away from his face as he declares, "I have been entrusted with the protection of your baby's soul."

"So it means..."

"Yeah, you are one of my humans, as you say. Well, you are not human, but your baby is, and I am here to protect it. Therefore, I am here to protect you. From now on, until this baby is born, I can be with you in an instant without breaking any rules or figuring out how to arrange a meeting through someone else I protect."

"Wow, that's amazing!" I exclaim, unable to contain my excitement as I jump up a little.

I adore Tubiel; he's been my favorite person in this new supernatural world, always so friendly. But it's been almost impossible to just get in touch and talk to him, as he's bound by angelic rules. But now, it will be so easy—all thanks to my baby. My human baby.

My enthusiasm wanes as the realization sinks in. Tubiel's assignment just confirmed it. My child won't be a supernatural being, blessed—or perhaps cursed—with eternal life.

It will die.

No, it's *supposed* to die, and I'll do anything to change that fate.

I push away the dark thought threatening to overwhelm me and force myself to stay composed.

"I didn't realize unborn children have guardian angels too," I say, keeping my voice steady, trying to shift the focus of my thoughts.

"They usually don't," Tubiel explains. "Normally, it's humans with souls who get pregnant, and they already have their guardian angels. Since the two souls share the mother's body for a time, there's no need for additional protection—they are always together, sharing the same fate. But you..."

"I don't have a guardian. I get it... But why you? Of all the angels?" I ask, unable to shake the feeling that this is more than a mere coincidence. I don't understand their system, so I can't be sure as anything seems possible, but it still seems a bit strange that the guardian angel of my unborn baby would be the only angel friend I have.

"Well, it's kind of a punishment," he says, waving his hand dismissively, as if it's not worth discussing. But he forgets how curious I am.

"What do you mean? You seem happy about this. How is it a punishment for you?"

"It doesn't matter," he says with a shrug. "I am happy. Very happy about this."

"I don't understand." I shake my head. I would love to leave it at that, at him saying he's happy, but I like understanding things.

"They said I need to learn my place. I don't want to talk about it. Please, just let this one thing go." He pleads with his words, his eyes, even the energy around him seems to want me to drop this and let him be happy instead of focusing on the bad side of this all. The side I don't see.

"Okay," I agree reluctantly. I want to know what's going on, but maybe it doesn't matter. He's still an angel, he didn't fall for me, and now we can be *normal* friends since we can meet whenever he has the time. I should focus on the positives, just like he's doing.

"So how does it work? Are you linked to me now? Can I call you with my mind whenever I want? Will you know if something's wrong?" I flood him with questions.

"First of all, you were always able to call out to me with your mind," he replies with a cocky tone, raising one eyebrow.

"Yeah, but I don't fully control that power yet, and it's not easy," I admit, recalling my failed attempt to connect with Ezra this morning. It's much easier with Tubiel or Ben, people I like and share a bond with. I know that's why he's using that cocky tone—he knows it too.

"If you say so." He studies my face, noticing the change in my emotions, yet he chooses to answer my previous question without prying. "But yes, now if you talk to me in your mind or out loud, even when I'm not with you, I will hear you. I'll know when you need my help, when you feel distress. I'll feel everything you feel, if it's strong enough. Even without you having to use your own powers."

Everything I feel? *Everything*? Tubiel has never hidden his special connection or affection for me. Is this his punishment—to feel my happiness with Ben, my feelings for Ben? That seems cruel. Will he also sense when I'm intimate with him?

"It will be the same as it was for you and Yabbashael," he adds, breaking into my thoughts.

"Yeah, well, I haven't spent much time with her since I found out I was a Nephilim. She was always so busy; we barely got a chance to talk. How come you have so much time?"

"She was facing an unusual number of demon attacks at the time. Usually, guardian angels aren't *that* busy, but we are busy enough."

"I see."

I try to recall what it was like having Yabbashael around. She always seemed to appear at the wrong times—either when I was with Ben and sought privacy, or during moments like being in the shower. She was also giving me her opinion about what I should do with my life. It felt like having my parents around all the time again.

Remembering this, I am starting to feel less thrilled about having another guardian angel around, but I must remember the positives. Even before knowing about this world, I sensed her presence, and losing her left an absence in my heart I didn't expect. Feeling that void filled again is oddly comforting.

"You don't seem happy about this anymore," Tubiel observes.

"Oh no. I am. Really," I assure him, forcing a smile.

"Don't worry. I know the difference between you and a regular human. We don't see humans as equals, as women and men. We see them as our children to protect. We're not attracted to them; we just observe, guide, and protect them in *many* situations. Too many, I guess. But with you, it's different. You're part angel, not human, and I will respect your privacy. To me, you are a woman."

His cockiness makes me nervous, and at first, I try to ignore his words, pretending he didn't say anything. Yet, I can't help but feel a flicker of enjoyment at his attention.

"So you see me as your equal?" I ask, raising an eyebrow. Angels usually don't like Nephilim, at least not the Nephilim who accepted their powers and gave up their afterlife, so hearing one say he sees me as an equal is... well, it's shocking and oddly comforting.

"I don't see all Nephilim as equals, but I see you that way." Yes, *comforting*.

After a brief pause, he surprises me with a piercing question. "But you don't see me as a man, do you?" His straightforwardness makes me bite me lip and shift from one leg to another. How can I answer without hurting his feelings?

"You're an angel," I respond, trying to keep it vague.

"So...?" He waits for me to elaborate. But I don't want to!

"Well, of course I see you as a man, a handsome one at that," I begin, choosing my words carefully. "But I'm not attracted to you.

It's not because of your looks or lack of charisma, but..." I trail off, hesitating.

He raises an eyebrow, a slight smile playing on his lips. "Don't worry, I won't get offended."

"... but what is there to be attracted to?"

His smile falters slightly. "I might have spoken too soon," he says with a forced chuckle.

"What I mean is, I usually like someone for their personality, but what is yours really? You're just like any other angel, just more goofy."

His eyes widen in surprise. "You're not the first person to call me goofy, but you're definitely the first to say I'm like any other angel... like ever."

"What do you do besides your angelic duties? You watch over human souls, but then what? What do you do in your free time? Scratch that, I know you don't have free time. What makes you 'you'? What do you like to do? You don't play volleyball, tennis, or badminton. Do you listen to music, watch movies? And not just over your human's shoulder. Do you do, or can you even do, something not all angels do? You're a good person, truly, which has always been the most important trait to me, but that's your angelic nature, not you, is it?"

He looks taken aback, struggling to find the words. "So basically, you think I don't have a unique personality because I'm an angel? That's insane. I'm different from others, just like they are different from each other. We are all special, unique."

"It's not that you don't have a unique personality. It's that I can't see it because I'm not from your world. The things that make people special in my world are different from yours. I've never lived a life like yours. I couldn't possibly understand it, understand you, or see what makes you 'you,' unlike other angels."

Tubiel remains quiet, his expression thoughtful.

I take the opportunity to continue. "You don't smoke weed, you don't complain or stress about things, you don't hate..."

"So it's wrong that I don't have these negative traits?" he asks, a hint of irritation sneaking into his voice.

"That's the point. All these things—the good, the bad—they make people interesting. It's about uncovering, understanding, discovering their qualities and flaws, trying to untangle who they truly are, growing together, learning from each other, appreciating differences. You don't love someone for being flawless. People are perfect because of what makes them different."

"See, that's it! With each other, we have a whole new world to discover. We can learn from each other, from each other's worlds. And we can grow together. I am not perfect, far from it," he argues passionately, his eyes lighting up with hope.

"Well... You can't even spend time with whomever you want. You have to do your job 24/7. You're with me now only because you're guarding my baby's soul. You wouldn't be allowed otherwise."

"Forbidden love. Isn't that exciting?" He smirks, finding a silver lining.

I chuckle. "Not in this case. It's like love between a mermaid and a monkey. It's both impossible and imaginary," I offer the most bizarre example that comes to mind, highlighting the absurdity of the conversation.

He scrunches his nose and shakes his head in disagreement, clearly not buying it.

"It all sounded too harsh, didn't it?" I say, realizing my mistake. "I didn't express myself clearly. I really like you, much more than other angels. I see you differently, and I know you're special. I just don't know what to look for in you that I would normally look for in a guy—a human guy with a human life, which is all I know."

For the first time, Tubiel *frowns* at me as he takes my words in. "I can't believe you're so superficial."

"That's so mean."

"*You* are mean," he retorts, sounding a bit childish, though he's right. I was the one who was mean first, but I never expected him to be mean to me. I didn't think it possible. He's too perfect for that.

"You said you wouldn't get offended," I argue.

"Yeah, well... I was wrong. Look, a personality flaw. I guess I'm not your perfect, super nice, good angel after all," he says in a tone I've never heard from him before, his usual confidence replaced with something raw and vulnerable.

We both take deep breaths, pausing to think. Tubiel breaks the silence. "I was wrong about you. I thought you cared about what's in a person's heart more than about what he does."

"I'm still just a human."

"No, you're not."

We start bickering like children again.

"You know what I mean," I exclaim, frustrated. We were having a perfectly nice conversation—how did it come to this?

He regains his composure and speaks softly, "I know. You've been human for practically your whole life. You'll learn to understand what's important with time."

"Perhaps, but remember, I'll never be an angel. I will never be a part of that world, of your world."

"You're right, but I can be a part of yours..."

"Don't say that," I cut him off, feeling a pang of fear. He can't fall for me, not in that sense.

"I have to go," he says, turning his back to me.

"Are you upset?"

He takes a deep breath, then looks back at me with a calm, crooked smile. "Of course not. You told me your opinion. I have mine. We don't always have to agree. I'll see you later, you hairy monkey." He winks.

"I was the mermaid in that scenario!" My voice echoes through the air, but he's already gone.

chapter 32

SILVER SKIES

I toss and turn in my bed for hours. I was hoping to find some peace in the darkness, but my thoughts seem to be the light in it, too bright to let me rest. Its Tubiel's words that echo in my head, casting a storm of uncertainty. Am I superficial? What am I really looking for in a guy? Is the thought of a Nephilim and an angel as a couple so crazy?

And of course regret seeps in too, as if it wasn't all enough. I know I shouldn't have said all those things. Maybe I should have kept my thoughts to myself. I curse my habit of speaking openly without organizing my thoughts first. I need to learn to filter my ideas, sharing only the ones that matter. Or the ones I am able to give a comprehensible form to first. Sometime it feels like I say things to try them out and realizing they are not true only after I give them life outside my mind.

But that is not important right now.

It's Ezra. Finding Ezra is crucial.

But I fail at redirecting my thoughts to the one thing that truly matters. These trivial musings shouldn't distract me; after all, I'm with Ben. Yet I blame Tubiel. He shouldn't have brought up this topic.

I can't take it anymore. With a groan, I thrust my fists into the mattress, the dull thud doing nothing to quiet the chaos in my mind. I lie there for a moment, staring at the ceiling, my chest tight with agitation. Finally, I give up. Sleep isn't coming.

With a resigned sigh, I throw the covers aside and swing my legs over the edge of the bed. I need to move. I need to do something. My mind drifts toward Ezra's room—a place I've only seen once, in the memory he shared with me. Until now.

It feels strange, even creepy, to go inside, but I do it. I knock even though I know no one's there, no one to invite me in, no one to disturb. I open the door, slowly peeking in. When my eyes confirm what my brain already knows, I enter.

I approach his bed, *their* bed, and inhale the scent of Ezra's pillow, trying to recall his smell. It feels invasive, and I hate doing this. I'm not one to sniff other people's belongings, but what choice do I have? The pillow's faint scent could trigger some memories of him.

I glance around the room, but nothing except his smell reminds me of him. Seeing his things—like the signed baseballs neatly displayed on a shelf—I'm struck by how little I truly knew him. I sigh, not seeing much more that could help me in my little quest.

I return to my room feeling worthless. I had hoped for more from this visit, thinking it might foster a deeper connection with Ezra. Instead, I feel a sense of inadequacy. I long for a ray of sunshine, a voice of encouragement, a hand to lift me up.

And just like that, out of thin air, there it is. Not just a hand, but a whole body.

Tubiel.

I let out a startled yelp, my body tensing like a frightened kitten. He smiles gently, but my shock keeps me from responding in kind.

"Sorry, I didn't mean to startle you."

"It's okay," I manage to reply, my breath catching. "I just didn't expect you here and now..." I had forgotten that through my baby, we're connected. He mentioned he could sense my feelings, especially when I'm stressed—I should have been expecting him.

"You need to talk?" he asks, his tone gentle and understanding.

I didn't think so, but if he sensed something was wrong, then... "I guess I do."

I sink onto the edge of my bed, my hand trembling as I place it over my chest, feeling my heart race beneath my fingertips.

"So what is this all about?" he asks.

"I need to find Ezra. I need to connect with him. But I just can't. We were never close. I can only connect with someone if I already have a strong emotional bond with them."

He doesn't seem surprised that I'm looking for Ezra, so I guess the word must have already spread. About him, about Abaddon, and maybe even about Ethan's wings.

"You were able to connect with *me*. Didn't you see Ezra more often than me?"

"Yes, but you and I are friends... or at least friendly. With Ezra, it felt like he didn't like me. I always tried to push him away, I guess... trying not to feel the negative emotions he had towards me."

"That makes sense. But still, you said you can connect with those you have a strong connection with." He pauses, waiting for me to catch on. "Does this mean you feel a special connection with me?"

I roll my eyes. I don't like admitting my feelings for anyone and I don't want him to get the wrong idea. Plus I thought we covered this topic just a few hours ago, and it didn't go that well. I wonder if he might be intentionally disregarding our earlier conversation in hopes of a different outcome.

"I felt an instant connection with you, that's true. I felt like you're my kind of person, someone I knew I could be *friends* with."

He lets out a loud sigh and walks over to the window, fiddling with the blinds. The fact that he's touching things means he's physically materialized. I guess he can do that often when we're alone, especially when there are no humans around who shouldn't see him.

After a moment, he turns back to face me.

"I'm sorry I don't know how to help you. I bet you've already heard it all—open up your mind, imagine talking to him, feel the connection, believe in yourself..."

"I did. You're right; it's all up to me now."

"Maybe a distraction might help. Come look out the window, the moon is huge tonight."

I hop up and hurry to the window like a child running to presents under a Christmas tree. The sight of the moon, so large and luminous, captivates me instantly. I could stare at it forever.

"Wow," I breathe, my mouth open in fascination.

"It's a full moon tonight."

I'm surprised I didn't know that. I usually keep track of these things, but lately, my mind has been too cluttered to remember the things I used to enjoy.

"I love the moon," I say, unable to tear my eyes away from its glow. "It's my favorite object in the sky. I'm like a werewolf."

"They hate the moon," Tubiel chuckles softly, shaking his head as if I've just said the silliest thing.

"What? Aren't they always howling at it like they're worshiping it?" I smile widely at him.

He scowls at my words, but his mouth twitches, hinting at a smile at the sight of my curled up lips. "The full moon controls them, it takes their free will to change forms. No one likes losing control or the thing that takes it away, of course."

I pause, considering this new perspective. "I guess I never thought about it that way." I turn my gaze away from him, drawn back to the moon. "I like the moon though. I am the opposite of a werewolf then. I feel like it gives me power."

Tubiel's laughter fills the room, light and teasing, making my cheeks warm with embarrassment.

"What about the sun? People usually say the sun gives them energy."

"Well, the moon's light is just the sun's reflection, so I guess both give me energy. But the moon is easier to watch. It won't burn my eyes out like the sun."

"You've got a good point," he says, nodding in agreement with a serious expression, but smiling underneath.

I watch the moon in silence, captivated by its distant allure. It hangs in the sky, so far yet close enough to reveal its detailed surface. Much better than an ordinary lamp, it gleams in the night, casting a magical glow across the darkness. The mere idea of standing on its surface, gazing back at Earth, fills me with a sense of wonder.

I glance at Tubiel. He might be able to actually go there, flying wherever he wants. "Have you ever been to the moon?"

"Why would I go there? There are no humans," he replies matter-of-factly.

And there it is. He's proving exactly my previous point. His entire existence revolves around his job—no room for fun, just for the sake of it.

"That sucks. You have so much power, yet it's so limited by your duties."

"Yeah, but if you go there, I can follow you," he says with a cunning smile.

I sigh, looking wistfully at silver object in the sky. "I wish. I've often dreamed about going to space, being an astronaut. But the thought of being cooped up in a tiny ship makes me claustrophobic. And honestly, the idea of those rockets terrifies me. I wouldn't like to explode or burn up in the atmosphere."

Another amused sound escapes his throat. "Nothing can happen to you, you're a Nephilim."

"You're right." I huff at my own silliness. "I totally forgot about that. Huh." I pause, then add with a wry smile, "But still, accepting my Nephilim powers didn't cancel out my claustrophobia."

Our conversation drifts effortlessly from the mysteries of space travel to the bravery of those who venture into the unknown, until, somehow, we've moved from standing by the window to sitting on the edge of my bed. Time seems to blur, slipping through our fingers, and before I realize it, the clock reads two a.m. My eyes grow heavy, and I stifle yet another yawn.

"You should go to sleep," Tubiel murmurs softly, his voice as gentle as the night surrounding us.

I stretch, my body heavy with fatigue. "Yeah, I sh-yaaawn-ould. Thank you for distracting me. I really needed that."

"Glad I could help. Good night."

"Night," I sigh, my eyes fluttering closed as exhaustion finally washes over me. I'm not sure if he's still there, but sleep pulls me under before I can care enough to check.

chapter 33

PULLS IN THE DARKNESS

The city sprawls beneath me, a shimmering maze of lights and shadows, but all I see is the path ahead. The full moon hangs high in the sky, its silvery glow my only guide as I soar above the rooftops. The wind whips against my face, and the sensation of flight feels as natural as breathing. Liberating. Every beat of my wings is driven by a singular purpose—finding Ezra. I'm not flying for the thrill. I'm flying because I have to.

But the sense of freedom is fleeting. Without warning, darkness swallows me whole. I can't tell if I'm in a lightless room, or if my eyes are blindfolded.

My hand instinctively reaches up to my face, but there's no blindfold, no obstruction. Just endless black. A void so complete, it snuffs out every flicker of hope, leaving nothing but suffocating obscurity. The air itself feels thin, barely enough to breathe, as if even the atmosphere conspires to choke out any sense of life or hope of escape.

Desperation swells inside me; I hate being here, even for a moment. I want to flee this pitch-black realm, but I'm helpless, lost in the dark with no clue how to break free from its grasp.

Stones bite into my skin, piercing the darkness with sharp, jagged pain as I lay sprawled on the unforgiving surface. I stagger to my feet, sharp rocks beneath and around me leaving my body sore and scraped. Disoriented, I take a few steps forward, only to stumble over a larger rock, crashing back to the ground.

I stay on all fours, determined to avoid another fall, and urgently explore my surroundings, desperate to find a way out. My hands and knees sting, battered by the unforgiving rocks, their sharp edges drawing blood.

I search relentlessly, only to realize I've probably circled back to where I began. Frustrated and exhausted, I collapse onto my back, the jagged surface aggravating my injuries. I exhale heavily.

How did I end up here? I was lying in my bed one minute, then flying above the city, then... Oh, *of course,* this is a dream. But why am I stuck in here? Why can't I wake up? Taking a deep breath, I try to focus, willing myself to end this nightmare.

Before I accepted my powers, controlling my dreams was nearly impossible. Being aware of dreaming was a rarity. But since embracing my abilities, I've gotten better at recognizing and manipulating them, and at avoiding slipping into dreams of other people.

However, it's clear that today, in my desperate attempt to find Ezra, I left my mind open, forgetting to close the door. Vulnerable, I failed to maintain the vigilance Ezra always emphasized. I don't know if this is someone else's dream I slipped into, or just a nightmare of my own subconsciousness. Either way, I want out.

Taking a breath of the stifling air, I try to regain control. I need to get back to my body, back to the real world. As I concentrate, I feel the connection to this dark place beginning to weaken. My real body is still immobilized but faintly perceivable, like a distant sensation. Yet the oppressive air lingers, clinging to me. As if not ready to leave, my dream hand moves reflexively, grasping something solid. My fingers trace its surface—rough, with two large hollows and a small, distinct ridge in between.

A skull.

The realization sends a shock through me, and I jolt awake, literally jumping out of my dream's body.

I wake up in the middle of the night, panting. My hand instinctively gropes around, searching for my phone, but it's not within reach. Propping myself up on one elbow, I stretch my arm further, fingers brushing against its cool surface.

The screen reads 4 a.m.

I debate closing my eyes, but the thought of slipping back into that nightmare makes me hesitate. Sleep feels like a risk I'm not willing to take. But if I want to find Ezra, I need full strength.

A sudden wave of calm settles over my racing thoughts, easing the tension in my chest. Lowering the phone, I spot Tubiel standing quietly in the room, his figure barely visible in the dark room, yet unmistakably comforting.

"What are you doing here? Have you been here all night?" My voice comes out softer than usual, thick with fatigue, as if even speaking requires more energy than I have.

I quickly make sure the covers are pulled up over my body, suddenly aware of my usual habit of sleeping naked—a habit I might have to reconsider now that Tubiel can apparently check in on me at any time. Luckily, since I was talking to him before bed, I actually stayed in some clothes for once. Maybe that's why I slept so badly.

"Of course not. I just got here," Tubiel says, his eyes scanning my face with concern. "I felt your stress."

"Just a bad dream. You didn't have to come," I say with nonchalance I don't feel.

"Do you want to talk about it?"

"No." I shake my head. "There's nothing to talk about. I should go back to sleep." I wonder if he'd do this if any other of his charges had a bad dream.

"I always check up on my souls when they're in any kind of stress," Tubiel says, as if reading my thoughts. "I see some of the souls under my protection ten times a day. The difference is, you can see me; they can't."

I raise an eyebrow, caught between suspicion and curiosity. Sometimes I can't help but wonder if Tubiel and Ethan can read my thoughts without me knowing, though it's more likely that angels are just exceptionally skilled at picking up on emotions and drawing conclusions. They should be, after all—they've had centuries of practice.

After a simple "Okay," I close my eyes, trying to drift back to sleep. Tubiel's presence fills the room like a quiet balm, easing the frayed edges of my nerves. There's a calm that only a guardian angel could bring.

The fear from my dream fades, giving way to gratitude—though it's tinged with a small flicker of annoyance at his unexpected visit. I take a deep breath, giving way to the sleep that's pulling me under once more.

I drag myself out of bed just before noon, heading downstairs with thoughts of brunch. As I step into the kitchen, the smell of coffee fills the air. There, leaning casually against the island in the middle of the room, is Ethan, a steaming cup of coffee in hand—a sight so unfamiliar it makes me pause. I've never seen him drink coffee, not once. My eyebrows raise instinctively, and I can't help but wonder if there's something a bit stronger than caffeine in that mug.

"Good morning," I say, offering a smile.

Ethan scowls, his eyes shadowed and tired. "What's good about it?" he growls. His gaze locks onto mine, and it's only then that he notices my smile. His expression hardens even more. "Did you give it another try? Do you have any news on where Ezra might be?" His tone is sharp, impatience etched into every word.

"No," I admit, the smile fading from my lips. "I just woke up."

Instant regret washes over me, knowing how little he wanted to hear that.

"You just woke up? Oh, nice." He crosses his arms, glaring at me. "I haven't slept for weeks, and you sleep till noon."

"I'm sorry," I whisper, my voice barely louder than a breath. Guilt knots my stomach, making the emptiness there even more painful. "I just needed rest."

Ethan has been a real downer lately. I understand where it comes from, but it's getting under my skin. If we don't find Ezra soon, Ethan and I might end up driving each other crazy. The heavy, negative energy he emits feels like a solid wave crashing against me, and I can't stand it much longer. Also, it can't be good for the baby.

"Eat your lunch, or breakfast, or whatever," he says, glancing pointedly at his watch. "Then, get to it."

"I am meeting Ben after lunch, he's coming over."

The moment the words leave my mouth, I regret it. Regret making plans with Ben, regret even considering it. Right now, after seeing the look on Ethan's face, I just regret being alive. Fortunately, my comment leaves him speechless.

"You know what? I'm not really that hungry. I can give it a try now. Let's go."

"You need energy," he growls, each word forced through clenched teeth. He turns away slowly, his movements stiff, radiating anger with every step.

I stand there, frozen, unsure of what to do, afraid that even breathing might provoke him further. When Ethan finally strides out of the kitchen, it's like he carried all the darkness with him.

The calm quiet is punctuated by the low rumble of my stomach, a sharp reminder of just how hungry I am. I open the fridge, hoping to find something edible, but am greeted by a musty, unpleasant odor.

"Are we living in a cave or what?" I mutter under my breath, wrinkling my nose in disgust.

After tossing a bag of moldy tomatoes and taking out the trash, I head back inside, straight to the sink. As I scrub my hands under the cool stream of water, the faint scent of mold still lingers in my nostrils, stubbornly clinging to me even though the trash is long gone. It's strange how smells can do that—how they cling to the edges of your mind like shadows of a memory.

And just like that, the dream that jolted me awake in the middle of the night comes rushing back, the musty odor triggering the same heavy, suffocating air I felt in that dream. It settles over me again, thick and unsettling.

I also remember that same heavy, oppressive air when I tried to connect with Ezra yesterday in the living room. Is it just a coincidence? Open windows, Ethan's complete obliviousness—none of it adds up. Was it just me? Or is there something more to it? Could this be a clue in finding Ezra?

I try to reconstruct the entire dream, playing it back in my mind. It was immersed in darkness, the surroundings felt harsh and jagged, and the air seemed to suffocate, making each breath a struggle. The walls seemed natural, not man-made; it might have been a cave of some sort.

But the image that haunts me most is the skull. Its meaning slips through my grasp. Could it be a symbol of Ezra's fate? A warning? Or was it his potential passing, projected into my dream?

"What are you doing?" Ethan's voice pulls me back, nodding toward the running water.

"Oops." I'd forgotten I was washing my hands, lost in my thoughts about the dream and Ezra. Quickly, I turn off the tap but try to keep my thoughts flowing.

"The skull..." I mutter, trying to push through the distraction of Ethan's presence and stay with the memory.

"What?"

I wave him off with a quick "shh," knowing I'm risking a reaction, maybe even a punch, but I can't lose the thread now.

"The rocks, the scratches..." My voice lowers as I try to focus. "Were those even rocks? Or could they have been broken bones, cutting my hands and legs?"

"What the hell are you talking about, Pandora?" Ethan demands, using not my real name, but the name he chose for me at birth for its meaning and the impact my life should have, as he had foreseen it. However, he knows I hate when he calls me that, which shows he's not playing around anymore. He wants his answers straight away.

I meet his gaze, hope shining in my eyes, my mouth opening as realization dawns. Maybe I did connect with Ezra after all.

"You did it, didn't you? You know where he is?" Ethan asks, reading the expression on my face.

"I might." A smirk playing on my face. "Do you know of a cave full of skeletons that is completely dark and where it is impossible to find your way out?"

Before I can finish, Ethan is already gone, not waiting for the word "out" to escape my lips. A faint breeze brushes my face as his wings flutter, leaving me standing alone once more.

With Ethan gone, I suppose I've done my part; it's all up to him now.

I can't go to the caves with him. The spell over the place would trap me inside. Only the ritual chamber where he gave me my powers allows safe entry and exit, but even then, one wrong step could lead to an inescapable fate. Unlike me and unlike most fallen angels, Ethan has wings. He can simply fly out of there, no sweat, or even dematerialize and pass through walls, trees—whatever gets in his way.

All I can do now is hope that I'm right about Ezra being in that cave. But there could be dozens of similar caves around the world. Hopefully, as a twisted joke, Abaddon hid him right under our noses.

chapter 34

HOLLOW

Ben's visit to Ethan's house marks a significant moment. For the first time, I decided to show him where I currently live, even though he won't understand all the strange things around. After everything that's happened, I chose not to move back to my apartment—I couldn't bear to leave Ethan alone, even though he had been gone until yesterday, and, honestly, I've kind of gotten used to the house.

I'm done trying to live two separate lives. Separating Ben from my life as a Nephilim won't work—not for him and certainly not for me. I want to share as much as I can with him, within the limits set by the Spell.

Leading Ben downstairs to the gym-bar, I caution him, "Please, just don't ask. I wouldn't know how to explain it anyway. This is all Ethan."

As we step into the basement, the ghosts of its vibrant past whisper around us. The vast space, large enough to fit a whole basketball court stretches out before us. Ben's eyes trace over the half of the room covered in sand, specifically laid out for the countless hours Ethan and Ezra spent training in Kalaripayattu. The echo of their swift, fluid movements and fierce clashes still linger in the air. By the bar, I can almost see Ezra and Marve lounging and sharing drinks.

As Ben steps into the room, his eyes widen at the sight, and he instinctively moves towards the weapon-laden wall, drawn by the allure of Ethan's prized collection.

"Do you know what these are?" Ben asks, gesturing toward the weapons.

I stare at him, puzzled. They're just weapons, I think. What is he really asking?

Seeing my confusion, Ben clarifies, "I mean, do you know their history? How old they are, who crafted them, their former owners?"

I chuckle softly, shaking my head. "No," I reply, considering his question more as a joke while also feeling bad for disappointing him.

I stand beside Ben, gazing at the wall of weapons. Despite Ethan's occasional stories, I never paid much attention to them. But now, with Ben's keen interest, they seem to come to life.

"I know this one," I say, pointing to a spear that has already captured Ben's attention. Its spearhead, shaped like the tip of a flame, gleams with a silver wire wrapping around the base and upper edge, while a gold shield encircles its center. "It was made by Tubal-Cain, a descendant of Cain. You know, from the story of Cain and Abel."

Ben snorts. "I know the story."

"Tubal-Cain is supposed to be the first smith ever. And this is why I remember the story: Ethan said the spear was forged from a meteorite. Isn't that incredible?"

"Yeah, incredible. And it's the real thing?" Ben's snort is louder this time, his doubt clear.

"Ethan believes it."

"He must be very rich then. And powerful! And influential! This spear must be priceless," he exclaims.

"I guess," I respond, avoiding Ben's probing eyes.

I turn and head towards the bar, eager to escape the conversation. Discussing Ethan's true identity, the mysterious origins of his wealth, and the reasons behind his low profile is a can of worms I'm not ready to open. How could I possibly explain that Ethan is a fallen angel who has spent centuries, maybe even millennia, amassing these treasures? It's a secret too heavy to share, and one I'm not even able to share for that matter. Thanks the Spell.

After about ten minutes of exploring the spears, swords, crossbows and other collectibles, Ben finally strolls up to where I am by the bar. His eyes land on the drink in my hand, eyebrows knitting together as his lips twitch in uncertainty.

"Is that a mojito?"

My cheeks flush instantly. I'm so used to everyone having drinks in this house at any hour that it didn't even occur to me how Ben might see it.

"It's a virgin one," I say quickly, forcing a casual smile, though lying never sits well with me.

Ben leans in, sniffing the air around my glass. "It smells like alcohol."

I shrug, trying to appear nonchalant. "Maybe you just associate the smell of mojito with alcohol. Or it could be this place—my *cousin* and his friends drink a lot and spill a lot, so..."

Ben hesitates, clearly not entirely convinced. "Ehm, okay," he mutters, dropping the subject but not his suspicion.

It slipped my mind that in his perception, I'm seen as a delicate, pregnant human female who should avoid alcohol. But being a Nephilim, I can't even get drunk due to my super-powered digestive system. I assumed it would be harmless for my baby because of it, but I have to admit, I hadn't even considered it before I made myself the drink. I feel terrible. What kind of person am I? Who does this? Being an immortal can't be an excuse for everything.

I place the drink on the table. Better to be safe in case it could affect the baby.

"Oh, sorry," I say, suddenly aware of my lapse in hospitality. "Do you want a drink?"

Ben shakes his head, but his eyes briefly flicker toward the abandoned mojito. "No, thanks." After a pause, he glances back at me. "So what do you want to do?"

I shrug, the past few weeks pressing down on me, leaving me with no original ideas. "How about a movie?"

Ben smiles faintly, nodding. "Yeah, sounds good."

But even as I suggest a movie, I don't really care what we do. The past few weeks have blurred into a long, drawn-out haze—each day consumed by the wait. I've been tethered to the house, unwilling to stray too far, convinced that any second Ethan would return, Ezra at his side.

My world has shrunk to these four walls, the soft brush of Berry's fur under my fingers, the television casting faint shadows on the walls. Everything has become a distraction—a meaningless routine, hollow and endless. Just waiting, always waiting.

I feel guilty, and it makes everything feel wrong. How can I live a normal life when Ezra's disappearance is my fault?

And If I'm honest with myself, I don't even want to spend much time with Ben. I'm exhausted from pretending to be just a regular human, hiding the truth about my life. It drains me. The lying, the pretending—I hate it. And I can't explain to him why I'm so on edge, why happiness feels impossible. I don't want him thinking it's only because of the unexpected pregnancy. Though deep down, I know it's part of it.

I was once head over heels for him, maybe like my teenage self, but now it feels like that rush was fueled by hormones, blinding me to who he truly is. I didn't see any of his flaws, only the good things. I thought I'd have time to get to know him later and find out how real this thing is once the initial euphoria settled. Now that I feel bound to him without truly knowing each other, the fear of attachments that used to hold me back starts kicking in.

And maybe it's not just me. As I watch Ben, it's hard to ignore the change in him too. When we first met, everything was alive—his laughter, his energy. Now, there's a disinterest that clouds our moments. His spark is dimmed, as if the initial zest for life has vanished.

When the movie ends, I hint that it's time for him to leave, using pregnancy fatigue as an excuse. But the truth? I'm not tired at all. I'm just terrified that Ethan might reappear, wings and all, with no way to explain it. And I'm not sure the Spell would cover that.

chapter 35

CRADLED ON WINGS

For three agonizing days, I exist in a state of relentless anticipation, each moment stretching into an eternity. I wait for Ethan, praying for news of Ezra, but doubt creeps its way back in. If my connection to Ezra had worked, wouldn't Ethan have found him by now?

Ugh, this is unbearable.

I've tried so many times—closing my eyes, reaching out, focusing every bit of my energy—and each time, nothing. No scent, no image, no trace of him. I hate waiting. I hate this feeling of helplessness.

Desperation pushes me to try again, to seek out a connection with Ethan instead, but the void between us remains as stubborn as ever. It's maddening. I thought I'd be getting better at this, not falling backwards. With each failed attempt, I feel my confidence unraveling, like I'm losing control of the very powers I once thought were growing.

"You know, stress isn't good for the baby."

I nearly jump out of my skin, hand instinctively clutching my chest at hearing Tubiel's voice cut through my attempts at concentration. "And the heart attack you almost gave me is?" I retort with a playful glare.

Despite my teasing, Tubiel's presence is a comfort. I know I can talk to him about anything, and so I let my frustration spill out. "Why can't I control my powers and use them when I need to? Why am I so bad at this?"

"You're certainly not bad at using your powers. You are just new to this, you can't expect yourself to become a super-powerful Nephilim overnight. You need more practice." His voice is soft, gentle.

"I just thought I'd be getting better little by little, not worse."

Tubiel tilts his head, his green eyes sparkling with curiosity. "Why do you think you're getting worse at it?"

"I was just trying to get in touch with Ezra and Ethan..." I start, but he interrupts me.

"Why? I thought you already figured out where Ezra was."

"I thought I did, I hoped I did... But Ethan hasn't come home since I told him, and I'm starting to doubt myself."

Tubiel lowers himself to the floor beside me, crossing his legs in smooth, unhurried movements. He doesn't speak right away, just studies me with a quiet intensity, as if letting my frustration settle before responding.

After a beat, he exhales softly, the calm in his voice matching his steady gaze. Then, finally, he says, "Have you considered that maybe Ezra isn't open to you anymore? Both Ezra and Ethan are powerful, strong in their mind abilities. They don't just let anyone in at any moment. My theory is that Ezra wanted you to find him before. He let you in by choice, giving you chance to figure out where he was. I don't know him well, but I don't think he's the type to let you in more times than necessary."

"So, you don't think it was the full moon that gave me so much power the last time I tried to connect with him?" I ask, half-kidding, half-hoping the moon has some special influence on me. It doesn't make any sense—my world is already magical enough—yet my life-long love for the moon and the wish to be a werewolf or some other supernatural being still linger. Suddenly, being a mere Nephilim seems so boring.

He laughs, eyes crinkling with amusement as a grin spreads across his face. "No, I don't. I think Ezra just made himself open to you that time. He chose to let you in."

"Or maybe we never really connected," I mutter, voicing my doubts once again.

"No, Tubiel is right. And I won't let you in again, not after what you did to me last time." The voice, one I haven't heard in weeks, flows through the air like a gentle breeze.

"Ezra!" I spin around, his familiar face coming into view. Instinctively, I take two brisk steps toward him with the urge to hug him, but I stop myself. We're not that close, and affectionate gestures like hugs aren't exactly the norm in this house. Besides, he looks—and smells—like he's been living on the streets. His clothes are worn and torn, covered in dust and tiny smears of blood. The pungent stench that clings to him is beyond description, it's so overpowering that it turns my stomach, and I have to fight the urge to gag.

Ezra's eyes catch the direction of my gaze, and a crooked smirk spreads across his face. "Admiring your handiwork?"

I blink, tilting my head in confusion. "What do you mean?"

"You did a good number on my body after I let you in," he replies, lifting his hands to show faint scars. "Cutting my hands and legs on any rock or broken bone you could find. Luckily, I heal quickly."

"I'm sorry," I say, rolling my eyes playfully. "I'll be more careful next time I'm saving your ass. It might take a bit longer to find you, though. But I guess it's more important not to break any of your pretty nails."

Ezra lets out a low chuckle. "Relax, I'm messing with you," he says, his voice light but carrying a rare sincerity beneath it. "It was worth it. Thank you."

"You're welcome... but I didn't do much. It was all you—you let me in."

"Don't be so modest. You did most of the work. If it wasn't for you and your abilities, there'd be no one to let in in the first place."

The unexpected compliment catches me off guard. Kindness from Ezra isn't something I'm used to—there was always an unspoken tension between us, like a shadow of disapproval over my decision to forsake the afterlife, to bind my body and soul indefinitely. But I guess most of it was just fear I was putting Marve in danger. A fear now gone.

Part of me wonders if this sudden warmth is just a fleeting byproduct of the overwhelming relief of coming home—something I had a hand in. Still, I can't help but hope this change between us is lasting. I could get used to this version of Ezra, one who doesn't see me as a liability. Having his support as I work on developing my powers again, without the cloud of silent judgment hanging over us, would make all the difference.

I'm still amazed I managed to connect with him at all. I didn't really believe I could do it. Those few lessons we had together must have been more valuable than I realized. I was able to slip into his body, feel things, smell things...

I frown, replaying the memory of the dark cave. "But one thing doesn't make sense. I should've been able to see. We can both see in the dark."

"I guess you weren't able to take over my body completely. Or maybe I am just not very good at being vulnerable and didn't let you. But perhaps it was because you were asleep and if you opened your eyes, you would have woken up..." he suggests one plausible option.

"Why is it easier to get into someone's mind when I'm asleep anyway?" I ask another question, excited my tutor is back.

Ezra grins, a mischievous glint lighting up his eyes. He seems to savor the moment, enjoying his role as my teacher more than I'd expected.

"It's easier to take over someone else's body when you let go of your own. Which is basically what happens when you fall asleep."

"But don't worry," he declares, his voice booming with playful bravado. "The teacher is back! You'll be controlling people while you're wide awake in no time."

Ethan, clearly tired of the conversation, jumps in. "This is all very touching, but seriously, go take a shower already. I know I need one after giving you a ride home." He wrinkles his nose.

Ezra rolls his eyes, though a grin tugs at the corner of his mouth. I catch the faintest glint of amusement flickering in Ethan's eyes—something playful, almost like he's holding back an inside joke, and it piques my curiosity.

I love seeing them back to normal, the familiar banter that dances between them as they playfully mock each other and everyone in their orbit.

"If you ever mention it again…" Ezra's voice is low, carrying a weight that could almost be mistaken for a threat. But the sparkle in his eyes gives him away, undercutting the seriousness with a playful edge, as if he's daring Ethan to push further.

I can't help but lean in. "What happened?"

"Nothing at all," Ezra replies, attempting to brush the topic aside, but Ethan isn't about to let it go so easily.

"Oh, yeah, nothing happened… except I had to carry Ezra in my arms like a baby to fly him out of there." Ethan's grins stretches wide, his eyes wrinkling.

Despite the severity in Ezra's gaze, I can't help but burst into laughter at the image of Ethan carrying Ezra in any manner possible. It's just too much. Ezra's piercing stare tries to smother my amusement, but it only fuels the laughter bubbling up inside me. Even with Ezra's menacing expression, I find myself unable to suppress my laughter for more than a fleeting moment before erupting into giggles once more. And seeing Ezra hate this whole situation only makes it that much funnier.

Ezra narrows his eyes, struggling to maintain his stern demeanor, but even he can't help the slight twitch at the corners of his mouth. Ethan, grinning from ear to ear, leans back with a satisfied sigh.

"Alright, alright, laugh it up," Ezra mutters, though his tone is more resigned than angry.

His grudging acceptance only fuels our laughter further, and for a moment, the room is filled with a lightness that had been absent for far too long.

I fight back the tears threatening to form.

This is home.

chapter 36

STRIKE TWO

After Ezra takes a much-needed shower—something we're all grateful for—changes into fresh clothes, and grabs a bite (meaning he eats everything he sets his eyes on), we gather in our old hangout spot—the gym. Since moving in, I've made sure to keep the kitchen well-stocked, so I wouldn't have to rely on takeout every time I get a craving. Looks like I just lost my entire supply.

I glance around, my heart swelling with gratitude. After so long, I'm finally surrounded by my favorite people. Well, almost all of them—Ben and Raya aren't here.

As I look at Ethan and the boys, it strikes me how much we

resemble a family, with our shared brown hair and sharp features that evoke an elven elegance, while the boys tower over me like protective big brothers. Well, more like one father, one uncle, and one... let's just say 'not a brother,' given that he's made it clear he has romantic feelings for me.

We lift our glasses together, the soft chime of crystal ringing through the room, a shared note of joy marking Ezra's return. Tubiel stands quietly beside us, refraining from joining in the indulgence, a silent observer to our celebration.

"What's this guy doing here anyway?" Ethan asks bluntly, his eyes finally landing on Tubiel, who's been with us for half the day. It's as if, only now, Ethan's tunnel vision has loosened just enough for him to notice Tubiel's silent presence at the edge of our gathering.

I whip my head toward him, eyes flashing with irritation. "Hey, don't be rude."

Ethan's brow furrows as he realizes his mistake. "Sorry," he mutters, rubbing the back of his neck. "The more, the merrier, of course. What I meant to ask is, how come you can even be here?"

Tubiel doesn't flinch or seem offended; he knows just how hard these past weeks have been for Ethan. Besides, he's too happy about becoming my guardian to be brought down so easily.

With a calm smile, he says, "I am Dora's baby's guardian." For a brief moment, his lips tighten, the corner of his mouth twitching before he quickly composes himself. A flicker of something unspoken flashes in his eyes—there and gone—before his expression smooths over again. But in this room, filled with perceptive former angels, nothing escapes unnoticed.

Ezra's eyes widen, the pieces falling into place. "Ah," he murmurs, his gaze shifting to me, then to Tubiel. "Because she doesn't have one, and her fetus is unprotected."

Ethan's expression softens further, his earlier bluntness giving way to guilt. "I didn't know," he murmurs, almost to himself. "When did this happen?" His voice drops lower as the realization sinks in—it wasn't just Ezra who had been absent, but him as well.

"It kind of just happened." I wave a hand dismissively, hoping to downplay the weight of it all. I don't want Ethan to carry any guilt for not being up-to-date on every little detail of my life. His mind had been consumed with finding Ezra—taken because of me—and if blame should fall on anyone, it's on me.

Ethan's brow furrows slightly, as if still grappling with what he's missed, but before he can say more, Ezra steps in. "Did anything else happen while I was gone?" Ethan's eyebrows shoot up, eager to catch up on the threads he'd lost track of, his eyes locking onto mine with quiet intensity.

"I'm afraid I have to disappoint you," I reply, keeping my tone light. "Nothing else happened. Actually, the past few weeks have been pretty boring." I throw in a casual shrug, hoping it covers the void I've been feeling—the waiting, the uncertainty.

But something shifts in the air the moment I finish speaking. Ezra's expression hardens, his features going from calm to ice-cold in an instant. "Tell me about that," he mutters, almost to himself. There's a chilling edge to his voice, as if those weeks of nothingness had carved deeper scars than anyone could see, the memory of that darkness trailing after him like a ghost.

"I'm sorry, I didn't mean..." The words slip out, tangled in embarrassment as I realize how ridiculous it is to complain to *him* of all people.

Ezra doesn't let me finish. "It's okay," he cuts in. The forced half-smile he offers feels brittle, like it might shatter if held for too long. His eyes, however, remain as distant as ever—untouched by the gesture.

Before I can scramble for something to say, Tubiel's hand rests lightly on the small of my back, a quiet, grounding gesture. It's just enough to remind me I don't need to dwell on the awkwardness

"So... what's the plan now?" Tubiel's voice breaks through the quiet tension, steering the conversation, offering Ezra a way out of the dark corners of his memory, and pulling us all back into the present. Or, actually, the future.

"Now," Ezra announces with a spark in his eyes, looking forward to the not-so-boring future, "I feel like hunting some demons."

Ethan's head snaps toward him, his reaction immediate, eyes widening in disbelief. "Wait, what?" His scowl deepens as he studies Ezra, clearly trying to figure out if this is some sort of a joke. "Since when do you want to get involved in any fights?"

Ezra's smile fades, replaced by a hardened gaze, his tone turning cold. "Did laying low and doing nothing bring us any fruits?" He pauses deliberately, his stare locking with Ethan's, holding the moment like a challenge—more than just a rhetorical jab, he's daring Ethan to answer.

Ethan clears his throat, glancing around awkwardly, his eyes darting between Ezra and me. "Um, no, I guess?" He gives the answer Ezra expected but doesn't stop there. "But what fruits do we want? Go to the store, buy an apple! We enjoyed life, didn't we?" He gestures grandly around the room, as if to remind us of the comfort we've had here.

I suppress a sigh, unable to imagine spending eternity cooped up here, drinking away the time and achieving nothing. Besides, Ethan had promised we'd go after demons and other monsters together if I accepted my powers. So why is he pushing back now?

"Enjoyed life?" Ezra echoes, a bitter laugh escaping his lips. "What life? We didn't enjoy life; it passed us by. We didn't pursue any goals or experience what life has to offer. All we did was lie low, surviving on alcohol that doesn't even affect us! I just don't see the point in that anymore. There is no joy in our lives and we already had thousands of years of it."

Ezra's eyes blaze with passion as he continues, striking his palm with his fist for emphasis. "Let's do something! Finally, let's do something for the good of humanity, as was our purpose in the first place."

Ethan stands there, his fingers twitch at his sides, and the wrinkle between his brows deepens, betraying the unease he's trying to suppress. "And hunting demons is the best thing we can do?"

Ezra lays his palms flat on the bar, staring Ethan down. "Got a better idea? I'm all ears."

Ethan, narrowing his eyes, pauses to think. After a moment, he sighs, his shoulders slumping. "I guess not... But do we really want to risk our lives?"

Before the question fully lands, Ezra cuts in, his voice sharp as a blade. "Our lives don't matter."

"If we die, we die for good—no afterlife," Ethan reminds him.

"Can it actually be worse than living for thousands of years without a purpose?" Ezra makes a valid point, leaving Ethan speechless. He opens his mouth slightly as if to respond, but no words come out.

Before Ethan can gather his thoughts, Ezra presses on. "And who's going to kill us?" He shrugs, almost dismissively, his tone dry. "It's practically impossible."

"Yeah, that's what you told me too, Dad," I interject, my gaze fixed on Ethan's face, searching for any hint of deception. Immortality was his selling point for this life, the promise of being practically unkillable his rationale for exposing me to dangers that could jeopardize not only my current life but also my afterlife. Was he lying about that too? Does he know something more, something he's been hiding about the weapon that can kill us and the creatures that possess it? I only the angels have it but does he know more?

And I still know nothing about the vulnerabilities of fallen angels or how they can be killed. Ethan just doesn't like to share that information. What is he afraid of—that I'd kill him? Did it ever occur to him that I might need to protect myself against another fallen angel one day? No, of course not. Information is power, and he obviously doesn't want a powerful daughter. Maybe he's afraid I wouldn't need him anymore.

Ethan's posture stiffens, but his expression remains calm, the same unflappable mask he always wear. "It is," he says, his tone unwavering, like the idea of our deaths is a distant myth. He pauses, eyes flickering briefly, clearly hunting for a new angle.

"But let's set us aside for a second. You're right, we've lived long enough. But by doing this, we'd be putting Dora's unborn child and her human boyfriend in danger too, you know?"

My body twitches involuntarily at the mention of Ben and my unborn child. The mere thought of putting them in danger makes my heart ache. I hadn't expected Ethan to drag them into this as an argument against Ezra. What do they mean to him, anyway? He's using them just to win an argument, too much of a coward to go along with Ezra's plan.

"You already know where I stand on that," Ezra replies, his tone flat.

We all understand what Ezra means by this—he doesn't care if a human with a soul dies, as long as the soul lives on and fulfills its purpose set by God. I believe Ethan shares this view when it comes to ordinary humans, though not half-humans like me. That leaves him without any real counter-argument against Ezra's proposal.

Ethan's next sigh is loud and prolonged as he realizes he's been cornered. "Okay. Let's do it! It's what you always wanted, too, isn't it, Dora?" Ethan's eyes flicker with something beyond resolve. Is it doubt? Uncertainty? Either he's hoping I've changed my mind because of the pregnancy, or maybe he secretly wishes I've reconsidered because, deep down, he doesn't want to go through with this at all. He might prefer retreating to his bar, drowning in drinks, pretending the world is fine when it's clearly not.

"Actually, I have my own plans," I announce, and the room goes still as eyes widen in surprise.

"You do?" Ezra and Ethan ask in unison. Tubiel remains quiet, but the furrowed brow and the deep wrinkles between his eyebrows say enough.

"And might I ask what they are?" Ethan's voice drips with condescension. They've always assumed control over my life choices, never considering that I might have my own thoughts, my own plans, or even the option to reject their proposal—though, in truth, I'm not rejecting it entirely.

"I need to find Baal," I respond, taking a deliberate breath into my chest as I straighten my posture, trying to project firmness and command respect with both my words and my body.

A heavy silence blankets the room, stretching out uncomfortably.

"What for?" Ezra's voice cuts through the stillness, his eyes locking onto mine with a fierce intensity, as if he's daring me to say anything he doesn't like. I can sense the tension radiating off him, a storm brewing beneath the surface, ready to explode.

I don't see the Ezra who just returned home today, the one whose eyes sparkled with relief and happiness. Instead, standing before me is the old Ezra—the one who couldn't mask his disdain, the one who treated me like I was nothing more than an unwelcome burden. His familiar scowl replaces the warmth I had hoped for, and it feels as if a shadow has fallen between us, dimming the light of our earlier reunion.

I take a slow deep breath, stealing a brief moment to brace myself for their reactions. "He's supposed to be the most powerful being after God, right? I think he might be the only one with the ability to make my child immortal."

Ethan's face twists. "What? Are you out of your mind?" he

blurts out, his voice tinged with panic. "It's too dangerous. Baal is too dangerous. You don't want to get involved with him."

"I, for one, agree with Ethan," Tubiel interjects, voicing his concerns out loud for a change.

But it's Ezra's voice that makes me feel truly small. Calm yet heavy with unspoken emotion, it rolls over me like a storm waiting to break. "How can you be so selfish?" His words slice deeper than Ethan's outburst. He doesn't seem surprised by my revelation, but the impact is clear in his eyes.

While the others fear the danger of the mission, the danger I would face, Ezra's apprehension lays in the potential success of my quest, which could endanger my child's soul.

To angels, or at least most of them, human existence serves merely as the cornerstone for soul judgment before the transition to the afterlife. They view the prospect of becoming immortal, of dooming oneself to eternal wandering on Earth, as the ultimate loss—akin to extinguishing the essence of life itself. This principle holds true for Nephilim like me. In contrast, for other beings—demons, vampires, shapeshifters, and even angels—the absence of a soul is innate.

Ordinary humans, to the best of my knowledge, lack the means to attain immortality. Yet, deep within me stirs a hope that somewhere, someone possesses the power to alter this fate. Unlike angels, human life and existence on this plane hold profound significance for me; it brims with potential and opportunity. And it's the only thing I know, of course.

Though it may be the most selfish decision I could make, stripping the child of the chance for an afterlife and fulfilling its soul's purpose, I cannot bear the thought of having a child only to watch it pass before my time. I have to find a way to grant my baby immortality.

As the shock begins to fade, Ethan steps forward, his expression earnest. "Ezra, you don't know what it's like to have a child. You don't understand..."

Ezra's eyes flash with a storm of anger and sorrow. "I understand more than you think," he retorts, his voice trembling with suppressed emotion. It's true; Ezra once had a son, and in a heart-wrenching decision, he chose to let him die, to allow him to ascend to the afterlife.

"But it's still selfishness, nothing more," he continues. "If you truly wanted what's best for your child, you would let them live, allow them to die when their time comes, and find their purpose—ascend to something greater. Something we can never have."

He turns to me, his expression laden with meaning, as if to remind me that such a future could have been mine as well.

Yet Ezra's eyes reveal even more—an ache that cuts deep. I can see the shadow of his past responsibility as a guardian of unborn souls, children souls, a role he took with utmost seriousness, until he couldn't bare it anymore.

I open my mouth, ready to apologize, but he cuts me off. "You've already made up your mind, haven't you?" He doesn't wait for my response, his words rushing out in a torrent. "You're as stubborn as your father. If you two had souls, I bet you'd both rot in hell for this." Bitterness drips from his voice, stinging like a slap.

With that, he turns his back on us, walking away—a gesture

heavy with finality. His decision is clear; he won't be part of this.

The room falls into a heavy silence, Ezra's words lingering like a shadow. Ethan and I share a look, both momentarily frozen.

After a beat, I discreetly clear my throat, breaking the awkwardness. "I don't think he's going to help me," I say, forcing a small, nervous laugh in an attempt to lighten the mood. I turn to Ethan, my expression earnest. "Will you help me?"

Ethan's face softens, conflicted emotions playing across his features. "Ezra is probably right; you are selfish, but so was I." he admits. "I made you this. It's my fault that you'll spend eternity on this earth without the possibility of ascension to heaven. So who am I to say no to you? I am not a hypocrite."

His words aren't entirely true, though. The decision to accept my powers and immortality was mine alone. He merely offered me the choice, opening the door to a path laid out ahead. True, he portrayed it in a more positive light, deliberately omitting a few potentially discouraging details, but ultimately, stepping over that threshold was my choice.

I nod, grateful for his willingness to help. Without Ethan, I'd be lost in this world. I don't know anyone or anything, and I have no leads on how to find Baal.

"Learning from your mistakes and preventing others from making the same ones isn't hypocrisy, Ethan," Tubiel says with the wisdom of an owl.

I study Tubiel's expression, trying to decipher his intention. Is he trying to dissuade Ethan from helping me, or is it merely a patronizing remark? I remind myself that his primary duty is to safeguard my baby's soul; that is the sole purpose of a guardian angel.

"Are you going to team up with Ezra on this?" I ask him. I know he won't violate the rules or betray the mission entrusted to angels by God, but I need to know where he stands. What he'll do.

Tubiel meets my gaze as he silently contemplates his options. "I am here for you..." He begins after a brief pause, shifting his gaze around the room, as though seeking the answer from anywhere but his mind.

Taking a deep, unsatisfied breath, he continues, "...until there is an actual and direct threat, until someone tries to take your baby's soul or alter it in any way."

Ethan snorts, a playful smirk curling his lips. "What an unexpected twist. You really are good at finding loopholes. I just hope you're not too afraid of falling, either. You're getting one step closer..." His words drip with irony, each syllable a playful jab at Tubiel's predicament. Yet, beneath the joviality of his laughter lies a sharper edge, a subtle desire for Tubiel's downfall fueled by the underlying grudge against the angelic order.

Tubiel's expression remains stoic, unfazed by Ethan's teasing remark. He simply nods, accepting the challenge that lies ahead.

Then, in a light tone as if shifting gears, Ethan poses the obvious question—the one I dreaded: "So, what's our first step?"

More silence.

More arched eyebrows.

More mouths opening without letting any words out.

I find myself adrift, thoughts swirling like leaves caught in a gust of wind, but no clear direction emerges to guide our next move. "I... I don't know," I confess, feeling a rush of pink creep into my cheeks.

Ethan and Tubiel exchange a glance, their eyes communicating a silent agreement that diffuses the tension, if only slightly. We may not have all the answers, but we have each other, and for now, that has to be enough.

Printed in Great Britain
by Amazon